A Tale

of

Two Avrahams

Other Books by Avraham Avi-hai

Ben-Gurion, State-builder: Principles and Pragmatism (available in English, Hebrew, French, and Spanish); Transaction Publishers, 1st Edition 1974.
Danger: Three Jewish Peoples, Schreiber,Shengold Publishing, December 1997.
Ma'aseh Bishnei Avraham (*A Tale of Two Avrahams*, Hebrew version), Carmel Publishers, 2008.

Copyright © Avraham Avi-hai 2013
Printed ISBN 978-0-9894169-0-0
Ebook ISBN 978-0-9894169-1-7

2nd printing September, 2013
Printed in the U.S.A.

Appletree  Publishers

Editing, interior design, cover art, and production:
Harvard Girl Word Services
Cover artwork: Oceanside Design

To order copies of this book from the author go to:
www.avi-hai.com or email 2avrahams@gmail.com

A Tale of Two Avrahams

Avraham Avi-hai

Reactions from Amazon.com Reviewers

"Imagination, scholarship, and conviction flow easily through Avraham Avi-Hai's pen in the writing of this masterpiece of a novel spanning 400 years of time and hundreds of miles of space. This is historic fiction at its best. ...A great story in and of itself, replete with adventure, romance, passion, and mystery, the kind of book that when one puts it down one feels an intimacy with amazing characters whose menaced lives, though far apart, are intertwined in a common destiny." (Ambassador Yehuda Avner, bestselling author of *The Prime Ministers*)

"A thoughtful, provocative novel that artfully examines political obstacles to Jewish spirituality." (*Kirkus Reviews*)

"*A Tale of Two Avrahams* is intelligently written history and novel. The writing is marked by considerable erudition and good description. . . . Footnotes illuminate translation issues and what otherwise might be inscrutable or at least mysterious. A passionate reader of historical narratives, [I find] this one offers insight into critical periods of Jewish life, both in relation to Christian civilization and Islam, and also into forces that forge the dynamics of Jewish continuity." (Herb Krosney, *NY Times bestselling* author of *The Lost Gospel: The Quest for the Gospel of Judas Iscariot*, National Geographic Books)

"*A TALE OF TWO AVRAHAMS'* IMPRESSIVE RESEARCH merges seamlessly into this excellent read."

"A JOURNEY WORTH TAKING. *A Tale of Two Avrahams* blends a contemporary thriller with a pivotal moment in Jewish history, some 400 years ago in Italy and Greece. Particularly striking is outstanding research combined with considerable literary skill."

"AN EXCEPTIONAL BOOK BY AN EXCEPTIONAL AUTHOR."

"GREAT READ. I had the pleasure of reading this book several years ago before the English version was published. ...Everything from adventure and action to philosophy and romance. I was riveted, and highly recommend it to anyone who enjoys historical fiction."

"THRILLER, HISTORY, AND ROMANCE. In spite of his in-depth research and erudite writing, Avi-hai is a wide-eyed innocent romantic, making this sophisticated and complex book a good and easy read."

For Violetta

... Keep Ithaka always in your mind.
Arriving there is what you're destined for.
But don't hurry the journey at all.
Better if it lasts for years,
so you're old by the time you reach the island,
wealthy with all you've gained on the way,
not expecting Ithaka to make you rich....

from *ITHAKA*, Constantine P. Cavafy, (translated by Edmund Keeley
and Philip Sherrard. *Greek Quintet: Poems by Cavafy, Sikelianos,*
Seferis, Elytis, Gatsos, Harvey & Co., 1992)

Chapter 1

Sandor came alone, unannounced, unexpected. The night was dark and moonless; he had chosen the lower entrance that was unlit, knowing that the family used the brightly illuminated one in the back. The doorbell rang, and there he stood.

Unusual in this neighborhood, a hasid in full uniform: shtraymel tilted a bit rakishly, but shtraymel it was. Long coat of shiny gabardine—black; black suit, white shirt, no tie, black beard. Hasidic rabbis never go anywhere without an escort—only if there is a death in the family or someone is in the hospital does the rebbe come to you—but he came alone. When he moved upstairs and sat down in the parlor a black yarmulke, large and round, was covering his still-black hair; looking closely, though, showed he was probably closer to fifty than first glance would suggest. His build was slight, but the beginning of a rabbinical belly was showing.

I call him Sandor, a diminutive of Alexander, someone much admired by the ancient rabbis—but no longer to his face. Others call him Rackover *rebbe*, Rackov being a tiny town in Poland where his grandfather had once carried on their small but respected dynasty. It is therefore out of respect that I avoid using his first name, though I used to carry him in my arms when he was just a tiny baby. His followers speak to him in the third person. I use second person, but no name.

I made him a cup of strong tea, sliced some lemon, and brought cube sugar. He looked at the cup, his eyes aslant, almost like a Tartar or Mongolian. He took it from me and nodded to himself. Normally, in his milieu, the tea would come in a glass. I sat, bare-headed, waiting. Sooner or later he'd tell me why he came. In the dark of night. Alone.

I waited. He sighed. I saw his lips move as he made the blessing over the tea.

He said nothing. Finally I spoke. "I'm listening."

"*Rodef.* They are talking about *rodef. Moser.*" It was uttered in a conversational tone, but hushed. I sighed as well. His tone was not accusatory.

Rodef means persecutor—a Jew who persecutes his own people. *Moser* is the one who betrays you to the authorities. Over the centuries, the *moser,* or *moyser* in Yiddish, and the *rodef,* have both been considered the lowest of the low. If a Jewish court of law passes a sentence of *moser* on a fellow Jew, the non-Jewish government carries out the execution. Either way: death for a *moser.* Death for a *rodef.* Sandor looked at me and then lowered his eyes. Perhaps he was apologizing for their decision.

Who are "they"? you ask. A group of rabbis, loosely organized— if at all—but powerful enough for their decisions to carry weight. Influential enough to get the word out. The same decision that condemned Yitzhak Rabin to death, though not necessarily the same rabbis. The killer only pulled the trigger; "they" triggered him.

I studied Sandor's face. "You placed yourself in danger tonight."

He shrugged.

"Am I so important?" I asked. "Am I a prime minister?"

He looked steadily at me. "They think you are a *moser,* father of the fathers of all *mosrim.*" His tone was even, flat. "Don't put them to the test. Go!" The term he used, "father of," is equal to another rabbinic term—"father of the fathers of impurity."

I sat like a stone. Not rigid. Just settled—a stone in its rightful place doesn't want to move.

He spoke. "I won't come again." Or maybe he said, "I can't come again." I can't be sure. Of course, he had broken the code, the inner code of the inside rabbis. "I won't come again. But I could not stand silent on your blood."

I shuddered. I knew the verse to which he was referring. *Thou shalt not stand silent on thy brother's blood.*

He asked me to let him out the way he came. I did not turn on the stoop light. He did not offer me his hand before melting black on black into the night. I was too stunned to ask why he wore a shtraymel on an ordinary weekday, one neither Sabbath nor Holy Day.

Which Sandor was here tonight? The warm, almost-nephew requiting childhood love and adolescent affection? He had not even looked at me. Was he sealing over the closeness we had shared since his youth?

I realized something else, too, another chilling detail. He had not said hello. He had not said good-bye. He had waited for me to speak first. He had followed the protocol for visiting a house of mourning. I was already being mourned. And I was also the mourner, mourning my own future death.

Had I been visited by Sandor the almost-nephew or the other Sandor, leader and counselor of the Sages? Perhaps he hadn't come of his own accord. Perhaps he had been sent. Perhaps by the gentler rabbis who abhor bloodshed. Perhaps by the haters who nonetheless don't want to kill a fellow Jew if there's another way.

I packed during the night, when the aching calls of the muezzins rang across the Jerusalem valley below the Turkish walls of the Old City. I wondered whether it was just one muezzin, echoing across history and the valley, or all the muezzins of all the mosques within hearing radius. The loudspeakers were at full Islamic pitch.

The few remaining hours till daylight passed with me dozing and thinking and twisting. With false dawn the church bells tolled from the Armenian church just inside the wall, and from the Dormition on Mount Zion, echoed by tinnier sounds from within the Christian quarter itself.

The next morning I cancelled some appointments and took ten thousand in cash out of our savings. The bank clerk raised his eyebrows, but I told him—innocently, I hope—that I needed it to buy a used car. By noon, I was on a bus to Haifa. *Rodef* means persecutor, the one who pursues. But I was the one being pursued, I thought, as I faded into the bus and through the port.

Even though the bus was comfortable and air-conditioned, and the ferryboat's cabin modern and clean, if small, I felt uprooted, torn from the comfort of my home, from my routine. The adrenaline that came with being hunted had reinvigorated me, but now, in the embrace of a ship's cabin, gently rocked by the sea, I fell asleep.

I dreamed of my wife and making love; of strange women walking by, exuding desire, but of making love to my wife. And I dreamed also of fearsome death figures waiting for me, and killers with knives lurking around corners. I dreamed of horses riding through a steamy land I did not know, and of a beautiful figure of a woman whose speaking voice rang as true as a tuned bell in a perfect belfry, in a synagogue whose cupola had a cross on it. People in shrouds reached out to me, but I knew my wife's arms were waiting and death would not claim me.

I awakened refreshed, ready to make some decisions. The first had been made: I had fled. Should I now go into hiding? How far did their threat go? If I stopped my work, would they call off the hunt? Or would they, pursue me still, relentless? Would they become the rodfim, the pursuers, the persecutors, and I the nirdaf, the pursued? Was I under a death sentence in all circumstances, or would staying in Israel be the basis for my execution? Would remaining abroad mean a stay of execution?

I must begin to weave a web of lies. Lies are always more certain than the truth. All my life I have tried to fight lies and lying, but I must learn a new skill and adapt quickly. Will I be able to?

I am faced with a much more immediate problem, however: where to go right now.

Chapter 2

Heraklion rears up from the Mediterranean, rolling off into the Cretan hills. The chants of ancient rites pulse through the olive-laden air onto mysterious mountains where Zeus himself was hidden from his father.

Heraklion made me sad, though not as sad as Athens, into which I dashed for a quick visit between ferries docking at Piraeus. Athens is a déjà vu of the old coastal Tel Aviv-Jaffa of decades ago, with some modern buildings, parks, the Parthenon and Acropolis, and not quite up-to-date buses in a smog-laden happy clime of *tavernas* and *ouzerias* and good beer. A few hours to revisit, to delight and sorrow in the old and the new, and then on to Piraeus and the ferry.

The ship to Heraklion was laden with some local holidaymakers, but even more with North Europeans—Swedes, Danes, Germans—traveling in organized hordes; no longer Huns, no longer Teutons, but kindly middle-aged tourists in search of the Mediterranean sun. They drank nonstop for the entire sixteen-hour voyage, and played cards carefully and in small sums through the night on the (again, disappointing) too-modern white, black, and polished chrome floating hotel, steaming slowly to give the deck passengers incentive to pay more money for a cabin. Where was the romantic barque of old? Why flee from ancient blood rites without at least enjoying the instruments of olden days? If we can no longer have the slave-driven rhythm of a "quinquereme of Nineveh from distant Tarsus," why not at least a medieval barque skimming across the waves to Candia, or sloughing into the rolling roughness, as the wind whips the waters toward the rocky black shore?

I stayed away from everyone, slept, and tried to recreate Crete in my mind, scraping through the little I could recall from reading, long years past. Crete....

The city rose steeply above the inlet and harbor, white and blue and red brick, its heavy medieval black-stoned Venetian fortress and humming Mediterranean town center lined with shops and cafés and restaurants. Nearby, I had found a medium-priced hotel. In registering, I dropped the surname, using the middle one, so the card read:

Last name: ASHER
First name: Avraham

It was clumsy, but at least a first step. I decided to spend a few days there, try to find a new passport.

The next morning, after an excellent breakfast—if you like yogurt and honey, as I do—I mingled with tourists milling about the local museum, and saw that most of its contents came from Knossos. So, on to Knossos.

It was a brief, bumpy fume-filled bus trip, which would reveal itself to be the turning point in my flight.

I had no chemistry with Knossos at first. Again, I experienced the sadness and disappointment of a true miss. It stemmed from the blatant intrusion of concrete on the ancients ruins, the removal of the artifacts to the Heraklion Museum, and the overhanging miasma of diesel from tired old buses as you enter the small Minoan valley. But the hills—verdant and thrilling to birds singing the old songs—and the excitement of the children and parents and the serious and pedantic young seekers with their backpacks, books, and maps, restored the magic. Slowly, slowly, the heart beats faster as the soul wings back in time.

I had sunk onto a bench, under a spreading oak, and screened out the irritations to return to the labyrinth, the Minoan bulls, the blood sacrifices. I was asleep/awake, dreaming of the palace, the tunics and gowns, the bowls and vessels, the red clay with the black baked into it. I felt the earthquake and smelled the dust of crashing buildings and short-lived fires of thirty-five hundred years ago. The invading mainlanders coming later—conquering, building, boasting, and strutting their nascent power. Suddenly I saw someone I knew.

I saw the face, and only then realized I was indeed *seeing*. It was a waking dream. A young woman in her late twenties, full-figured and round-faced, was standing in front of me. "I have seen you before."

"No."

"I have seen you before," I said again.

"Are you well? Do you feel alright?" She spoke with the clear vowels and consonants of Greek, in the matter-of-fact straightforward tone that is Cretan. "I am a doctor. I did not want to intrude, but you seemed...."

"I was in a dream of old Knossos, and it was as though I were there, and then suddenly I saw you in front of me."

"So, you are well. Well, then, excuse me. I will go back...."

"To join your friend, or friends?"

"No. I came here alone."

"Then join me, or let me join you."

That's how I met Ariadne.

I learned later where I had seen her face. I had given her a compliment. She had—again, perfectly matter of fact—rejected it. "I am not pretty. But my face is the face you saw in the museum. I have a Cretan face. You have seen it."

We walked in the warmth of Knossos valley. It lay huddled in a mantle of low rolling hills where the winter sun was swallowed by the dense green foliage of the olive trees and the orderly lines of grapevines, serried along parallel wire frames, in the middle distance. Knossos was timeless and the open square old digs—the remains of a house, a mansion of its time—exuded the remembered odor of the blood sacrifice of Man as a youth, and of Bull as deity.

Knossos preserves its own savagery, beauty, power, and civilization. Only the modes change with time. The themes are eternal.

Humankind never changes its essence: savage and power-seeking, shaping beauty and building a passing order that falls again into eternal chaos. Silently strolling, we shared the unspoken.

Ariadne drove me back to Heraklion in her VW Polo, papers strewn on the back seat, but otherwise shiny and quite new. It was a short drive. That evening, she took me to her favorite *taverna*, where we drank *raki* and good Cretan white wine, ate, and talked.

She was direct, intelligent, quick-witted, and grave, with flashes of humor that lightened the gravity. The educational system of Crete must be remarkable, for the young people—the young intellectuals, I suppose I should say—still read and love their literature. All I recalled of ancient Greek was the conjugation of the verb αγω (pronounced agOH), and the fact that it had a form for singular, dual, and plural. I told her that Hebrew had a dual form for pairs of body parts: ears, eyes, hands, and feet. And I asked her to remind me how Homer had said "rosy-fingered dawn." She told me and recited the first few lines of the Odyssey.

The meal ended. Direct femininity radiated from her. It was so natural, and she so unaware of it, that it was all the more endearing. As she had told me, she was the form from the museum come to life, and I feared to cross the barrier of decades and build a wall of destructive distrust. (I have not yet reached the stage of the ailing King David who, only when very old could bring a maiden to warm his bed, and "know her not." My namesake, Abraham our Father, did have concubines, but we know how badly that ended.)

We walked back to the hotel. It was on the bluff overlooking the harbor near the main square, which was really a circle large enough to cover a few acres. On the port side it was bounded by a small park and the Venetian stone ramparts.

In careful and delicately chosen English, Ariadne spoke fiercely of Crete, proudly of Greece, and gravely of her life, her village, her parents. Rooted as a peasant in the rich soil that gives forth its vines and olive trees, she was also at one with today, with electronic devices and medical machinery. But I saw her as a soul divided into three parts, to borrow from the classics: Minoan—a civilization close to three millennia old, with blood sacrifices and well-developed art; Cretan—a fierce, vengeful, rooted, and hardy race, tempered by heat and storm, heritage and battle, whose mustachioed warriors had struck terror in the hearts of invading Ionians, Dorians, Muslims, Venetians, and Germans; and finally Western—well read, free-willed, and melding rationality and science with innate humanity.

All these placed an extra burden on me, since she sought wisdom from me. A person of my age, white-haired and a Jew ("You are the first Jewish person I have met"), and on top of that an Israeli, what did all these mean to her? What did she expect? Why did she nod as if hearing the music behind my words, or as though recognizing some predictable or anticipated phrase when I uttered something out of the usual?

It was a strange night for me, and as I slept reality—fear, desire, sacrifices, and Golden Calves—chased around my head in flickering images, some color and some black and white. I did not want to be the sacrifice. In the morning, from the balcony, the Cretan Sea was divided, as was I, into two parts. Closer to me was the choppy bay, its dark gray waves capped with frothy white whipped by some freak wind rebounding off the mountains and churning the waters as they beat against the breakwater and shore. Farther out the sea was so blue, a Mediterranean happy blue, yielding to emerald green as the sun played its magnificent tricks of light. The words of an Israeli folk song of simpler days ran through my mind. Its tune was Slavic. So was its mood expressed in the self-pitying words of the idealistic pioneering period, when sentimental young lonely men and women tilled the harsh soil and yearned for their distant home and beloveds:

> *Flow on, O waves, breakers stream,*
> *Over hill and vale,*
> *My beloved, with peace hale.*
> *Bless her while I dream.*
> *Tell her, tell her, O breaker tell*

How love cuts as does a knife.
Without her what is my life?
My pain as deep as Hell.

With this came a wave of longing for my own beloved. The temptation to indulge in self-pity is a dangerous weakness. It was actually a blessing, a stroke of great luck that she had been in Los Angeles visiting her mother when Sandor came, and that she was now out of the loop. But she hadn't heard from me for four days, and we usually speak daily when we're apart. That, too, might be a blessing, because if she had been calling and leaving messages, and *if*, as I feared, my phones were tapped, her obvious lack of information would serve to protect her.

But I needed to find a way to speak to her. I needed a different passport. Ariadne did not look like someone who could help me get the passport, nor could I ask her to call Vi. That would only force me to tell her the tale of my flight, a reverse exodus. Uneasy, I woke up early, and decided to risk talking to the night porter who was still on duty. He was a stooped old man, white-haired, and his eyes shared brightness and cynicism in shifting quantities. Show me a night porter or concierge who doesn't know how to pull strings. He was, almost inevitably, named Nikos.

I gave him twenty Euro and asked him to bring a bottle of good ouzo and some ice to my room. He came in with a bottle bought at the all-night kiosk across the way, and ice in a plastic bucket from the machine on the mezzanine floor. I began in the usual way, which he knew well, but which would give him an out, if he turned me down. "My friend needs to avoid some unfriendly people...." I said, then paused to read his expression. He looked interested. "He needs new...."

"We all have such friends, sir, from time to time. Life today has complications."

I smiled. "Good. And it is good to drink ouzo while dealing with philosophy." I poured out two half-glasses and added ice. "*Yassas*," he said, toasting me in the formal form of address. "Cheers," I said.

"Nikos, what do you think someone would need to introduce me—for my friend, of course—to the right person?'

"Such an introduction, sir, might be possible for ten percent of the fee charged—to your friend, of course—by the specialist."

"Which would be?"

"He asks about one thousand Euro, but sometimes, if there is not too much work, a bit less. Or maybe one thousand U.S. You settle with him."

We gulped down our drinks. As he left, I handed him a fifty-dollar bill. "The rest when I meet the person." He nodded.

"*Kalhnyxta kyrie.*"

"Good night to you, too, Nikos. Remember—my friend trusts you, as do I." I gave him a piercing look. That was as far as I could go in warning him about going to the police. Well, if worst came to worst, I'd go home with a Greek police escort.

Late that evening, Nikos took me to a *taverna*, introduced me to the owner, and left to begin his night shift. The tavern keeper and I walked down the hill and along the port to a rough café. There were tables for six and eight set along two sides of a balcony lined with windows overlooking the harbor. The sea air was full of diesel and salt, with the clear smell of open waters coming from the prevailing wind. The men wore rough clothing, and were probably port workers, sipping small Greek coffees and smoking. Here and there a man sat alone, sipping the local Mythos beer and puffing on his cigarette, eyes turned inward because of fatigue or in search of a sought-after memory. The man we met introduced himself as Yiorgos-George.

He took me to a dingy, barely furnished flat in a run-down street leading up from the port. I doubt whether it was even his. He snapped my picture with a pocket camera, collected five hundred dollars, and said he would meet me at the cafe in two days' time with a "fixed" authentic passport. That would be another thousand. I wondered whose passport would be stolen in the next twenty-four hours, or whether he had a supply on hand. I also knew that the *taverna* man would get a cut. Fair enough. I paid George another twenty to make a phone call to my wife, to tell her that I was traveling and would call her at her aunt's home the following day at 10 a.m. Los Angeles time. The tentacles of the ultra-orthodox extremists are long, and obedience is unquestioned. They could have her mother's number and wouldn't hesitate to tap it. But I doubted whether they would tap her aunt's phone.

That evening, Ariadne was busy preparing for a qualifying exam of some kind, but joined me for a cup of coffee. I walked with her to the bustling city center, with its side-by-side cafés and restaurants. Out of the blue she said, "You do not seem like the usual tourist. You must have family, friends... but you are here alone, in the off-season, and you seem unsettled. I do not know you, nor do I have a right to ask about your circumstances, but you are from a different world. Please tell me about your world."

I told her part of the truth. "I am avoiding some people from Israel who have threatened me. I decided to come to Crete because of its proximity to Haifa by ferryboat.

"Please don't ask me why I am avoiding them, it is complicated. Let me just say, it is not criminal, it is political. I know something they do not want the public to know.... I am a journalist, which is part of the reason I am in difficulties. I am not sure whom I can trust there. Let me also tell you that my name is really Avraham. Asher—the last name I have used at the hotel—is my middle name, but I have never used it before. And finally, Ariadne, I am married and have children, but my wife is visiting family abroad and my children, with whom I am very close, are adult and married."

I paused. "I hope that I have cleared the air."

She nodded, saying nothing. She was thinking intently. Then she nodded again. "All right," she said, "you have been careful, but I believe the part that you have revealed is true. Perhaps one day, I will learn the rest."

I walked her back to her car, "May I kiss you good-bye?"

"Of course."

I leaned forward and carefully kissed her on both cheeks. Back at the hotel, I took a long time falling asleep.

Chapter 3

Armed with my new passport, I began driving westward. The eastern side of the sausage-shaped island is not for me. Its beaches, hotels, and discos are made for sun-seeking tourists. Besides disliking tourist centers, I was afraid I might be spotted by a visiting Israeli. Until I could figure out what to do, and where to go, I needed time to reflect, peace and quiet, paper, pens, a guidebook, a Bible, a computer.

I made another call to Vi from a phone booth, via her aunt's phone, and filled her in more coherently on what had happened. From that point on, she would write to me under my new name, Anthony Appleton, in envelopes mailed from the U.S. and Europe by various friends. I arranged to write her the same way. I didn't want to use faxes or email.

I was looking for a village called Vamos. It is strung out thinly on both sides of a two-lane highway that meanders down from the main Hania-Heraklion road. I ate some salad and a vegetarian dish I didn't recognize at a restaurant on the road—the facilities were clean and the food tasty—washed down with Greek (don't say that other word beginning with "t") coffee. The people in the restaurant directed me to the local tourist office, along a narrow cobblestone lane. I felt more and more at home in this geography that was somewhere between southern Mediterranean and the Israel of the 1950s. Provence with a Middle Eastern touch—men sitting in cafés and restaurants, women shopping in stores that were something like those in Arab villages in the Galilee.

The quarters I found were beyond my wildest hopes. A square handsome building stood at the top of the rise, just beyond the tourist office, surrounded by other old stone buildings intermingled with a few more recent ones. The Turkish Governor of the area had lived there, and now the local tourist authority ran a hotel in it: large plain rooms with clean modern bathrooms. The view was of a café and restaurant with vine-clad green hills running off into the distance.

Here I rested, and here I finally halted my flight and found time to think. I jotted down the main points on paper, studied them, and then burned them. Reconstructed, in a letter to Vi, they looked something like this:

- *I cannot trust any Israeli official body. If these rabbis have "pronounced my blood free" for the shedding [hefker in Hebrew], they probably can reach easily into the police, as well as the ShaBaK.*
- *Politicians are untrustworthy, can't keep their mouths shut, and will leak the story to their favorite (or most hated, but… if they "need" him…) newspaper person.*
- *Can these rabbis be called off, mollified? I have uncovered too much corruption. My team and I found millions of shekels that were embezzled via false registration of non-existent students in all sorts of yeshivot. Among them are yeshivot of almost all the right wing—the extreme right politically and the extreme right religiously. They even include women's schools, some set up for sweet young girls from overseas, as well as for the local, equally sweet bridal crops. As we uncovered the links and ties, we found a trail leading to many different types of rabbis. And among them, we stumbled on those specific rabbis who had sanctioned Rabin's murder. They are keeping other potential murderers up their sleeve for the future, as a reserve, on tap when needed.*
- *Should I even want to mollify them? Why ask the question? Crooks are bad enough. Crooks in the name of religion! And those evil few who spawn murder? Why should I want to mollify*

them? I can't negate myself and my beliefs. Those with blood on their hands do not deserve a thought. They can go to hell.

The only reason I asked this last question was to prepare myself for Violetta's asking me. Wives tend to not want their husbands dead. Most wives, anyway. Violetta certainly agreed totally with what I was doing, and we knew we were playing hardball. But to be hit by a hardball is not the same as being hit by a truck or a bullet. Anyway, in good marriages, the partners have to work at keeping one another fully in the picture, or as much in the picture as the other wants to be. So, this is in answer to her.

- *They will not forgive, and will not forget, and they know that I have proof of their identity. We know who the murder-encouragers, the truly guilty, are. They are not afraid of scandals over money. They know politicians can be bought by promises of support—of votes. Stealing is okay, if it does not carry too long a prison sentence. But murder and incitement to murder? That they must cover up. They will try to mollify me until they can rid of me.*
- *What about going to the press? I cannot document the threats against me. What happened that night in Jerusalem? Just a visit by a friend, not recorded. Trying to go public would lead to one reaction: this is a wild, unsubstantiated story. Scandal for a day.... But I would still be on the list.*

So, there's your answer, Violetta darling.

My first responsibility is to stay alive, BUT (very big but) to make sure I do not endanger my family. The children will be alright. By now, Sandor will have "happened" to bump into one of them. In his own way, without revealing all, or very much, he will tell them what they need to know. My second responsibility is to record this story, and some of the basic facts, and to ensure that all of this is preserved:

Preserved so that the historical truth will eventually come out.

Preserved for my children, and grandchildren, and perhaps those who come after them. They will be shocked not by my views, but by seeing the depth of disgust and hatred these people have evoked in me. The hypocrites, the poseurs, the careerists, the carpetbaggers, the plunderers of the public purse, the liars, the false, the fickle; I hated them all. Not because they were what they were. That I would merely despise. But because they did it shamelessly in the name of God, and what is almost as holy, some did what they did in the name of Israel.

I don't have faith and deep belief in everything the prophets spoke, but I am hopelessly intoxicated, possessed by their fervor for justice, and their hatred for the false and the hypocritical. Especially toward those who were priests or ruler—they were to be judged more harshly, their acts weighed more carefully.

Having unburdened myself on paper—at least temporarily—I felt much calmer. Now what, now where, now how? These were my next questions. I had been away less than a week. It seemed like months. I should lie low for at least several weeks to make sure that I am not was not being followed. It would also take that long to test my new identity. It would probably take that long to establish a safe way to maintain contact with Violetta, so that we could try to decide how to go forward from there.

Vamos sounds Spanish, but is as Cretan as can be. From there I decided to head on to Hania and get to know the country a bit. Ariadne recommended Melia, a tiny remote village where she might join me. She had bought me a portable phone and activated it in her name so we could be in touch. I was still too afraid to use it to call Vi, but I gave her the number in case of emergency.

To be a tourist in Hania and Melia, just sleeping, walking, and reading, seemed an appealing way to make time pass. I trimmed the three-day beard I had started, and decided to comb my hair differently and wear a hat whenever possible, resolving to buy a number of them so that I could change them often. Needless to say, I'd never had training in spycraft, but Le Carré was a good teacher. I really missed a laptop computer, something simple that I could write on. I was able to get English and French books in Hania, as well as a tape recorder to play language tapes, and a lesson book and Greek dictionary. I might as well use my time productively. I was angry—furious—that those gangsters had turned me into an exile. They would pay the reckoning one day. But for the moment it was better for me to keep my head down and wait.

It was in Melia that things began to happen. Life often brings surprises in clusters, as if once one leaves the normal groove everything and anything can happen. Ariadne had driven up through the rolling and somehow frightening hills in her little car along a deserted road that mounted from the seaside highway. She arrived looking frightened. The tavern keeper and some of her friends had told her that a man with a dark curly beard and dark skin had been asking about a tall older American "with a name different from yours."

"The man was looking for an Avraham Benheim. The description sounded like you, but the name was wrong. You have told me that something forces you to hide and I was afraid. I thought you should know that people are asking about you." She paused, and her silence was profound. "I don't see you as evil or criminal—you already told me that this is about politics. I will trust what you tell me."

Melia is a village that was wiped out by plague one hundred fifty years ago. It lay empty, hidden by mountain peaks and high hills over five hundred meters above sea level. Goats and small animals lived in the black stone buildings, and fear and foreboding inhabited the deserted homes. No one came to redeem it. A few years ago, a group of idealistic environmentalists rebuilt the houses, some that were merely freestanding little square structures, and then the few larger buildings that were perhaps once a monastery or home of the local patriarch. They repaired and renewed it all, leaving the wall indentations where the oil lamps had been placed, and building amenities and showers in each unit. With this, they adopted strict rules: no imported electricity burning fossil fuels. They heated their water and powered their generators with wood fires, and opened a hotel-refuge, with food and bread made there, simple hearty fare, and bunches of sage hanging from the ceilings in the dining room.

It is negative tourism at its best. No raucous music, no excess lights or sound. Hills and tended valleys, green, rounded hilltops close by, fading into sharper and higher brown peaks looking east and south. To reach the village, one has to travel six kilometers on an unpaved road that branches off from the north-south road connecting Kastali and the barren and rocky stern south. Few know Melia; few will come to it. The only visitors are fine young people, some backpackers, some from abroad who discover its secret charm and are willing to overlook its forbidding past. It offers hope for the battered city-dwellers of the West and for the refugees from the tourist hotels and raped landscapes of beach resorts.

Ariadne and I stayed in separate little buildings, each of us alone in our own private apartment. Ariadne told the "manager"—it seemed more like a kibbutz of the fifties than a hotel—that we were expecting a dark, bearded gentleman, but wanted to surprise him. The young man, by his accent Austrian or Swiss, promised to let us know when he arrived.

Ariadne was smart, street smart as well as intelligent. I hadn't bargained for that. She had also brought me some light brown hair dye, and suggested that I change my walk from my usual American stride to a shorter-stepping European city-dweller's pace. Could I manage without my spectacles? I could, and affected a trans-Atlantic upper-class accent, something between Southern England and the Northeastern American intonations of Roosevelt. She advised me to pitch my voice somewhat higher, or say little in front of others, because my voice had a special timbre that would give me away.

In Melia, the almost pitch-black night is clad in mystery. Gentle breezes stir the bushes and trees separating the stone houses. The first night we were there, Ariadne and I decided to go for a walk. She told me her life story, and I told her mine. She was open, critical, and amazingly frank. She had had a lover. A jealous man. "I gave him cause," she said.

That was fair. I skimmed the highlights of my life, playing down my public roles, and poking fun at myself. She saw through it easily, I think.

"You were born in Canada."

"I was not only born there, I was educated there through part of university."

"So, why did you go to Israel?"

"Simply because I was a Zionist."

"I do not know exactly what that is."

"I believed that the Jews, in order to be safe from the anti-Semitism, or Jew-hatred, in many countries, needed a territory of their own, and their own self-defense. I also believed, and still do believe, that in the modern world of mass culture, we need a place where we can develop our old culture in new ways...."

"Is there still hatred of Jews? I thought it existed only in the past."

"Ask your fellow citizens. Even the most liberal have been exposed to a couple of thousand years of blaming us for killing a Jew called Jesus. To you, it may seem unimportant, but even Kazantzakis's grandmother told him that around Easter, Jews put a Christian child in a barrel studded with nails to extract blood for our Passover bread, matzot."

To escape the heaviness of that topic, we decided to choose a subject each, to take our discussions away from biography of fact to biography of mind. Ariadne chose poetry, and quoted me a few poems by Kavafis and Kavvadias.

It had been so many years since I had really opened myself up to poetry. Too many years writing essays and speeches and pretending to be an academic had made me ponderous and heavy. Too much reading of biography and history and the recurrent and ongoing battle of the prophets against evil-doers had made me cynical. I told her that I think I am happiest when I study the Bible. I love the language and the challenge to understand, and the internal nuclear war that rages between the rationalist and the naïve young person of faith who is gone forever. I quoted her parts of the poems of Moses and Miriam at the Red Sea, of Deborah celebrating her victory, of David lamenting his beloved Jonathan and Saul, and promised to give her the text of the great orations of Moses and Isaiah, both calling on Heaven and Earth to lend an ear.

The next evening we ate dinner a bit earlier and walked again as the day drew to a close. In that hilltop valley, the setting sun casts the shadow of the mountain across the village so it becomes darkling, obscure, and the sharp shapes of the houses fade into the hillside. The tops of the eastern ridge are still bright, and then the lambent orange touches the range of rolling hills and lights the tops with the warm glow of the last sun. Then it too fades, until the undulating backdrop becomes just an opaque cardboard cut-out against a deepening blue, a blueness slowly dying to black, pitch-black, until the moon rises.

At the darkening hour in Melia, the wood-generated electric power faintly lights up the lamps set into black shale and Cretan stone. I wondered whether I could unravel for Ariadne the social and historical forces that created this war that has turned me—who had been close to the founding fathers—into the prey, the hunted, the exiled. As the shades of night drew down, hundreds of kilometers of land and sea away, I tried to make sense for her of what my history teachers called the underlying causes. I had been—and still was—so angry, uprooted, and usurped from the kind of country we had been. These people are total believers and can do whatever they want, all in the name of God... fuck us however they want because they have a monopoly on God's word. I didn't know how I was going to be able to say all this to her, leaping across history and culture without terrifying her with my flaring anger and consuming hatred.

"It's very hard to understand Israel. It's such a mixture."

"Of what?"

"Of people, history, religion, languages. I'll give you an example. I was born in Canada. Canada is my land of birth, upbringing, and education. Western values, English, literature, French, all these flow from my being Canadian."

"But you are an Israeli."

"Yes. Israel is my homeland by history, religion, and choice. In Israel I am considered a Canadian or an English-speaker or a Canadian Israeli Jew. So, in our homeland we are all, in a way, displaced people."

"I don't see how, if you chose to be there."

"I said before, maybe not in these words, that I had left home to come to the homeland. Well, that's part of our duality. Our home, once left, is never our home again, and, at the same time, it's always home, the virtual home of our dependence, of cushioning support and love and high expectations. So, it is forever home."

"You mean that you are dual. That should enrich you."

"It does. But let me try to explain how complicated it is to be an Israeli. Every few years different groups of Jews return to—that is, choose to go to—Israel, or sometimes are forced to come, by being pushed out of their original homelands. So they come to an ancient dreamed-about homeland with very many different visions. Some just want a roof and food and job. Some want to prepare for the Messiah. Some are idealistic socialists, trying to create a model society and model Jews. Some were ejected by Hitler from Germany before World War II and wanted to live in a Germanized Western European Israel."

"I thought that these were displaced persons—DPs, I think?"

"DPs are those who survived the war and were held in camps for displaced persons until they could find where to go. Those who tried going back to Poland in 1946 were greeted by pogroms. Do you know that word?"

"I think it is when the Jews were attacked by their neighbors."

"So, we have a homeland that is home and not home because we are all displaced as it grows and changes and prospers and takes in the myriads of wanderers."

"But you have Arabs there."

"Yes. Even if they live here on ancestral land, the Israeli Arabs are displaced, because they are a minority in Israel where they feel they are the majority in the Middle East. To generalize...."

I continued. "Listen, Ariadne, here's the strangest part: the Jews, the majority, even if they have lived here for decades or centuries, or even if they have come 'home' as good Zionists—the Jews too are displaced. Not just the hundreds of thousands of Jews who came from the camps. Each wave of immigration to Israel displaces the previous. Language shifts. Modes of dress and thinking change all too rapidly, and so, too swiftly, do private behavior and public mores.

"You know, maybe an example would be best. The mixtures. A story."

"I am listening."

We walked back to the large verandah overlooking the dark hills. I got myself an Ouzo from the kitchen staff who were cleaning up, and brought her some tea.

"This'll take a few minutes. You have heard of Caesarea."

"A Byzantine city in Palestine."

"Yes. I'll tell you about a magic evening in Caesarea, in the renewed Roman amphitheater in the old city. The Bolshoi danced *Giselle*. Nina Ananeishvilla was the *prima ballerina*."

"We have no ballet in Crete," said Ariadne. "Just sometimes in Athens."

"In the fifty minutes of the first act, tears rolled from my eyes. I didn't weep, or sob. Tears just flowed. It was the setting, the fusion of dance and music, remembering where we were sitting, where all the splendor and cruelty of Rome and Byzantium existed on the wreckage of the Jewish Second Temple State.

"The orchestra too was perfect. The Rishon LeTzion Symphony. Orchestra of a minor town.... But the ex-Soviet conductor was leading an orchestra that was overwhelmingly Russian—all Jews or married to Jews or descendants of ex-Soviet Jews—they played as though possessed by angels. Perfect rhythm, perfect cues for the dancers, perfect balance, in that Roman theater overlooking the sea. No doubt most of the players, perhaps all of them, had not in their wildest dreams seen themselves playing for the Bolshoi. *The Bolshoi*."

She nodded. I saw on her face a combination of focus and almost of envy. She was seeing it with me. I went on.

"The Russian-speakers—perhaps one out of three in the audience—sat with their children, often in the expensive seats. Most had been in the country fewer than ten years. Blonde, quite frequently beautiful Slavic blonde, high-cheeked young women in party dresses, not costly, but levels above street clothes, sat with their pretty little well-dressed future ballerinas, sun-streaked hair pulled back into chignons held in white net.

"Their grandfathers may have been saber-wielding Cossacks, Ukrainian, and Russian *pogromchiks,* killers from the Black Hundreds, or even true followers of the now-dead Stalinist-Marxist god. But if they had one Jewish grandparent, or their spouse had—they could come in.

"Some of the Russian women, comfortably plump, wore shoddy CIS-made evening gowns. To me, that was a touching reminder that this was their best, and 'we *kalturnyi* always wear our best to The Ballet.' The women in gowns, their husbands in shirt-sleeves."

"What do you mean by Israeli—aren't the Russians Israelis too?"

"Exactly. They are the newest batch, and the people I called Israelis are older batches, who have lost their obvious previous ethnicity. Young and old Israeli couples, intense intellectuals, dressed in the leftist, would-be bohemian-fashion Sheinkin-Street mode, where these types hang out. Some wore *kippot,* small skullcaps indicating that they observe religious practices carefully. Then there were just people, those who came to see, along with a few social climbers who had come to be seen or so they could brag to their friends. Watching the people is a second show, a study in applied sociology."

I stopped. Enough. How much could she absorb? I closed my eyes for a moment. I could still see the people who had arrived in special buses and hundreds and hundreds of cars. Couples strolling along the paths from leveled parking lots, the Byzantine and Crusader and Turkish city behind the Roman theater next to them, the Russian ballet ahead of them. Each with his or her painful and prideful past; most with a danger-laden future. The streaming, strolling crowds pouring from all sides, past the cars and along the footpaths, converging on the entrance, like a great scene from Fellini or Eisenstadt.

Ariadne asked if I felt alright. I sighed, and said, "Just reliving it all. And homesick for that mad quilt of a country...."

She said, tentatively, "I am beginning to understand more. Before we met, I thought Israel was a great power with tens of millions of citizens, with a vast army which threatened the Palestinians and the whole Middle East. So I went to the library and looked in the atlas. It's tiny, and its name won't fit on its territory on the map, and just a few million people live there. It is amazing to me. I did not know this."

"But let me go back to the ballet," I said, "for that was the real experience, a night of joy and tears, a night of deep self-recognition. Innocent Giselle dies. The heart cannot live with betrayal. Bolshoi danced a lament for broken love, for recognizing too late that love cannot resurrect the dead, and that which dies, dies within us.

"So, I am sad to be away from all of this. But I am in the middle of a fight and I want to live."

Ariadne had listened without moving, but I saw her absorb every expression, every nuance, leaping across languages, cultures, civilizations, literatures to our common humanity. We walked back in silence. In the hills, silence means the soughing of wind and the shifting of branches, the skittering of small animals, the chirping of the cicadas in Greek or Minoan, and the round black contours of the surrounding mountains. I left her at her door. She turned to me, and at first shyly, then determinedly, kissed my cheek, said softly, "*Kalhnyxta*," and entered her bungalow. The door closed gently and I heard my steps across the narrow stone pathway as I dodged plants and branches and walked down the few steps to my own bungalow.

As I entered, I saw in the dim starlight a form sitting in the rattan chair in the corner. I looked around for a weapon. My kingdom for a blunt instrument. He spoke English, with barely a trace of an Israeli accent.

"Relax, Mr. Appleton. Manny Shiloh is my friend. Please sit down."

My blood pressure dropped from a rocketing spiral and I felt faint. I told him that I needed a drink of water, and then sat on the edge of my bed. "May I turn on the light?"

"Why not?"

Whoever my intruder was, he was not one of the stalkers. Manny Shiloh had been a senior official in the Mossad, retired like me. Once he had asked me to provide him with a cover on a visit to a European country, and I had allowed him to pose as my assistant. Someone had noted my presence in Crete, and someone else in the organization knew enough to relate me to Manny. Tenuous links, worrying links.

I let my breath out, and asked, "I suppose your name is Yosef Magen, or something as imaginative as that." He chuckled. Yosef Magen was one of the code names they gave operatives in dry runs and other training exercises.

I took out a bottle of Ouzo and poured us two drinks. "Yosef" was over thirty-five, maybe even forty, and trim, dressed in stylish leisure clothes. If he was armed, he could only have had a leg holster.

"How's Manny?" I asked him in Hebrew.

"Fine. Sends regards. But let's speak English, you never know who is where...."

"Yosef" told me that on his undercover visits to Europe, he regularly checked with his informants. A passport forger had told him about someone with a very Israeli name who had commissioned a passport. A bell had gone off in a coded computer check. Anyone who had once held high-level security clearance, no matter how long ago, was routinely included on an automated checklist. When I turned up, they checked with Manny, who vouched for me, but offered to come and find out what was going on. They turned him down. (Well of course they did, I thought to myself; the new boys don't want the old boys wandering around).

"If Manny thought it was worth his while to come here, we decided to trace you, and found out where you had been, and followed you through the car rental information." The young woman with me had thrown him off—he thought perhaps this was just a romantic secret tryst. Nonetheless, he still thought that he should warn me.

"Of what, of meeting young women?"

"*La-bri-ut*," he smiled, lapsing into the Hebrew slang meaning

"To your health," or simply, "Enjoy, it's none of my business." Come to think of it, a wonderful word.

"So?"

"So, Mr. Appleton, there was a man with a beard asking about you at the hotel in Heraklion."

"*Haredi?*" Ultra-orthodox?

"Right. An Arab *haredi*. The Hamas man here. The hotel desk or the passport forger, both are neutral about who pays for information."

I groaned to myself. Or maybe aloud.

"Your identity may be known to them, and they would love to kidnap you. An Israeli with a forged passport. Who knows what they might do to you? Kidnapping? You are a Canadian originally, your wife is American. The West and Israel—they would claim that you are at least Prince of the Jews, Master of the Western Hemisphere, agent of the Mossad, CIA, Canadian Foreign Intelligence.... Anything."

"You just came to warn me?"

"Yes, but Manny owes you one. He wants you to know that the Palestinian extremists will conduct the *intifada* under all circumstances. If not in Israel, then wherever they can. You are on someone's list, for reasons I don't know. You might. Manny does. We think you should get out of here before trouble starts. I'll have a clean passport for you. I will buy you a ferry ticket to wherever you choose, and want you to lie low. Change your appearance, change your clothes."

This was coming too fast. Two sets of danger, and one of them too close for comfort. The bearded man was a Muslim, not a Jew. Not much consolation. "Yosef" gave me a cell phone and electric charger.

"Keep it on at all times. If I call, I'll say 'Manny speaking.' If you call, say 'Manny's friend.' Keep everything simple, but if you are in trouble, state as calmly as possible where you are and what is happening. Just pretend you are back reporting again, and it's happening to someone else. Speak quietly, but don't slur words. The number keyed in as #1 will be monitored at all hours.

"You should leave Heraklion as soon as possible. In the meantime, use a different hotel there. I'll have your passport and ticket ready. Just call me to say where you are."

End of conversation, a handshake, and a bad night. A very bad night. I kept tossing and turning. Finally, I got up and copied out a few lines I'd found in a magazine.

> *Whether exploited by traditional religions or political religions, psychological totalism—the unquestioning fealty to one God, one truth, and one right, embodied in one faith, one cause, one party—has everywhere provided the tinder of persecution.*
> *—Jack Beatty, "The Tyranny of Belief," The Atlantic, September 13, 2000.*

Once I would have taken pleasure from such a neat formulation. But, when it's about you, not an abstract idea or a "they," that's a different story.

Chapter 4

The French call it *une nuit blanche*, a white night, sleepless.... The Israeli ultras were looking for me, because of what I did against them. The Arab ultras were out to get me just because I was here—my very existence was offensive to them. I now had them coming at me from both sides. I had visions of spending the rest of my life like some pigeon or hen, constantly jerking its head from side to side, alert to danger and attack. As Descartes would have said, *Sum, ergo mortiturus!* I am, therefore I must die.

We were being hunted again. My grandparents and their grandparents and theirs and theirs before them must have known this feeling across generations, centuries. My cousins and uncles and aunts in Poland knew it and lost. I would not lose. *I will not lose.*

It was time for cold logic and no emotion. After a silent breakfast, during which Ariadne cast questioning glances my way, I simply asked her to pack and leave. I would settle the bill, but would stay in my room for ten more minutes, and meet her at the car exit. She understood that this was not a time for questions.

In my heightened state of tension, I almost exploded with frustration when, as I was settling the bill, the young man in charge of the refuge casually asked to show me something. I was in a rush, I explained. I knew that I had to move fast and I really needed to use the hair dye Ariadne had brought. But life is a magician with a rabbit in his hat.

Jorgen, the Austrian manager, persisted, his pale blue, nearly washed-out eyes searching my face. "We were digging through the foundations of an abandoned house we want to renovate, and I found a batch of papers with what looks like looks like ancient writing. It had been packed away in a jar, sealed, and covered with wax. It's not Greek. It's not Turkish, because I've seen the old Turkish inscriptions, when they still used Arabic script."

He spoke unhurriedly, slowly, calmly. The ground was burning beneath my feet. In spite of myself, my curiosity was aroused. "Can I see it?" I asked. I almost regretted my request when he seemed to take forever to retrieve a package from one of the desk drawers and carefully extract a bundle of pages from its various layers of wrapping. But when he finally placed a thick manuscript on the counter between us, my heart leapt right out of my breast.

It was written in a squarish print-script I immediately recognized that had been used by medieval Spanish and Italian Jews. The cotton-based paper had held up well. Apparently the sealed jar, carefully coated in a wax preservative, had kept dampness from ruining the contents down the intervening centuries.

Jorgen looked at me. I felt myself pale, but said nothing. Perhaps this was a test. Perhaps he was working with the other side. I decided that his eyes showed curiosity and nothing else.

I said, "Look, I think this could be in a Semitic language. It could be Aramaic, or maybe Hebrew. It looks like things I once saw at university. But I simply cannot delay. I have to leave now." Still I hesitated, finally going on to say, "If you want, I'll take it with me, and ask some friends of mine about it. They are experts and will be able to tell if the paper is safe to handle. They will also know about the language.

"I can tell you that this may well be valuable and I may be able to help you sell it. I sometimes dabble in buying and selling old books. I know this place can use some money. Let me handle this for you and I will charge you fifteen percent as my commission. Once I do the research and establish its provenance and age, I might be able to get a handsome amount for you."

In his careful and almost excruciatingly meticulous way, Jorgan asked me what provenance meant. I mentally gritted my teeth and explained. And then, unusually for me, I played the role of the book dealer and pushed. "If you send it to the University in Heraklion, it will lie around for another few hundred years. It's not ancient—the paper and the jar prove that—so it is not covered by the antiquities regulations. I will give you a receipt, and will contact you here within two weeks."

Jorgen stood still for another minute, while he pondered my proposal, and then a charming little smile played at the corner of his eyes. "Why not? Why not? You look honest. How much do you think it might bring?"

I forced myself to stay still and reply. "Without an expert opinion, I couldn't say. As a curiosity, a few thousand euro. If it is unique, much, much more. Once I get back to Hania, I'll call some people who will know better." The smile moved down and spread across the Austrian's face. Again, he said, "Why not." This time it was a statement.

A handshake, and done. I rushed to the bungalow, performed the fastest hair wash in history, and hurried to the car with a hat pulled down over my head, still wet and itchy from the astringent coloring. I hoped that mentioning Hania to Jorgen might throw followers off my track.

Once we were on the road, I began explaining. "Ariadne, without meaning to, I have placed you in grave danger."

Again, she said nothing.

"At the first village or town on the northern coastal road, I'll take the bus to Hania and then on to Heraklion. In addition to my Jewish enemies, it looks like Arab agents, Hamas, are looking for me. That's all you need to know right now; we don't have much time till the main road.

"If you know some people who are high up in the police or security services, you can tell them this: you might be a target of Arab agents. Tell them that you have befriended an Israeli, whose original name (from the first hotel) is Avraham Asher. He has just told you that you are in danger because these agents are looking for him. They probably know that you have spent time showing him Melia.

"Tell them anything, but explain, please explain that these people would probably want to interrogate you. If they do, they use torture without qualms."

Ariadne spoke very quietly. "I only know traffic police who give me speeding tickets—" we both laughed a bit "—and security people. They must be so secret that if I ever met one, I wouldn't even know." I had to admire her sang-froid.

"Not too much time for jokes, Ariadne. If you have no such contacts, find some excuse to get back to your home village in the Plain of Messara. There, tell your father the same story. Tell him to make sure family and friendly neighbors know. Keep the armed villagers, cousins, and friends nearby. Make sure they're the kind who are willing and able to put any stranger through his paces.

"After all, you've told me that in these villages the *vendetta* is still alive." She had said that men keep firearms handy, and xenophobia—a good Greek word—was a given for village people.

"Okay," she said. "We use the word *vendetta*, which we learned from the Venetians. Makes sense," she added, "to go home for a while."

"I'm sorry I got you into this."

"Well, I asked you if you were feeling alright when I saw you in Knossos. So, the right question... wrong diagnosis...."

We both laughed, the tension eased for a moment. I said, "You know, on second thought, I am sure you'll be safer at home than in Heraklion. It should pass over in a few days. And they may not be on your track at all. I just want you to take care." I leaned across and kissed her cheek at a bus stop on the National Road.

I dozed on the bus to Hania, where I changed to another bus to Heraklion. At the stop just outside Heraklion, the passenger next to me got off, and his place was taken by another, younger-looking man, who nodded a greeting and smiled at me. I nodded and dozed some more.

As the smelly bus pulled into Heraklion, hours after I had left Ariadne, the man turned to me and said very softly, "I have a gun pointed at you. Just get up, take your bag. Do exactly what I say, or I will shoot you. There is a silencer on this pistol." He pressed something against me. It could have been a gun.

A second man took my bag from me as I stepped off the bus. Both were young, well built; they could have been Mediterraneans of any nationality. The accent was—I assumed—Arab. Or was it? I moved on carefully while a third man came up on my other side, taking my arm in a friendly fashion. I just kept going. They put me into the back seat of a car, one on each side of me. The bag lay on the front seat beside the third man who had taken the wheel.

"Close your eyes and pretend to rest or we'll need to bind your eyes." We drove a few blocks. I remembered from spy novels that the hero was supposed to keep track of time and the number of turns the car made and the types of noises and smells outside the car. But all I heard was the blood pounding in my ears. I wasn't afraid—it was more like paralysis.

If this were an Alistair MacLean novel, the next series of events would probably begin with something like, "Once I was safely out of the hands of Hamas...." What actually happened was stranger than anything in MacLean's fiction. When the car stopped I was taken—blindfolded—into a house. I could tell that it was in a town or city because I heard traffic sounds and the smell of cooking, as if from a restaurant in the same building or very nearby.

My captors didn't tie or chain me to the bed. They didn't handcuff me, and they treated me with care, except for one thing. My pleasant-looking seat mate from the bus told me with deadly calm, "Choose between this gag or a promise to keep quiet. If you make a commotion, we will kill you with either this—or this." The first "this" was a sharp six-inch-long hunting knife with a brown bone handle. The second "this" was a 9-mm. automatic, with a round silencer on its barrel.

I promised.

The interrogation had barely begun when the phone rang in another room, and I heard a voice murmuring, with pauses. One end of a phone call. While the conversation continued, I said to the two men who had stayed with me, "I'm an antique book dealer. I found this manuscript in Melia." The questions went on for about an hour. *Where did you come from? Where do you live? Who is your family? On and on....* Then the other would begin: *What is your real name? Where do you really live...?*

They went through my suitcase, and made no remark about the Hebrew script. Perhaps they wouldn't have recognized it anyway—it wasn't like Hebrew script used today, or like modern print. Abruptly, the interrogation ceased. The two must have been waved out of the room by the man I never saw, the third man. I heard him muttering something to them. I had no idea what was going on. I was exhausted from the rush and ebb of adrenalin pumping up my reactions and then crashing me down into almost unbearable fatigue.

Everyone has some way of handling too much stress. Mine is sleep. They let me use the toilet, gave me a drink of water, and I fell asleep on the bed. When I woke up, there was almost perfect silence. In the darkness, I made an accounting. So far, they had been kind captors. This could have been a technique to relax me, catch me off guard. It could have meant that they were inexperienced. Finally, maybe they just had orders to verify my identity.

After what seemed like hours, the silence suddenly spoke to me. I realized that I hadn't heard any sounds at all within the apartment. No one steadily breathing in his sleep. Nobody shifting position in bed, or flushing a toilet, sniffling, or coughing.

This silence was too silent.

I tried to still my own suddenly rapid breathing, and listened again. Nothing.

Kidnappers, especially would-be executors, do not leave explanations. I was alone in an unknown apartment, in an unknown street, in an unknown town. Perhaps it was a metaphor for life itself. I tiptoed across the room, still hearing nothing and, fearfully, heart pounding, tried soundlessly to check each room, each]dark except for slivers of light from the street lamps creeping through the drawn louvers.

Nothing. Nothing again. Nothing.

I made my way to the front door. Unlocked. I returned to the room where I had slept, took my small suitcase, and left. The night was almost gone and I saw a distant pink glow, heralding dawn. They must have put something into the water; I had slept deeply.

I saw that I was right. I was in a town, with three- and four-story apartment buildings rising around me, sounds of people speaking in hushed voices, and dogs barking. Bag in hand, I started walking, calculating that if the dawning sun, still below the horizon, was on my right, I was walking north towards the sea. I would find a main road there.

And so I made my way, finally arriving after half an hour's walk at the central square of Heraklion. We had never even left the city.

I found a large hotel, rang for the porter or duty manager manning the lonely night shift. He gave me a knowing, jaded look. How many men had he seen check in at dawn with dark circles under their eyes, pale, disheveled, and furtive?

I washed my face and drank tap water, too weak to shower or bathe, and slept another long deep sleep. At noon, I called Manny's man, the name I had mentally assigned "the Mossad operative."

I ate ravenously in a small *taverna* while he listened glumly to my story. He looked at me with cold eyes. "If it weren't for Manny's knowing you, I wouldn't believe a word you say. Hamas would either kill you, or dope you up and smuggle you to Libya or Syria. Then they'd use you a bargaining chip or trade-in for one of their people we have.

"This was not Hamas, I'll never believe that."

I looked at him incredulously. I was angry. "So, who was it? The Israeli ultras?" He shrugged. As far as I was concerned, I was a distraction from his main job, and he owed me no more time. He handed me another passport, a ticket to the ferry to Piraeus, and stood up. "By the way," he gave me as his farewell blessing, "you look good in your new getup."

I had to think for a minute about which new look I was wearing at the moment. Oh, yes, I was now presenting with a dirty-blond head, a baseball cap, and wrap-around sunglasses.

I reminded myself of the Parisian taxi driver, who said indignantly to me one day, "*Quoi, ils croient que je suis idiot?* What do they take me for, a fool, those spooks? They get into the car, give the exact address of their office, and think that behind the sunglasses and under the hat, no one will know what they are? Do they take all of us for idiots? They might as well make an announcement, wearing that uniform…."

Here I am now, the spook. I decided that it was more enjoyable to read about it than to be in the middle of it. Up to the neck.

By this time, Ariadne was my only ally. I wasn't sure about Manny's friend anymore. The weird episode with the kidnapping had left me wondering. Had I been given another warning? Were they Israeli ultras or Arab Hamas? Why did they let me go?

That evening, as soon as Ariadne had finished at the clinic, we left for Sfakia. She knew the area from her national service as a doctor, and believed I would be safest there.

This time she had exchanged cars with a cousin, found a wig, and wore a head scarf and dark, drab clothes. I, too, wore my French spook sunglasses and regulation baseball cap. Sfakia. I could see, as though still a pupil in Canada, the handsome *Sigma*, the unusual *Phi*, and the stately *Kappa*. Sfakia. Σφακια.

Ariadne began my introduction to the new area: we drove through brutal brownish mountains, crisscrossed by deep gorges. Herds of domesticated goats and their wild longhorn mountain cousins, the ibex, were leaping from rock to rock, where no man could follow on the steep crags and cliffs.

Sfakia sounded like the right choice, a region that no foreign conqueror had ever completely controlled. Its fierce mountain people had fought the invaders with a verve and dedication that was overwhelming. When there were no foreigners to fight off, they often killed one another. *Vendetta!* Ariadne told me a "once upon a time" story.

In the village of "A" there were perhaps thirty black stone houses, each with a fence and a yard and a vegetable garden. Chickens pecked for fodder, and roosters welcomed the false dawn with their call to renew living. Nearby were the fields on the plateau, across a deep gorge that ran some kilometers to the Libyan Sea. On a hot, very hot summer day, during the mid-day napping hours, a child played in his yard. Played, shouting and singing as children do. The irate next-door neighbor yelled at the child, scaring him into shocked, fearful silence. Then came the child's father, no less irate. The rifles were brought down from the wall, and by that evening there were eleven new graves in the small old graveyard next to the tiny church. Within days, the village had become a ghost town as whole families fled the vendetta.

"Once upon a time" was just a few decades ago. To this day, as I saw when we stopped to walk into that ill-fated village, goats graze through the deserted homes, the doors hang loosely, grass grows in clumps of soil carried inside by the strong winds and filling in the empty rooms, the empty windows. No furniture, no furnishings. Nothing. Death hangs over the ruined black houses, which echo with long-past gunshots.

Hora Sfakion is a small town sprawling down to the Libyan Sea, on the lapping blue waters of an inlet used for coastal shipping and a marina for fishing boats. We stopped for lunch at Giorgio's (pronounced Yorgio's in modern Greek). Ariadne vouched for the owner's discretion. "Call me George," he said. He was swarthy, in his thirties, slim, resembling—for all the world—an Arab from the Galilee or a third-generation Jewish Yemenite. He was open, friendly, ready to prepare whatever we wanted. I had a beer and invited him to join us. After we had chatted for a while, I asked my question: "And how do people get along here?" Possibly a stupid question, a tourist's question....

"Very well. Good."

I mumbled some encouraging word or other, which he ignored.

"They have to. If not, they *khill* you!" He made it a guttural "kh" or "ch" like the Greek letter Chi. Kill you, chill you. The point was clear. He smiled, a closed smile.

The car climbed the stark hill and cliff, rising steep and high. Behind us, the evening sun turned the sea orange, red. We sped through a sprawling sleepy town and crossed the bridge over a deep gorge. Ten minutes later we came to an isolated cluster of well-tended houses overlooking small vineyards and olive groves that had been hacked out of the hills millennia ago, or at least centuries ago.

The headman of this little area, close to eighty, was a walking advertisement for the Cretan diet, (the original model for the famed "Mediterranean diet") and he could have modeled mustachio wax as well. Naturally his name was Ioannis. Ariadne had nursed his old mother, then a mere ninety-five, during her last days. Yogurt and honey, *raki*, and a small amount of wine every day prolongs life. If the genes are right, of course. That's how modern man says, "God willing." Ioannis also smoked. Well, at his age, as Golda Meir once said about herself, he won't die young anyway.

Ioannis arranged for a private little house to be cleaned up and put at my disposal. It was spare—if not Spartan, then at least Cretan. "His son used to live here, before joining a monastery," Ariadne translated. "An old woman will come to cook and shop and clean. No one will mention your presence. Ioannis's word here is binding," she explained.

I asked her, "Otherwise, they will *khill* you?" She shrugged. I said, "Here and now, that's a reassuring thought."

To seal the bargain Ioannis handed me an old, well-oiled, long-barreled Luger with two full cartridge clips. Ariadne looked at me with wide eyes. He had adopted me, indeed. Later she told me the pistol had been taken from a Nazi officer he had killed after the Germans decimated all the men of Anogeia and ten more villages, which they then pillaged and razed to the ground. (They had wiped out dozens of men mercilessly on suspicion that they had, in 1943, harbored a small band of local partisans and British officers who had kidnapped the German commanding general, Major-General Heinrich von Kreipe. The general, who was taken unharmed, had been spirited away on a British submarine to Egypt.)

"The Luger is not a gift, only a loan. I know that Ioannis always carries a small revolver." She smiled at the recollection.

"How do you know?"

"I danced with him at a wedding here, and I touched it at his waist."

I asked why. She laughed a little girl laugh. "It's hard to believe, but he always carries it. You see, forty years ago his brother killed a man. Ioannis thinks that the dead man's family might still be carrying on the *vendetta*."

Ioannis had shown me how to click off the safety, draw back the slide to get the first bullet into the breech, and warned me to shoot for the body, instinctively. No fancy grips, no fancy stance. I haven't had a hand gun since my old French revolver, a St. Etienne 1892, that I used on the range, with great accuracy I still boast, right after the 1956 Sinai campaign. In my time in the army, we had fired only ancient Mauser rifles—some with German and Nazi markings from the two world wars—and the then-new wonder weapon, the homemade Uzi.

A middle-aged man strung an electric cable from Ioannis's house to my stone hut and installed light bulbs—bare, but adequate—and made sure the switches and power outlet worked. While we ate Sfakian pancakes and drank cups of coffee, the old woman, Ekaterina, cleaned the house and set out the linen and bed coverings. I could hear her pumping water, and washing dishes, pots, and pans.

No one who came after me would be a match for my hosts. After the vaunted Germanic thoroughness, mere Hamas or Israeli ultras would be easy prey. Years had passed, but Ioannis was still armed, and the younger men were now the age he had been when he killed the German major. And, in the last resort, I was armed as well. Finally, I felt safe. Even the Mossad would not find me here easily.... Maybe that was good, too.

We ate a quiet meal at Ioannis's table, set under spreading grape vines that created a leafy entry-way into his house. A cool breeze wafted in from the Libyan Sea. Twilight slowly descended; day melded into a velvety night with myriad stars visible in the darkness, unhampered by city glow. The same stars that Apollo and Venus had seen, and Abraham and David.

I slept heavily and toward dawn dreamed that Ariadne had come in under the covers, to give me warmth and comfort. Later I half awoke to see the hazy dawn beginning to light up the window, and heard her car starting. Was my dream a reflected memory of Abraham and David's starry night?

Now my biding time could be filled easily. A new road in my life: uncovering an unknown historical manuscript. I leafed through it. I could handle it. I began reading the writing carefully. Amazingly, I coped well with the script, and with the language. There were some Italianisms that were a bit over my head, and some funny grammatical forms, but my early familiarity with some Bible and Talmud helped me think my way into the style. I was bedazzled by what I read. I felt like running naked into the open, shouting *Eureka!* like Archimedes. I could hardly wait to get it copied and smuggled somehow to Applebaum, my old friend and specialist in Jewish history.

It was as though my favorites Salamone de' Rossi and Rabbi Leone da Modena were talking to me. Who are they? This is another case of the amazing coincidences life produces. On occasion, I'd heard de' Rossi's name on the classical music station, and listened not too carefully to his duos, to the *madrigaletti, canzone,* and trio sonatas. Then, on another program, I heard his synagogue music. This fired my imagination. Who was this man who crossed the end of the sixteenth century, the legendary *cinquecento,* and lived into the seventeenth? Who was this de' Rossi who wrote music for both synagogue and for the "others?" This Salamone—*Shlomo* in Hebrew—a violinist and composer who could move both the music-loving Italian nobility, whose creations would also be sung in the ghetto synagogues?

He was a court musician to the Duke of Mantua. I found a CD, whose notes told me that de' Rossi's innovations influenced the mainstream of European musical composition. I also learned that his synagogal music had created a furor among the Jews in the houses of prayer. The old-timers would have none of his newfangled polyphonic singing, which required professional, or at least trained, singers, all male, of course, and this was an innovation that traditionalists fought. The debate led me to Leone da Modena, rabbi, profligate gambler, teacher of Hebrew, Bible, Talmud, music, and dance (!) in his beloved Venice. Probably the greatest preacher in an era of preachers. Priests and prelates, nobles and academics made their way to hear him in the ghetto synagogues, where he would preach in perhaps three or five different synagogues during each Sabbath. He, of course, favored good music in the synagogue, and fought for it; he wrote the preface to *Songs Which Are Unto Salamone,* the collection of de' Rossi's Hebrew music. He supervised the printers, a complicated task, since the notes ran left to right and the Hebrew is, as we all know, the opposite.

Now, a contemporary of theirs was talking to *me!*

מגן אברהם

Magen Avraham:

The Shield of Avraham

Manuscript written by Avraham de' Pomi about 1600 CE
Discovered by Avraham ben Hayim, Melia, Crete 2000 CE

Annotated by Dr. S. A. Applebaum

CHAPTER THE FIRST

With the help of Heaven
The 5th Shevat, 5360
corresponding to January 23, 1600

I, Avraham de' Pomi, write this memoir for my grandchildren, as well as for the other members of the House of Israel, and for men of wisdom from among the Gentiles. May it be the will of the Father of All that this writing be preserved and found.[1]

It is not, I hope, a vanity, an attempt to cling to immortality in this world. Having been in the courts of princes and dukes, popes and prelates, I know how swiftly the glory of this world yields to forgetfulness, and how the praised of the day become the reviled and cursed of the night.

Night, though, is not always synonymous with darkness. It was night when this began. I was in Mantua to wait in attendance on my lord, the Duke. (I will not always add phrases like "May his Excellence Increase, Amen," and all the others we are wont to add. I do not know whether paper is scarce where I go, and, for safety and secrecy, less is probably wiser than more. Suffice to say that, wherever warranted, these honors and blessings are implied.)

But enough of a digression. I will try to control this tendency, inspired by so many years of explaining texts. It was night when my tale begins, wintry and damp, with the river giving off odors of the contents we spill into it. The horse-balls

---

[1] Annotated by Dr. S. A. Applebaum, a Jerusalem scholar and relative of Avraham Ben Hayim. These notes will help clarify the learned references of the author, Avraham de' Pomi.

on the streets raised steam, and walkers were swathed up to
their eyes in woolen mantles, some in furs, striving to keep out
of their bones the cloudy moisture that hung over us.

I sat at the Sabbath table of Isaac de' Piatelli, one of the
wealthy bankers of the city, rumored to be connected as well to
the truly powerful banking houses of the Gentiles in Florence
and Venice. Not only a great financier, he was an able diplomat
to harness two such unpaired animals, not an ox and an ass,
forbidden in Deuteronomy, but rather a lion and a wolf.[2]
Withal, most of his time was spent in scholarship, and he was a
full doctor of Jewish lore, entitled to be called to the Torah for
the readings of Sabbath and special days in his synagogue, and
worthy of the honorific Morenu HaRav Rabbi Isaac.[3]

Rabbi Isaac has a beautiful wife, younger sister of his
late and beloved Pomona. The young woman was heavy with
her first child; around the table sat the four young children of
her sister, nieces and nephews who were now her stepchildren
as well. The house, necessarily crowded in the cramped
Jewish neighborhood was well appointed, occupying the first
three floors of a good but narrow property on Via Governilo.
Christian serving-maids worked there by special dispensation
to Rabbi Isaac, in exchange for the Hebrew and Bible lessons he
gave the Duke's almoner.

We were lucky that the Duke had not gone into residence
at his country villa, but January was not too attractive in the
open, windy, and occasionally snow-bound hills near Mantua.
Lucky, because two men summoned me from the table. The
serving-girl came into the dining room frightened and white,
having answered their determined knocking. They refused to

---

[2] The lion was the emblem of Florence; the wolf, of course, suckled Romulus and Remus, founders of Rome.

[3] Literally: Our Teacher, the Master Rabbi Isaac; the highest title for ordained rabbis and masters.

speak to her. Give this to Doctor de' Pomi, they said, and thrust a piece of paper into her hand. On it were three Hebrew letters:

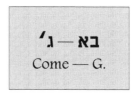

בֹּא — ג'

Come — G.

I recognized the hand in which the note was written. I did not want to explain to Rabbi Isaac's family. It must be a matter of urgency and of discretion. Until I understood, better not to involve them.

I excused myself, saying that a former patient had heard I was in the city and begged me to attend on him, a matter of urgency. I uttered a shortened grace after meals, bowed my thanks and Sabbath greetings to my host, hostess, and the assembled, and took my leave. Not without a tremor of fear, and almost foreboding. Someone writing Hebrew, and dispatching messengers to the home of Rabbi Isaac, on Friday evening, at the Sabbath meal — these were all evil omens. I was not awaiting good tidings from any quarter that I knew. This summons could only herald bad to come.

I passed through the room I shared with the younger boys, and strapped on a short sword under my outer garment. Though it was the Sabbath, I preferred to be armed, hiding the sword beneath my heavy woolen coat, which had a special opening in the lining through which I could, heaven forfend, draw the weapon if needed. I was permitted to wear my doctor's berretta, instead of the orange-banded Jew cap required by law. Permission for hat and sword required powerful intervention with the authorities, and a not-insignificant payment to the official coffers. However....

The two men, similarly swaddled, walked silently before me. They led me quickly through the long street lined mainly with Jewish homes, past the Chief Rabbi's four-story house with its beautiful wrought-iron balconies. The streets were quiet on this damp night, though as we came closer to the Ducal Palace, the noises of revelers and gamblers came out of the tawdry taverns. In minutes we had passed the Rotonda da San Lorenzo, and the Tower of Santa Andrea, and made our way through the pungent Piazzetta dell' Olio. The church buildings lining the Via della Dottrina Cristiana reminded me of the dangers I sensed lay ahead. A few streetwalkers forlornly sought custom in the damp, shivering under the eaves of the *palazzi* along the remaining short route.

The escorts exchanged some murmured words with the Duke's armed bodyguard, and we entered the precincts of the labyrinthine Palazzo Ducale, and continued on to a small section of the long house on the edge of the sumptuous central halls of the main palace. The fog and moisture steaming off the road and the walls of heated buildings mingled with the smoke emitting from the dozens of fires—two chimneys to a room— and made my head spin and my vision unclear. We entered the simple house, simple indeed by those sumptuous standards, yet furnished in good taste. A fire had been laid and lit, and in front of the flickering red-and-yellow flames stood G.

Madama Gloria, reputed mistress of the good Duke Vincenzo, daughter of my friend and kinsman, Jacopo da Pisa. Gloria was justly named; indeed she was full of glory, beautiful of limb and fair of face.[4] Her long blond hair was enhanced with colored ribbons twisted through her tresses. She wore a gown, tightly cut, its pences of white satin enhancing and exposing her perfect white breasts and clinging to her waist in

---

[4] An echo of the description of the Matriarch Rachel: "beauteous of form and beauteous of appearance." Genesis 29:17. (Annotator's translation.)

a shimmering silk made by the expert craftsmen her father had trained.

Gloria had not converted to Christianity, but rumors flew. She hovered between two worlds thanks to her magnificent voice, rivaled only by the great Madama Europa, sister of Salamone de' Rossi, the court musician, known to me as the Haver Shelomo.[5] Both had singular voices — their tones could break a heart of stone — both were singularly beautiful, and both participated in the dramas and concerts for which the Mantuan court was justly famous. To tell the truth, had I not been two generations older, and had she not been the daughter of a friend, I would have been tempted by her unbelievably creamy skin and by the femininity she exuded. I sighed. There are blessings one makes just for the looking, and not for the tasting. The Duke knew what he was about.

Gloria had summoned me and so I waited for her to begin. She took my hand and kissed it, whether because I was an almost-uncle or a doctor and rabbi, I do not know. "Rabbi Avraham," she said in the Hebrew pronunciation, "Rabbi Avraham. Shabbat Shalom." I responded to her greeting in the same words.

She continued, "Your enemies have prevailed." Like a smitten ox, I looked at her, my eyes wide with the inability to grasp what she had said. "The Bishop's spies have discovered a letter you wrote. The letter will be used to show that you spread anti-Christian sedition."

It is true that I had written a letter in which I had quoted the critique proposed — two hundred years ago — by one of our Spanish doctors and rabbis in a letter to an apostate Jew (who later became a Bishop).[6] Our Rabbi had stated that logic could

---

[5] Haver means colleague or associate. In this sense it dates to Talmudic times as a member of the inner circle of the learned keepers of the laws.

[6] Dr. Joshua Lorki to Solomon of Borgos, who later was known as Pablo de Santa Maria. Lorki later also became an apostate.

not perceive of One God who was Three, nor could it embrace the possibility of a virgin—in Nazareth or elsewhere—being impregnated by the One and Incorporeal God. This I had quoted in a letter to Picoletto della Mirandola (a grand-nephew of the famous philosopher Pico della Mirandola of Ferrara), who, like his illustrious ancestor, had learned Hebrew. As a matter of fact, for a time I myself had been his teacher.

Apparently it was this missive that had been intercepted by the spies of the Bishop of Mantua, an ignorant and bigoted churchman who owed his rank to his rich father, who had canceled a debt owed by the Pope. With the help of learned priests and his tame apostates, he had had the letter translated, and had accused me of insulting the Trinity and the Virgin. He demanded, so Gloria told me in considerable agitation, that I be handed over to the Inquisitor, in spite of the fact that the blessed rulers of Mantua had long opposed the power of the Inquisition within their lands.

Pope Clement VIII had a reputation for great Christian piety that included reviving harsh edicts concerning the Jews.[7] If that were not enough cause for woe and travail, Gloria added bitter news to the bad already conveyed. Doctor Joseph Roghel, a master schemer and slanderer who was jealous of my medical achievements, had warned the Duke that I was preparing a potent poison. He claimed that the Medicis of Florence were plotting to have me—me!!—poison the Duke himself. Was I not staying in the home of de' Piatelli, known to consort with the Medici agents? On reflection, Roghel was probably behind the entire operation against me, to remove me, a newly arrived and—forgive me—more famed practitioner—from competition with him. My cures for the Duke's stomach pains and spells of nausea were already proving to be effective, after years

---

[7] Clement VIII (Ippolito Aldobrandini of Florence (1538–1605) reigned 1592–1605.
[8] Both reflect learning. As noted earlier, the first means colleague or associate; the second, man of wisdom.

of Roghel's useless potions. And Roghel was a pillar of the synagogue, a Haver soon to be elevated to the title Haham.[8]

All this Gloria told me in the Italian-Jewish vernacular, with key words in Hebrew so that the retainers who stood nearby would not understand. In truth, my blood ran cold: one Jewish doctor had already been murdered by a rival Jew over patients. And the Christians were being incited by Dominican preachers who painted us as the Satanic anti-Christ. Could our kind and liberal ruler, lover of Gloria, long withstand such pressures?

"Therefore, Rabbi, I broke upon your Sabbath pleasure at the table of a friend, because—Sabbath or not—you must leave now." I was struck dumb for a long moment. I had only just arrived in Mantua, still missing home and hearth, and seeking peace and tranquility. Finally, I was able to ask, "Leave for where? How? With whom, with what?"

"The Duke does not trust the Bishop, nor does he believe the doctor who slanders you. But he is now at odds with the Papal court over a matter that need not concern us. He does not wish to give the Pope an opening to attack him through the Inquisitors. The Bishop is the Pope's man. Therefore, the Duke wants you out of the way. He wishes to send you tonight, with an escort of horsemen, mercenaries, French and Swiss, to Venice. There you will stay incognito in the palazzo of his kinsman and agent, Laurenzo, known as Monsignor Philoxenus, who will make arrangements for you to leave for safety."

"My books? My manuscripts? My prayer shawl and tephillin? My clothing? Money for the trip?"

"We will arrange it all. I shall also swear de' Piatelli to silence, and he will spread the word at prayers tomorrow that you are ill, and cannot teach. Later we will find another excuse for your absence."

And so into the night, on the Sabbath, by horse, escorted by twelve armed Gentile mercenaries, I left another town, another city.

To where? God knows. If He cares to know....

CHAPTER THE SECOND

With the help of Heaven

Never before had I traveled on the Sabbath. A sickly
feeling held me in its grip, but even a child knows that life-
danger overrides the Sabbath day. This, fortunately, passed,
however, and was speedily displaced by alertness to danger.
The mercenary captain, face covered with a scarf and hat
pulled low over his forehead, introduced himself as Jacques.
I had no reason to believe that was his name. He was swarthy
and squat, more like a man of Languedoc than of Burgundy,
where the people look more Germanic. Could I trust him, or
was Gloria part of a ruse to get me out of sight so a poignard
could pierce my heart or guts?

Captain Jacques had a spare outfit for me, and made me
remove my doctor's cap. The horses trotted at a fair clip, and
the road was blessedly not muddy. Fog eddied above us as we
rode past the lakes of the Minci river valley. By the time we
arrived in Venice, pushing hard, it would be late Monday or
even Tuesday. As long as it took Abraham and Isaac to reach
Mount Moriah from Beersheba. Isaac had gone willingly,
trusting his father. Whom could I trust?

We stopped a few hours later at a rough shepherd's hut
that had been abandoned for the winter — probably on land
owned by the Duke. Now I would see what they had in store
for me.

Jacques made his horse and *condottieri* comfortable,
and then looked to me. He brought out a special package of
aliments and wine: courtesy of "milady Madama Gloria." I

breathed easier. If Gloria had sent *kasher* food and good wine,
I was not likely marked for assassination, not on her part,
anyway. Jacques spoke Italian in the Roman dialect, yet with
a French accent; I spoke to him in my Italianate French, and
then in Provençal. His face lit up at the sound of the familiar
cadences of his native tongue. The captain's demeanor was
matter-of-fact, and so I eased my clutch on the sword under the
cloak. Much good it would do anyway, outnumbered as I was.
Thus I resolved to act as usual, and even went out of the camp
to ease my bowels, trusting that this, the most vulnerable time,
was not when I would die. I was glad of that: one wishes to die
in cleanliness if not in purity, and unbesmirched by decay of
self or food.

   And so we reached Venice, where, as it would come to
pass, I would find life. Would another need to die in my stead?
Is that how the Divine plan and balance works? One side of
the scale up — life; the other side down — floating in a canal? If
so, may my God and the God the other believed in have mercy
upon him, amen.

   This is what transpired in Venice. Captain Jacques took
me to the *Casa dei Catacumeni*, the house for converting Jews.
Once having entered this dread place, a Jew may only leave as
a former Jew, a convert, a Catholic. To prevent undue influence
by family, friends, or rabbis, no Jew may pass by the *Casa*, or
even look at the building, under pain of torture and death by
the Inquisitors.

   I refused to enter — indeed, could not enter.

   "Captain Jacques," I said, calling him aside in the
twilight hours on the third day, standing outside the "Jews'
House," the dreaded *Casa*. Again we spoke in Provençal, and
this created a certain almost conspiratorial bond.

   "Captain, this is the *Casa* where apostates — whom the
Christians call 'converts' — are held in isolation, without contact

with other Jews. The Duke did not expect me to convert, nor shall I. Therefore, sir, I may not set foot in that house, under pain of torture or death."

"Indeed, that's why the good Duke wishes to lodge you there. No one will look for you here."

"Once I go in as a Jew, I must come out a Christian. I fear the converts there will betray me, or the priests who are their instructors."

"You will be held separately."

"'Held'?"

"I mean 'kept.'"

"Captain Jacques, night is falling, and I will go with your men to wherever they lodge. If they are loyal to you, swear them to silence."

Finally the swarthy Frenchman gave in, conditional on his reporting to the Duke's diplomatic representative at *la Serinessima*'s court.

We made our way to a foul-smelling lodging, half stalls, half beds of straw, next to a canal that stank as well. Ah, this was not the Venice I had loved when I lived in the home of my friend Leone da Modena da Venezia.[9] However, exhaustion, fear, and aching bones brought sleep swiftly to Jacques and his riders, including this anomalous, disguised Jewish doctor.

The morning came quickly. I could not pray openly, with *tallit* and *tephillin,* but I could recite the shortened prayers for times of danger. I did make a good breakfast of warm milk, bread, cheese, and an apple and pear. They were brewing a bitter brown drink called *cioccolata* nearby; even when sweetened with sugar, it was not to my taste.

The captain of the *condottieri* told me he would return soon, and left on foot. When he reappeared a few hours later,

---

[9] He is known as Leone da Modena, where his family lived, but he preferred to see himself as a Venetian, the city he truly loved. In Hebrew, he is known as Rebbi Yehuda Aryeh miModena. Aryeh=Lion=Leone; a Biblical description of the tribe of Judah is "Judah is a lion's whelp...."

he asked me to be patient until dark. Once more, wrapped and muffled, we moved at night through the dark streets. Two of Jacques's riders strode before us, hand on hilt, and two behind. He did not tell me where we were going. After an exchange of numbered knocks, we entered a palazzo through the postern door. I was certainly not back at the Jews' House. Waiting for us in full priestly regalia, well-tailored cassock, and skullcap stood a stately man, obviously a person of breeding, with the look of the scholar about his eyes and of the thinker across his wide, lined brow.

"I am Monsignor Philoxenus da Paolo. My lord Vincenzo of Mantua is my mothers' kinsman, and I am his *bailo* and represent all his interests here, both diplomatic and more mundane affairs. You will be at home here until I am able to arrange passage for you. Meanwhile, come and take some wine with me. Have no fear, it is neither sacramental nor blessed, and I shall give it to you sealed, so you yourself may pour it."

Now I was deeply troubled and even afraid. The Monsignor knew our customs and practices well. Even those few rabbis who permitted Jews to drink the wine of Gentiles would not permit sanctified Church wine, especially wine that had been handled and poured by a priest of whatever rank. My host knew even this....

Monsignor Philoxenus dismissed Jacques, whom I thanked most warmly and commended to my host, who would doubtless so advise his master and kinsman, the Duke. A serving-girl stood at the end of the room, the blush of youth upon her, and followed everything with keen eyes. He beckoned to her, and told her to bring a sealed bottle of wine, along with some bread and fruit. I lifted my eyebrows. This was a man who understood some of the turmoil in my head.

"In both our religions, one feeds the body before the soul, for have your sages not written, 'If there is no bread, there is no teaching?' First sup."

I washed my hands in a laver the girl brought. She lowered her eyes, out of respect, and then glanced at the prelate. He nodded to her, tilting his head toward the door. She must have been there long, or had had other occasions to learn his ways. I poured myself some wine.

The Monsignor now read the turmoil in my soul. Immediately, then, he told me that the Duke wanted me to be sent to safety.

"You may choose, either to go the Court of the Great Turk in Constantinople, who has always welcomed Jewish doctors, and where the hand of the Inquisition will not reach. You may also choose Candia," which we call Kritim, almost like the Greek Kriti, "where the Duke has large holdings of olive groves and vineyards.

"There, in Candia, you will be sent to oversee the Duke's interests, and be protected by his people and in his villages."

Were that not in itself a sufficient guarantee of safety, the Monsignor said he would send a sealed message to the Venetian Governor, the Duke of Candia, holding him responsible for my safety.

"But," he added, "Venetian territory is Catholic, the people of Candia are Greek Orthodox, and the infidel followers of Mohammed strive to return there. For you the danger might be that the Church could try to reach out its hand toward you. Either way the decision is yours."

"The Duke is most gracious toward me and saves my life."

"The Duke is a man of honor, less given to evil and betrayal than the Florentines or the Venetians. It is also perhaps the influence of the beautiful Madama Gloria, who is — I am led to believe — your kinswoman. But, in truth, if you are away in a safe place, the temptation to hand you over to the Church at some time in the future is removed. And so I counseled him."

"The Monsignor will let me reflect....But may I ask you, how is it that you are so familiar with our customs and the rules of Judaism?"

"I will tell you more tomorrow, with your kind indulgence," he replied. "Now, Leonora will see you to your room. She is entirely trustworthy — she is of a ducal village where my father was in charge. She is bound to secrecy by the constraints of man and the oath of Heaven."

There must have been a bell-pull or similar invention because before I could say "Constantinople" Leonora led me to a small well-furnished apartment, separated from the main halls and parlors by a double door. A small bathing-basin had been prepared, and a change of linen and clothing. In the luxury of the small bath, I nodded off, and barely managed to keep awake long enough to fall into a soft bed, the words "Candia or Constantinople" still circling through my fevered cerebrum. Too much was happening, too fast, for a man my age. Any age, for that matter. Candia, the mythological Knossos, Irakleion, or Constantinople, in Hebrew Kushta, the city of truth....[10]

---

[10] Kushta is the Aramaic word for "truth." The use of the word as a name for Constantinople actually stems from the Arabic way of pronouncing the name: something like Kustantiyya.

CHAPTER THE THIRD

With the help of Heaven

The next day, clean, rested, renewed, I rose to the shouted greetings of gondoliers and snatches of conversation from the canal beneath my window. I knew Venice well. I had studied here as a young man, as well as in nearby Padua, under our Master, Rabbi Samuel Archevolti. Medicine I had studied later in Padua and Bologna, but my abilities in Hebrew grammar, and rhyming — such as they are, and through no fault of my teacher — are due to my premier teacher, the same Rabbi Samuel. Of course, I would never see him again, whether I chose Candia or Constantinople.

This was a great dilemma. Although there are a few learned and even distinguished scholars in the Venetian isle of Candia, no doubt the great Kushta has more. Yet, surely the ancient Grecian myths still reverberate through the air of Candia from Knossos and out of the dark mountains where they believe their main god (may we be forgiven for using the word in such a context) Zeus was hidden from his devouring father. To oversee olive groves and vineyards would be almost Biblical, "each man under his own vine and under his own fig-tree." Perhaps, with the peace and quiet of the rustic island would come the opportunity and conditions conducive to the return to study and learning that I have pursued insufficiently in these later years. There, too, I could study Greek and read the wise men of Athens in the original texts.

Kushta has more scholars, more rabbis, and more doctors. It also has the Sultan's sycophants and the powerful

who intrigue in the corridors — all with a healthy respect and
sometimes even awe of Jewish medicine. And which ruler
anywhere has welcomed in finer and more hospitable fashion
our persecuted and expelled brethren from Iberia than the
Grand Seigneur of Constantinople, whose court is called the
Sublime Porte?[11] But the Sublime Porte must be a center of
intrigue and plotting, where, although each embraces the other
with sweeping wide arms and greets his fellow with sweet
words, the wise man will remember that the poignard may
be in that very hand that claps his back and the sweet words
may be dipped in poisoned honey. As we study in Fathers, "Be
cautious with those in power, for they bring a person close only
for their own advantage: seeming like loving friends when it is
to their benefit, and deserting him in his time of need."[12]

I do not need more thought. I have seen enough intrigue
and suffering and have lost dear ones and friends through the
travails of nature and powerful men. Now, too, I must flee
for my life. Therefore, my heart says Candia. Even there we
have seen emerge scholars and men of erudition such as the
Delmedigos and Capsalis, doctors, rabbis, and philosophers.
Indeed Picoletto della Mirandola, to whom I wrote the letter
that has brought me into so much trouble, is a grand-nephew
of the great Pico who studied Hebrew with Elijah Delmedigo
of Crete, who later served as professor of philosophy at the
University of Padua. Thus even the Cretan air can support our
scholarship and synagogue; manuscripts and books will all
be within reach. And since Candia is Venetian, letters to my
family and friends can traverse the waters swiftly, and in a
matter of weeks, letter and response will have been exchanged.

---

[11] The Grand Seigneur (Great Lord) in modern language—the Big Man, the Sultan; the
Sublime Porte—also a French term—is the translation of the High Gate (Baba Ali) in
Turkish, which was the "chief office" of the Ottoman Empire. Much as "Downing Street"
or the "White House" or even better, "Buckingham Palace," are used today.

[12] Babylonian Talmud, Mishna Avot (Ethics of the Fathers), Chapter II, Mishna 3.

At worst, in a matter of months, if pirates and weather
intervene, which fate may God forbid and save all who take
ship over the deep.

There was a knock at the door. Leonora entered bearing
bread and honey and hot water. Monsignor would expect
me at my pleasure in his study, where we met last night. I
washed my hands and recited the prayers, missing my tallit
and tephillin. The prayers were no problem: I had no need of a
prayer-book. From age three I had read the siddur; the words
of our ancient rites came as naturally to me as breathing. Yet I
missed the comfort of holding it in my hand, an old friend, and
seeing its handsome square letters and punctuation.

Monsignor had prepared a replacement for the square
Hebrew letters, or so it seemed, for another friend awaited
me, none other than dear Leone da Modena, may God guard
and save him! This indeed elevated my spirits, which began
to rise as soon as I saw the smiling face of my host, the good
Monsignor, and the lovely works of art that covered the
tapestry-lined walls of the "informal" parlor used for receiving
favored visitors and personal guests. Leone and I fell into one
another's arms. In truth, our friendship antedated ourselves.
My distinguished blessed ancestor, Davide de' Pomi and
Leone's father, Isaac, both of blessed memory, were good
friends.[13]

Leone was younger than I by some twenty years, but
through visits and correspondence we had drawn close to one
another. Also the age difference was in many ways less: when
only two-and-a-half years old, Leone had read the concluding
portion from the Prophets in synagogue on Shabbat. Though all
of us went swiftly to the books — as mere babes almost — Leone

---

[13] Davide de' Pomi, of ancient Roman descent, as were the de' Rossis, was an outstanding
physician, linguist, political activist, and writer (1525–1593). He lived in Venice for most
of his life. Leone da Modena's father Isaac had to leave Ferrara, due to an earthquake
in 1570. A year earlier, a Papal edict had expelled the Modenas and all other Jews from
Bologna. Isaac da Modena died in 1591.

had done so earlier than most of us, and the report spread through our towns and hamlets like wildfire. Thus as a mere youngster he also studied under our Master Rabbi Samuel, another bond that tied us together. Even then, he already had the learning and bearing of a young man. At age 14, his tractate against card playing and games of chance was already written and published, and read, too, I might add. But gambling is an addiction, and my young friend, such a talented preacher, teacher, and decisor[14] of Jewish law, had not paid heed to his own words — alas!

Monsignor made us both welcome, and left us. I asked Leone in Hebrew if he knew what had brought me to Venice. He nodded, compassion and sadness showing in his wide-spaced eyes. He was not a handsome man, Leone; there was a Socratean look to him: wide face and wide nostrils, like the bust of the Athenian, but without the latter's thick lips. He nodded, and without words handed me a small packet. In it were a prayer-shawl, in the *Italiani* mode (fine silk instead of the northerners' Ashkenazi wool), and small phylacteries, well used, and with supple leather straps, perhaps for use of his students.[15]

I thanked him, and assured him they would be sent back to him as soon as my belongings arrived. Again, though, he was silent. That was unlike him, for his golden tongue drew many a noble, scholar, priest, and prelate, as well as visiting traders and even royalty to come to our synagogues in the Ghetto to hear his sermons.

"I have a heavy heart." Everyone knew of the heartbreak he had already endured when his beautiful and pious

---

[14] "Decisor" is not, as it sounds, a tooth, but the usual translation for posek, the rabbinical authority who decides matters of Jewish law in all areas of life (business, personal, religious). His decision is respected.

[15] Italiani is the Hebrew word for the Italian prayer rites and customs, which were different from the Sefardi or Spanish rites, the Ashkenazi or German/Polish (Central and Eastern European) rites, and the French Provencal rites.

betrothed, Esther, died shortly before the marriage was to take place. "Not for me, dear friend and haver, but for you. Before I continue, let me tell you that you are safe here, and even my visit to this house will not be remarked on. I teach Monsignor Philoxenus the Holy Tongue and some of our Laws, and once a week attend upon him here. He is a good student who reads texts well and correctly; and also will understand our speech in good part. Therefore let us continue in Italian, which is more suited to the plots and plans with which we are presently concerned.

"I have a heavy heart because you must once again flee to a place of safety. But, further to set your heart at ease," Leone continued, "a rumor will be spread throughout Italy that the great Hebraist and doctor Avraham de' Pomi had to leave Mantua to treat a wealthy Florentine banker in Geneva, and has taken the hazardous trip over the Alps. In addition to the attraction of Florentine gold from your supposed Genevan patient, you will be searching for Hebrew manuscripts. Supposedly, you have sent word to Provence and to the Rheinland provinces in Germany and the bordering French communities about your search for manuscripts. This the Monsignor has commissioned me to do, both among our coreligionists and among the Gentile circles. Naturally, I can do so, because the de' Pomi name is so well known in our city.

"One more thing," he added, hesitantly. "To further confuse matters, Monsignor has 'arranged' that when the next corpse is pulled out of the canals, a rumor will be spread by the authorities that it was a Jewish doctor from Mantua." He held up his hand as I began to reply. "No, no, have no fear. No taking of life is commissioned or condoned. But we all know how many scores are settled with a knife and the canal…." He sighed, and I sighed along with him. We Jews are well versed in the matter of sighs. But, a true Venetian, he also shrugged his shoulders.

I thanked dear Leone warmly and raised with him
my doubts, questions, and thoughts about Candia versus
Constantinople. From mention of the great scholars and rabbis,
we went on to doctors. Leone warned me that Jewish doctors
were active both as diplomats and secret advisors in the court
of the Sublime Porte.

"Dear friend, they will not be too welcoming of someone
with such an illustrious family name as yours."

That only confirmed me in my leanings.

The young woman came in with fruit and nuts over
which we both recited the blessings, and this inevitably led to
discussing Leone's latest decisions. In secrecy, he told me of
discussions with Salamone de' Rossi on the latter's visits from
Mantua and by correspondence (under the ban[16]) regarding
the creation of modern music for our synagogal prayers. He
thought there would be a terrible outcry from the ignorant
conservative rabbis: "those who had never read a book outside
of sacred literature all their lives." I embraced him warmly for
that felicitous, and tragically, all too accurate description.

Leone is very clever, as well as being wise, but for his addiction
to gambling. (Who knows how many hundreds and thousands of
florins he has lost, condemning himself and his family to poverty?)

He counselled me to take a new name. In his wisdom, he
reminded me that the four original families who had settled in
Rome some centuries before the Christian calendar included
my own, the de' Pomis, and my former host in Mantua, de
Piatelli. The families across the centuries must certainly have
intermingled and intermarried. (The branch to which my host
in Mantua belonged was called de' Piatelli, an Italian word for

---

[16] "Under the ban" of Rabbenu Gershom, who ruled that it is forbidden to open or read
another's mail. In brief, Leone was saying that a trustworthy fellow Jew, one who would
not dare face the ban of excommunication and probably a banker or peddler, would
convey his mail to and from de' Rossi.

"grape." He suggested I call myself Modesto. This was a play on words from the Hebrew: two similar words, one meaning grape, and the other, modest or humble, the latter being the very word used to describe Moses our Master who led us out of Egypt.[17] And instead of Avraham, why not Amico, for was not Abraham known as the Friend of God — the Yedid? Amico Modesto. Perhaps it is too resounding and makes too many claims. Possibly Amico de' Modesti is less bombastic, yet still conveys a sense of — what — quasi-nobility? We shall see, but I certainly shall need a *nom de guerre* or, at the very least, *a* nome di viaggio.

Leone promised to return within the next day or two with sacred texts and books, and I promised that he would remain privy to my travels, in order that we could correspond.

"A final word, dear Master Avraham," Leone said. "You may need to hide among the Gentiles as a Gentile. Be like the reed that bends to the storm, but is not broken because it is too stiff, or proud. 'And thou shalt choose life,'" he cited....

We embraced warmly as he took leave of me, and wept on one another's shoulders. We were probably at our last, our final meeting. As the elder, I blessed him with the blessings of health, prosperity, and peace within his household. (The entire world knows the sad tale of his bitter marriage with a shrew.) He in turn blessed me with the blessings of Isaac to Jacob, "Those who curse thee shall be cursed, and those who bless thee shall be blessed," for I too had to flee out of fear of Esau.[18]

---

[17] Anaw'im means grapes; anavim, the humble or modest. The four families used the Hebrew word "min" (of) as the Italians used "dei" and the Germans 'von." They were min Ha-Addumim (the Red, "Rossi"), min Ha-Neurim (the Young) and min HaTappuhim (the Apples, "Pomi," possibly "of the Orchards???") Thus min ha-'Anavim would sound like "of the Grapes (Vineyard), playing on "of the Modest."

[18] For the reference to Leone of Modena's early love and her death, see Chapter the 7th, endnote 11. Xantippe was the shrewish wife of Socrates; I have often wondered whether he so willingly took the cup of hemlock because he lacked the true love of a woman. The blessing of Jacob is in Genesis 27:29. The citation is apposite because Esau is seen as ancestor of Edom, which became a code name for Rome and thus for Christian persecution of the Jews.

That conversation left me warmed, yet sad. I would
be losing such opportunities, to meet and talk with sages,
of whom I have a wide choice in Italy. I was not at all sure
whether I could meet with sages or learned Jews in Crete.
Who knows whether I dare reveal myself to them for fear of
spies and mosrim? Heaven knows that just as enemy disposes
of enemy with a murderer's swift silent knife in Venice, and
bodies often float through the canals, so too they could find me
in Crete. I shall need to have my own reliable guards. And who
can rely on mercenaries, for silver often blinds their eyes, and
blandishes their heart? Much thought and painful reflection
did I give to the question: whether to be a proud oak only to be
brought down by a tempest, or to be a reed bending and rising
once the storm subsided. Of one thing I was sure: I would
never worship false gods.

I rang for the young lady, who came quietly and swiftly,
and returned with the requested paper, ink, and quills. And
thus I passed the day, recording that which is written above.

This time, I was able to say my afternoon and evening
prayers in peace, though — ironically — sheltered under the
wings of a monsignor, in a house replete with symbols of that
Jew whose followers cause us so much pain. Again, I supped
on fruits and bread and cheeses. I retired with the One God
in my heart, but suddenly rose to add to my scribblings the
citation of Petrarch I love so well:[19]

I was noting the substance of thought — the pettiness
of this life, its brevity, haste, tumbling course, its

---

[19] The great Italian poet of the 14th-century flowering of language and science is
described in a magnificent brief essay by Morris Bishop in The Italian Renaissance,
American Heritage Library New York, 1961, ed. J. H. Plumb reprinted 1987; the
quotation is from p. 162.

hidden cheats, time's irrecoverability, the flower of life
soon wasted, the fugitive beauty of age, the wrinkles,
illnesses, sadness, and pain, and the implacable cruelty of
indomitable death.

In spite of all that certainty about our end, "I shall not die
but I shall live."[20]

I continued writing, for the thoughts that moved within
me had not yet been appeased by paper and ink. This tale
began at night. This should not be a surprise — after all, it was at
night that many miracles took place (if they are in the manner
of nature, as the Teacher, Rabbi Moses ben Maimon[21] taught;
that is, that miracles may occur only in accordance to the laws
of nature). But, let me not digress. Though my purpose is
didactic, it is not to teach Torah and tradition in this tractate,
but rather to preserve witness of a full — possibly strange — life,
while I can still write and think and recall.

I will risk writing the truth. Though I write in our Holy
Tongue, there are Jewish betrayers, mosrim, and even — may
their names be erased — apostates who have kissed the cross.
For money or for glory, they would as soon translate these
words as I would quaff a good cup of wine right now. And
once translated, they could fall into the hands of enemies, or of
friends who would become enemies once they read my truth.
Regardless of that danger, though, I will write the truth. What
good will it do my grandchildren to bequeath them not only no
material inheritance, but to enhance that nothing with a pack of
lies? Caring for the dead is called the loving-kind act of truth,
for the dead cannot reward you for washing their soulless
bodies, dressing them in shrouds, and bringing them to burial

[20] Psalms 117:17.
[21] Maimonides, 13th-century doctor, philosopher, and master of Jewish teaching in every
field. He was called Ha-Moreh because of his great work Moreh Nevukhim: A Guide (or
Teacher) of the Perplexed.

in a Jewish cemetery. For me, the loving-kindness of truth is caring for the living, those who follow me, and who deserve only truth as best one recollects and preserves....

A warm bed, a safe haven, paper, pen, ink, and a prayer. How protected I feel tonight. And so, speedily I fell asleep for a dreamless restoring night.

CHAPTER THE FOURTH

With the help of Heaven

Finally, as our ship hugs the Adriatic and Ionian coasts and crosses the Cretan Sea, I can once again record my thoughts and memoirs. During the day, curiosity kept me from writing, as did the all too frequent rocking and yawing of our craft over the waves. I watched the shores of Italy yield quickly to those of Illyria, and then to the more savage lands of the Slavic tribes. Small fortified towns, most of them ruled by Venetian governors, dotted the Adriatic coast and we breathed easier knowing that pirates would think twice before attacking our vessel within hailing distance of Venetian territory.

White beaches and rocky promontories occasionally marked by walls and church spires punctuated the fierce mountains where the "other" Christians, the Orthodox Christians of the old Byzantine persuasion, lived. I must learn more about this variety of Christianity: Italy, after all, is Roman and Catholic, or Latin, as opposed to Greek Orthodox. As we passed between the Adriatic and the Ionian Seas, the wild and rugged mountains, dark and more brooding, rose up in the Turkish lands of Macedonia and Albania. Here the possibility of danger was much stronger.

The Grand Turk and his governors usually honor the lions of St. Mark, the emblem of Venice. Venice though has become weaker in its economy and has participated in too many wars; therefore the Venetian galleys, powered by sail and two hundred rowers, no longer inspire the great fear and respect that they had in former years. Pirates — both Christian and Muslim — prey more daringly on them. The pirates are an international group of brigands: their ships manned by Englishmen and Scotsmen, Aegean Greek-speaking islanders, Turks, and Arabs sail from Malta and hungrily ply these waters. Besides plundering the cargo — a highly lucrative business — they sell the captive passengers as slaves in Afrikiya or the farther lands of Asia and Arabia. The nubile or attractive women are often placed in harems. If, for lack of pulchritude, the women were not considered worth saving, they were used by the sailors and then sold as kitchen or even field workers.

For voyagers like us, traveling under warrant of the Doge of Venice as well as of my benefactor, the Duke of Mantua, were we to fall into pirates' hands, there was another option: Venice would redeem us. Being a Jew, which I would reveal only as a last resort, gives me an even more favored position: all pirates know that Jewish communities were bound by our holy laws to redeem captives. Much chastened by history, we know that no matter how we squabble among ourselves, no Jew is foreign to us, and every Jew in captivity is our fellow. What would happen, I wonder, if Jews were never again to be subject to captivity, and we would live as free and equal in the lands of our Dispersion, or even, after the Messiah comes, in our own Land? Would we still save our fellows, or does comfort lead Jeshurun to "wax fat and kick"[22]?

Despite the circumstances that led to this journey, I find that I am excited to be on the sea and safe from the hands stretched out against me. In the thrill of novelty and adventure, what is perhaps a childish dream has been awakened. Who, as a child, has not seen in his mind's eye the landfall of a Cristobal

---

[22] See Deuteronomy 32:15. Jeshurun, used here ironically, means the "straight" or "righteous" people. It may also be a play on the word Yisrael. Moses, in his farewell oration, predicts that wealth and ease will lead Israel to leave the straight path: Jeshurun grew fat and kicked…and forsook the God who made him.…

Colombo, Amerigo Vespucci, or Vasco da Gama in their
search for the Spice Isles and Cathay, finding the Indies, east
and west? Who has not imagined being with them in strange
climes, meeting strange people speaking unknown tongues?
And, as a Jew, I feel another bond with those voyagers. Who
did not hear the whispers regarding both Colombo and
Vespucci, that they were of our blood and stock? Could it be
just coincidence that the wicked expulsion or forced conversion
of our brethren by Isabel La Catolica and Ferdinand, leaving an
eternal blot on the escutcheon of Spain, occurred in that very
same year of the explorers' great voyages across the Atlantic?

These digressions are taking me far from the telling of
my own story, of my own travels. Perhaps it is the invigorating
sea air. Perhaps it is because there is no one with whom to
share these hidden thoughts. I know I am enthralled with
my people, and their lives; what else should I be? From my
mother's milk and my father's recitations I breathed the air of
Abraham, Isaac, and Jacob together with the air of my land of
birth. And how often did my land of birth remind me that I
should have been born elsewhere?

So, let me return to my tale, in which I am no longer
Avraham de' Pomi, doctor, rabbi, refugee. I am now Amico
de' Modesti, an expert in viticulture and former bailiff of
the Duke of Mantua's estates where olives and wine grapes
grow in abundance, en route to supervising His Excellency's
holdings in Crete. These properties—villages and orchards and
vineyards—he obtained in a strange and unusual barter with
Venice as part of a diplomatic agreement.

I am dressed now in the colorful garb of a city dweller,
but am equipped as well with more modest and simple used
clothing, as befits my profession. Well hidden are my prayer
accoutrements and holy books. In my new home I will be

unable to pass off the Hebrew writing in this diary as Greek or Turkish. The literate people there may know these scripts, having seen them on old buildings, monuments, and former mosques. I have thought of a solution: I once saw Armenian writing in a letter coming from far off Kushta-Constantinople, from the Armenian partner of the Baruh family there, who imports fruit from the Turkish lands for all of Italy. Now I also know Armenian! Another falsehood. Sin does lead to more sin.

Thus I am a Mantuan farm manager, a not too observant Catholic but Catholic nonetheless. What religious disputation could not achieve, the Bishop could accomplish — outwardly, anyway — by threatening my life. I have not and shall not leave the beliefs of my people, but will cloak myself with the appearance of Christian ways, as just another suit or perhaps a second skin. This is a good lesson for me, for now I shall truly feel on my flesh the essence of being one of the "forced ones" in Spain or Portugal, the anusim whom the Spaniards, with true Christian love, call marranos, pigs....

~

The captain, Signor Caponegro, must have been given special instructions and a good purse as well, because his attentions and kindnesses surpass normal courtesy.

He is not a learned man, but for the principles of navigation and the use of such arcane instruments as the astrolabe, for which he had little need until we stopped skirting land and set our across the open sea. He has risen from the ranks, as a devoted man of the sea, and as captain is the only one aboard whose woman travels with him. She is blonde and well-endowed — a Slav, by her looks — and though she is probably a slave, he treats her with kindness.

This is the first time I have ever found myself living in an entirely non-Jewish environment, pretending not to be a Jew. In this Gentile milieu, there seems to be less interest in others, in strangers like me. And I find among these sometimes rough seafarers as much kindness and as much lack of it as in our own closed society and community. As it is written, "From all my teachers have I learned."[23]

And thus, rocking, bobbing, and sometimes heaving-to, to ride out a sudden squall and unfriendly winds, we sailed on by Greece, its islands and peninsulas causing us to navigate with great care. Here we were more prey to attack, but here too were both pacific Turkish vessels, plying the trade routes to Venice and Ancona, and naval vessels under the direct command of the Turkish admirals. They have passed us, each barque warily keeping a fair distance, each signaling with a dipping of flags, salutes of peace and safety. The true test of our security would come when we embarked across the cruel and long Cretan Sea separating the Peleponnesus from Candia, a hundred leagues away.

The closer the coast's rocks, the grayer and darker the waters swirled when the stiff winds rose. Further into the sea, the waters were that heart-penetrating blue that the authors call "Mediterranean"; often in the quiet of sunset they turned emerald, in magnificent tricks of light. At those times, my heart fills with awe, and the prayer rises from my lips, "How great are Thy works, how deep Thy thoughts."[24]

I paced the deck from one end to the other, past the two masts, puffed out under full sail, and then back again. The challenge of travel and the thrill of novelty indeed took years off me, and while the sea air diffused my fear and anger, it added to my loneliness. The world knows great travail,

[23] Ethics of the Fathers, Chapter Four, Mishna 1, quoting Psalms 119:99.
[24] Psalm 92:6.

as I have in my own life, but much beauty, joy, and fleeting moments of happiness.... As I paced, I told myself that in Candia I must find time to record for you, my descendants and, perhaps, other readers, some of those illuminated moments, lest my tale be but a pale copy of those who have suffered even more.

Breaking into these thoughts, Captain Caponegro called me to his side, a long brass eyeglass in his right hand. "No land in sight yet, but I already see land-birds and seagulls far off. Tomorrow morning, I shall post a look-out, and we should make landfall that day." I nodded my satisfaction. The captain took my elbow in his hand, steering me away from the helmsman and suggesting with a wave of his hand that we walk towards the prow. His face bore a serious, almost embarrassed look.

"Esteemed Signore," he began, in formal tone I had not heard before. "I wish to raise with you a matter of great delicacy, if I may...." I nodded, and with a gesture asked him to continue. "You may not know that before my family moved to Venice, where we had business interests, we lived in Linz, in Austria, where our original name was Schwartzkopf."

I kept my silence.

"In Linz, and on my travels, I met many...Hebrews. I learned that all men are men; and in spite of the tales we read or hear, they know love and revenge, as do we all.[25] I also learned something else." He was obviously sincere, and embarrassed. Could I question his good will? Where was this leading, my heart asked? But I held my silence. As Rabbi Akiva said, "A fence for wisdom is silence...."[26]

---

[25] This might—with a stretch—refer to Shakespeare's Merchant of Venice, which was first played in 1596. However, the story in one form or another had been known long before.

[26] Ethics of the Fathers, Chapter Three. Mishna 17.

"I learned that Jews do not cross themselves," the captain went on. "Nor do they go to our churches, or eat certain foods. I noted that most Jews had a look about their eyes, often in their eyes, of very careful observation, of wariness, coupled with great interest in what goes on around them. I find them often calculating, albeit almost unknowingly, the order of command or precedence among strangers they meet, for obvious reasons. And, I also observed the ability of many of them to show warmth and sympathy to strangers who do not threaten them.

"Signore, forgive me if I say, in truth, I find these traits in you. If you are a Hebrew, you need not fear me. Money and favors might hold my silence for a time, and fear of the Duke of Mantua and Monsignor Philoxenus might keep me silent even longer. But I see you are an honorable man, with more distinction than a rustic manager of villagers and vineyards. Thus, from one man to another, both made in His image, you need have no fear concerning my continued silence. I therefore wish to warn — no, that is not right — I wish to exhort you to pay heed, for perceptive people may suspect the truth about you."

I kept myself in check, and held my features and body frozen.

"This, too, Esteemed Signore — silence, stiffness of body — this, too, is an admission. Take heed, Esteemed Signore. Forgive me if I suggest you change your food habits, and that you bear yourself with more hauteur and distance. Be not you, but act the role the Duke has commanded." He stopped for a moment. Then, "If I may continue, Sir?" I nodded tightly. "A manager of vineyards does not read a strange language he calls Armenian. But a man who studied law and literature, a man who was called to serve his kinsman and master before completing his studies, might have learned some Hebrew, especially at the University of Padua, or in Mantua itself, from the court Hebrews who serve the Duke."

In a world I do not know, in a world where the codes are different, and men are measured in modes my ancestors and I never learned, I am greatly at risk. In whom to trust and in whom not to trust? Putting everything onto the shoulders of the Creator, as it were, will not save me. So what does trust in God mean? And what did it mean to all my fellow Jews who trusted as they went up in flames or were cast into freezing rivers by armor-clad men who also put their trust in God?

I am learning from the black-headed captain. If I thank him, he will see it as admission. If I deny it, he will see the denial as a stronger admission, with the further insult that I do not trust him. Now I see why our nation has had to learn the arts of diplomacy. Thus, I replied carefully. "Were all you said correct, kind Captain, your interlocutor would have to respect your penetrating eye and discerning heart. Were it to be incorrect, your interlocutor would have to respect your desire to help, your open-hearted acceptance of a fellow man, and be grateful to you." I gave the captain my right hand, over which he bowed. We parted from one another with respect, and I with admiration for a true man.

This exchange, however, did not halt my racing thoughts. That night I retired knowing that sleep would perhaps await me in Crete. On board ship, the night would be consumed with planning my behavior, following the sage counsel of the good sea captain. Of all things to change, food and behavior.... I thought I had already taken care of the food problem. When I boarded ship, I told the men who waited on us at table and the cook that I had taken upon myself a voluntary fast of abstinence from meat and fowl in honor of St. Christopher, patron saint of wayfarers and sea-goers, bearing

us across the waters. The black-headed captain had seen
through that.

I pondered the question of how to act with more hauteur
and distance, without destroying any possibility of winning the
loyalty of those who had to serve me for the Duke's sake, and
those whose friendship and esteem I wished to inspire. Perhaps
I could have used some lessons in mummery and acting from
Leone de' Sommi Portaleone, so famous in Mantua — indeed
throughout the world — and the other lion, dear Rabbi Leone in
Venice.[27]

When I finally fell asleep I do not recall, but I sat up with
a start at the cry echoed from the others on deck: Terra, terra!
Candia, Candia!

---

[27] The latter, Rabbi Leone, in enumerating all his various 33 kinds of employment needed
to maintain his family and to feed his gambling habit, included acting and teaching
acting. The Jewish actors of Mantua were considered "world-class" for their time.
The first major book on stagecraft was written by the prolific de' Sommi, who was a
writer, poet, and producer/director. His Dialoghi in materia rappresentazioni sceniche
contains four "dialogues" on stagecraft, and is considered by historian Cecil Roth to be
"a memorable contribution by a professing Jew to general literature in the age of the
Renaissance." (The Jews in the Renaissance, JPS, Philadelphia, 1959, reprinted 1977, p.
262. More on de' Sommi ff. and preceding.)

CHAPTER THE FIFTH

With the help of Heaven

The stark hills reared up from the emerald waters and formed a shell around the black battlements surrounding the port of Candia, city of many names and many conquerors. Homer sang of the brave and powerful Heracles landing at the port, therefore named Heraklion. Then came the Arabic-speaking Saracens, naming it Rabd-el-Khandak, or just Khandak[28] When the Byzantine rulers reconquered it from the Saracens, they called it Khandax. Finally, the Venetians, wishing to protect their sea-routes to Kushta — or as it is now known, Constantinople — softened the name to Candia.[29] The whole Cretan isle they also call Candia.

The *Città Vecchia* was clustered along the shorefront, and stretched up onto the high hill around which heavy stone ramparts had been built. There were two harbors: one was military, with men of war, barques, bobbing at anchor, and the other had smaller smacks and fishing vessels riding the gentle waves. Around the city, the lush land grew olives and vines and other fruits. Green fields with young wheat sprouting and orchards gave way to hills and then to the mountains. All told it was a brave and stirring sight, and though the Città Vecchia showed traces of Byzantine, even hints of Saracen styles, this could only be discerned from a closer viewing.

[28] The Arabic has the connotation of a defensive position, which Candia proved to be in withstanding a 21-year siege by the Turks (1648–1669).
[29] Thus, Candia in religion was Greek pagan, then fell under rulers who were Islamic, Greek Orthodox, Roman Catholic, and again Islamic. Linguistically, Koine Greek was layered by strata of Arabic, Byzantine Greek, Italian, and Turkish.

As we made our way into port, there was an overriding Venetian cast to the buildings, which demonstrated what Venice's architects and builders could do without canals. Though it had none of the eye-catching beauty and grandeur of Venice, Candia held its own charm or even beauty. The houses higher up the slope hinted at the need to seek a place for cooler days and nights, when the hot winds from the Libyan desert swept across from the southern or Libyan Sea, as everyone warned they would.

I ordered the seamen who would escort me ashore to take up my bags and boxes, and made my way to the captain. With his permission, I stood at his side as he eased the vessel gently to dock with what seemed to me masterly ease. It made me fleetingly think of the musician's talent, bolstered by constant practice, which made Salamone de' Rossi's bowing of his violin, and the music he coaxed from it flow effortlessly, as though nothing at all were involved. I understood clearly then that talent may be distributed unevenly, but that it is practice crossed with talent that produces that seemingly effortless greatness. So it was, too, with other prodigies I have known in medicine and in Jewish learning, whose minds worked rapidly and unerringly to produce without effort exact citations, and their locations, culled from thousands of pages of text, as it were, in the wink of an eye.

As I stepped off the gangplank, I crossed myself. This was one of the resolutions I had made with regard to my need to exhibit Christian-like behavior. I will append these later as an explanation to my descendants, should this ever reach them. Captain Caponegro bowed me off his vessel with an ironic nod. I doffed my hat in a low bow of thanks—thanking man after I thanked the God of Abraham. Actually, both Abrahams, the patriarch, and the Abraham I had been. Now I am Amico. Amico.

The Duke of Candia had sent runners to receive the official mails; I knew that there would be a letter for him from Monsignor Philoxenus. I learned to my surprise, and even pleasure, however, that the Doge of Venice himself had asked the Duke to extend his hospitality and courtesy. So it was that I was taken from the handsome Venetian-style dwelling, used as an official inn for important visitors, to the Ducal Palace, an even grander stone building at the top of the hill, sheltered by the inner battlements and looking straight down upon both harbors. The Duke, Zuanne Sagredo, was a handsome and clever man, well dressed and surrounded by soldiers, equerries, and scribes in varying rooms of the three-story building. There were a number of wings — one for his household, another for the servants, and one for honored guests. That, with all due humility, was my status now....

I feel an impostor. When I dwelt with the good Monsignor in Venice, he was giving shelter to the Jew, Abraham de' Pomi. I had no fear of discovery, since he knew all. But this will be my first test; God grant it not be my last. And now all the hard questions raised by the kind Captain Caponegro will need answers. I pray the decisions I have made are correct.

Tonight, after bathing, supping lightly in my chambers, and arranging my belongings, a pretty young serving-maid, perhaps all of seventeen years old, presented herself. She explained in passable Italian that there were other services she was bound to provide, if I so desired. I did desire the services, having been without a woman these many days. However, her youthful appearance and innocent look mingled with my fear of showing a circumcised member, which would no doubt be new to her and occasion gossip among the maids. As the great

Hillel said, "The more maidservants, the more promiscuity."[30]
I pressed a coin into her hand, and in kindly tone, blamed the
exhaustion of the voyage on my muted response.

Here was one more test the kindly captain had not
envisaged.

I had planned to write the rationale for my Christian-
like practices and behavior that night, but fatigue and the
relief of arriving safely conquered my body. As blessed sleep
approached, my heart chanted, "Give thanks to the Lord for He
is good, His loving kindness endureth forever." In spite of my
safe arrival, still, in truth, even in the midst of all this sheltering
comfort, I felt as "those who sit in darkness and the shadow
of death, bound by affliction and iron...."[31] Dreamless sleep
swept me into her welcome embrace.

The following morning I mentally noted some
points about how I needed to conduct myself in this new
environment. When time permits, I will write them down in
detail.

On my second day in Candia, Duke Zuanne Segredo
welcomed me at his dining table. Not being accustomed
to all the niceties of diplomatic life, to my surprise — and
trepidation — I discovered that I was the guest of honor, seated
at his right. The table glittered with white-rose damascene
linen, figured with the lions of San Marco, knives and the newfangled silver forks from Florence, also stamped with the coat
of arms of Venice, glassware filled with flowers, and decanters
and goblets in crystal and colored glass blown in Murano.
The wines were, I discovered later, a good Cretan white, the
somewhat sweet malvasia, and the dessert wine muscato.[32]

---

[30] Ethics of the Fathers, Chapter Two, Mishnah 8.
[31] Psalms 107: 1 and 10.
[32] Named for the malvasia grape grown especially in the coastal area of Malevizia near
Candia. Moscato is "muscatel" and malvasia was called "malmsey" in English, and
became a major export to England. (See Molly Greene, *A Shared World: Christians and
Moslems in the Early Modern Mediterranean*, Princeton 2000, pp. 110–111.)

Liveried footmen lined the walls, and the guests numbered some twenty or so. In the hubbub and drinking, I could eat what I wished, with none the wiser. But I decided to take the bull, or at least the bull's meat, by the horns.

I had been greeted with great warmth and long toasts, most, of course, in honor of my master. In my response, I included some thoughts that would help protect my new identity. "I am a simple farm manager in a place not too close to Mantua, in the Gonzaga village area. It is naturally difficult for me to be up to date on the latest doings and modes in the urban centers of civilization. Mantua is some twenty leagues away,[33] and as to Venice society, well, all the distinguished lords and ladies here know it better than I. As such, I beg forgiveness for a country bumpkin who might not possess all the niceties of the illustrious, illuminated denizens of Venezia, la Serenissima.

"Second, I hope that in spite of my lack of polish, to find time and teachers with whom I could resume my study of medicine. These I of course interrupted when the Duke of Mantua found greater need of me to look after some of his holdings.

"And finally, before bestowing my richest and deepest sincere thanks to our host and his distinguished guests and compliments on his nobility of soul and deserved high rank, I apologize if I partake but little of the meat." In inventive mood, I related that while in the service of the Duke I had learned from one of the oldest land-working tenants, who lived in good health well beyond the age of eighty-five, that his secret to longevity was a diet heavy in greens, fruits, grains, and milk products. So, too, a famous doctor, de' Pomi by name, had expressed his opinion—similar indeed—to that of the old man.

---

[33] Today about 30 kilometers separate Mantua and the Ducal village of origin, Gonzaga.

All these tales were invented, though some of our sages do permit such invention if lives are at stake. In this case, my life.

I retook my place, amidst great applause and compliments on my Italian style, and harsh denials of my "country bumpkinhood." I realized that the showy humility I had demonstrated pleased the assembled, and was seen as tongue-in-cheek modesty, considering my educated language and polished manner.

Once I had finished, the subject changed quite naturally. Most people are more interested in their own limitations (and maladies). (You will, dear reader, forgive the egotism I displayed. Obviously I had quoted my other self. I add, however, with unabashed pride, that a few diners nodded when I mentioned Doctor de' Pomi.)

I knew that on the morrow all Candia would know, and thence it would fly as by birds borne to the very shores of this blessed isle, that the newly arrived Mantuan was a man of learning and a former student of medicine. My remarks about food would probably also take wing.

On the morrow, though, there was a certain price to pay. The resident Archbishop, Pius (a native of Sienna) sought me out in the ducal palace. A short dour man, unlike the high-living, not overly pious men of the purple I had met on terra firma, he was without social niceties. I could see that he had the short-sighted gaze and self-absorbed look of a scholar. Good, I thought, I'll have someone to talk with. As he advanced into the parlor of my apartment, I bowed over his outstretched hand and ring, planting a ceremonious kiss just above the symbol on his finger. He wasted no time raising what was on his mind.

"I note," he said, "that the doctor you mentioned is a Jew." I nodded. "You are aware that the Church has made it known more than once that we wish to reduce all contact with these people and their services." I nodded again and made some nondescript indecipherable sound. The Archbishop continued. "It has been forbidden a number of times, and has failed because prelates and dukes use them, in the false belief that they have special powers from one of their secret holy books, the Kabbalah, and from traditions handed down by the generations of doctors before them." Again, I nodded. "We even have some Jewish doctors here, particularly in Hania."

So the conversation spun on. I told him I had heard of a Jewish doctor — more than one — who had treated various dukes. When their noble patients died, the Jews who treated them were executed. The Archbishop surprised me. "This is superstitious stupidity and" — this truly amazed me — "heretical barbarism. One may not take life in an act of revenge against an innocent man. Only if the doctor is a poisoner and knowingly maltreats his patient should his life be taken. And that execution should be for murder compounded with betraying the Physician's Oath of Hippocrates."

As a doctor, I had long since learned that it is better to listen than to speak. So as our conversation continued, the prelate spoke, I listened, hmmed, and nodded, occasionally intervening with a brief comment or question. In truth, this was the first time I had had a conversation with an ordained Christian, as equals, so to speak, for in the past, as Jewish doctor before a priest, monsignor, or bishop, all meetings included lengthy discussions of the clash of doctrines between Christianity and Judaism. (The only other exception was Monsignor Philoxenos, but he was my protector and thus I was not on equal footing.) It was refreshing, but I maintained a careful if hidden guard, well knowing the dangers of my dual personae.

Finally, I asked if there were schools for doctors in Crete, and an Accademia or University such as those found on terra firma, which, I described as "the crowning glory of Italia." The archbishop told me that the profession was often handed down from father to son, or master to apprentice, except for the few who came from the mainland seeking less cultivated territory and fewer competitors. Nonetheless, the finest were to be found among the learned Jews of Hania, including the noted Delmedigo family. His face darkened when he said this, doubtless recalling the Papal condemnation of the use of Jewish doctors. I resolved to set my face toward Hania as soon as possible....

Archbishop Pius told me that the Cretans lived long lives, and that he too thought it was due to their relative poverty, since fruits, greens, oil, and cheeses were in abundance, but little meat. Near the coast, there was also fish, and some households kept chicken and geese both for eggs and meat. The occasional slaughtered goat or sheep were for festive meals on special days and holidays.[34]

We parted warmly, and the Siennese, himself perhaps parched for new faces (and more simulating ones?), bade me farewell with a compliment. "I see you are a truly intelligent and learned man. Such is Mantua's reputation, and your master has chosen well. I thank you for your good conversation, and will be honored if you call on me, or sup with me when you are again in Candia."

It was indeed a highly encouraging visit. I seemed to have passed a few difficult tests and been able to carry off my new role. Still, I was only too conscious of the fact that complacency could be fatal. And now, it was time to visit my new charge — the lands and farmers of my master and protector.

---

[34] To this day, the Cretan diet is considered a prototype of the healthy Mediterranean regime.

The next day I was to ask the Duke, my good host
Zuanne Segredo, permission to take leave of him the second or
third day following, once a small troop of my retainers arrived
from our holdings in the Plain of Messara. The runners had
returned and at my request Stavros Gortinopolis, the chief
steward for all our properties, stayed behind to supervise
preparations for our arrival. But the good Zuanne would not
let me go, he said, unless we had had a chance to speak of Crete
and its ancient history.

"Crete without Knossos," said the good Zuanne, "is the
Church without Jesus."

"What a strange metaphor!" I replied. "How, sir, in
the same breath, can one mention the myth of the sacrifice of
virgins and of valiant suitors stumbling through a labyrinth
to their death, offered up on the altar of a <u>bull</u>, no less,
and the idea of the Crucified One who gave his life to save
mankind?" In my heart, but held back from my tongue, was
the comparison with the Sacrifice of Isaac. The Sacrifice of Jesus
does not have the merciful Father send the propitiously placed
ram to spare his son.

"Surely," I continued, "these myths of Minotaurs and
labyrinths are like the other myths of the ancients, like the birth
of Zeus and Athena springing full-blown from Zeus's forehead,
and like the ancient gods frolicking with the daughters of man?
Surely, esteemed Signor Doge, there was no Knossos. There
was no labyrinth, there were no blood sacrifices."

"I do not share your assuredness, dear friend, Amico
in name as well as standing." I bowed to acknowledge the
compliment. And thus our debate continued, with great
courtesy and friendliness. "The religion of the Jews was a
religion involving blood, animal sacrifices; our own religion
sees the Son of God crucified by Roman soldiers when Pilate

ratified the decision of the Jewish court. In the name of the
Christian God, we have slain infidels for hundreds of years.
The Latins and Greeks, both members of the original Catholic
Church, have killed one another with dispatch and often with
desecration. The Protesters in the North and the true followers
of the Church in our Holy Roman Empire will readily shed
blood, each for his own truth. Mohammed conquered with
the sword, and we are locked in battle with the Turk — and
not just for trade and profit." He paused, as if to weigh his
words, perhaps to decide whether he could let me hear his next
sentence....

Finally, Segredo seemed to come to some decision.
He sighed, and very quietly almost whispered, "Where man
gathers in the Name of God, bloodshed and death are sure
to follow. And he who turns the other cheek will be a good
Christ-like believer. But what good will it do him? For...
he...will...be...dead!" He spaced the words of this last brief
sentence as though he wanted them underlined with his voice.
What a risk he took to speak so blatantly, but his words rang
true. He must have known I would never betray his private
beliefs to others.

The thoughts flashed in illuminating celerity across my
mind. They came with such rapidity that it took me some time
to amplify them, and I now set them down before you, dear
descendant or chance reader.

In ancient times, the Bull was worshipped. Is that why
the symbol of a Bull and its Calf were important to the
Egyptians, and to the Israelites who later danced around
it? The Bull has power — is power itself. But it is an animal,
nonetheless.... What a strange symbol to worship.

Knossos — lehavdil — Mount Moriah, and again —
lehavdil — the crucifixion all deal with blood.[35] Is human
and animal sacrifice and blood an essential part of placating
a god, and — lehavdil — God? In Christian parlance, the story
of Abraham and Isaac is called "The Sacrifice of Isaac,"
while in Hebrew it is known as Akedat Yitzhak, "The
Binding of Isaac." Is this not a basic difference? The Binding
is an almost-sacrifice, which then turns into a command to
live; in their religion Jesus must die. Thus, the Resurrection
is an attempt to turn Jesus into Isaac. But rising from the
dead after three days is an image I cannot accept. And the
form of the Hanged One on a cross is, in my eyes, not a
symbol of life, but of the very opposite.

The next day a band of armed riders, well clad in
Venetian livery, escorted us along the short route to the
supposed area of Knossos. Though Venetian in dress, a
good part of the troop had been raised locally. Their officers,
however — it was firmly and strongly stressed — were from terra
firma. Even riding slowly to accommodate me, the ride took
under two hours. The sun shone brightly, and the deep green
of the forests, enriched by the winter rains, surrounded us in
a glorious mantle of fertility. The green was reflected in the
silvery sheen of the olive trees stretching far and wide across
the valleys, rising over the slow slopes and gentle hills through
which we rode. Then a valley, in which nestled ruins of Roman
Knossos, built, , they say over Minoan Knossos, a civilization,
we are told, existing hundreds of years before the Patriarch
Abraham. But it has yet to be seen.[36] In my mind, I heard the

[35] The Hebrew word lehavdil means "in contradistinction," but conveys a basic lack of
desire to compare the two, because the innate superiority or essential difference. Knossos
is distinct from Moriah, where Isaac's Sacrifice is to take place. And Isaac's binding to
the altar is vastly different from the crucifixion and death of Jesus.
[36] Excavations on the site of Knossos were first conducted as late as 1878.

roaring of bulls and even smelt the spurting of hot blood from innocent young sacrifices. The ghost of the blood lust, freed in my conversation the day before, reared itself. I feared it might be, as well, a dread portent of what would come to pass.

~

Here I return to an earlier subject. As I indicated earlier, I have written in detail the rationale for my behavior in the guise of a Christian, especially for the edification of my offspring's offspring, may He grant that this come into their hands.

Resolutions Regarding "Their" Customs

The most recurrent problem will be with food. For over fifty years—all my life—I have never tasted forbidden food like pork or shellfish, have never mixed meat and milk in one meal. How can I begin now to eat what is forbidden? Rationally, I may do everything to save my life except the three forbidden acts.[37] Reason is one thing: long years of ingrained habit are another. Therefore I have resolved to find a way, even though it involves a level of prevarication (which nonetheless, will save my life!), to abstain from meat most of the time.

Originally I had thought that I would hint at some dark sin or crime in my past to atone for which I had pledged abstinence from meat all year, but for three days: Christmas, Easter Sunday, and New Year's Day. I hoped that the hints would add semblance to the need for contrition. But on second thought, I came to the conclusion that it is better to stay away from elaborate lies when a simple one will do just as well.

---

[37] One may do anything to save any life (pikuah nefesh) except: perform acts of idolatry or the worship of false gods, engage in forbidden sex (e.g., with a married woman, or incest), and commit murder. To die rather than perform these cardinal transgressions is considered an act worthy of Divine approval (kiddush ha-Shem: hallowing the Name of God). [Let himself be killed, and not transgress these. Babylonian Talmud, Sanhedrin 74a.]

Who will argue with a great doctor? I will cite one who has
prescribed a diet of little or no meat. I ate lamb at the Ducal
table the first night he invited me, as a sign of respect, and an
act of thanksgiving, and used the opportunity to announce my
general abstinence from meat of all types.

The problem of drinking wine produced by non-Jews
is less important, for some authorities permit it, unless it is
destined for Church use, in which case all forbid it. Even wine
touched by a priest is deemed sanctified for their religion.
There will certainly be priests and prelates dining at the tables
I shall necessarily frequent. Here, I will bow to the principle of
saving life. This, I am sure, will not be considered worshiping
false gods.

Participating in prayers in a church does, however,
present the problem of worshiping graven images and statues,
and of uttering prayers, crossing oneself, and kneeling. I have
on occasion joined my friend and teacher Rabbi Leone da
Modena when he has gone to hear outstanding preachers in
the grand churches of Venice. Though he has not—indeed
cannot—pray there, or join in the crossing and genuflecting,
he has attended Christian services. He explained to me that
he did so to enhance peaceful relations, for have not priests
and indeed bishops come to hear his magnificent oratory in
the synagogues of the ghetto? (With all my love and respect
for Leone, I believe also curiosity and probably vanity were
also at work, though only the Holy One, blessed be He, can
truly measure the workings of the kidneys and of the heart.)[38]
And, considering the tenuous situation of Jews in the Christian

[38] The ancients located emotions in various internal organs. The Hebrews believed
remorse lay in the kidneys, hence musar klayot, literally "the chastisement (morality)
of the kidneys" or figuratively "pangs of conscience." [The present annotator has seen
menus in a Tel Aviv restaurant showing "kidney" in the Hebrew listing and "remorse"
in the English translation!] In various High Holiday prayers, the form of language is a
reference to God as investigating or examining "kidneys (conscience) and heart is used,
based on Jeremiah 11:20 and Psalms 7:10.

principalities, whose very right of residence and livelihood depend on the renewal of the condotta by the local Christian ruler every few years, we need each precious modicum of goodwill.

Well, then, I shall attend church as often as the other men of my class do, and though I shall bow and cross myself I cannot kneel. In my heart, though, I shall be in the Holy Temple of Jerusalem, may it be established speedily and in our day. I will even make confession, for often the confessor may be a learned and intelligent man, whom I may befriend as an intellectual companion. Though this may indeed be skirting danger. And if I am ignorant of the words of some prayers, why, upper class mumbling often passes for superiority of breeding!

These will be the most constant and therefore obvious forms of behavior: food and prayer. There is another danger, one which I noticed as I left the confines of my previous life. Our people in Italy have our own Italian Jewish forms of speech, and sometimes use Hebrew words in our Italian. However, while yet a student, I learned to speak "outside" differently from how I spoke "inside," at hearth and home. Now, I shall need to be doubly on guard against such slips.[39] And it will take a bit of distance, a bit of hauteur, a colder bearing than that of the tolerated Jewish doctor.... We shall see.

Not desecrating the beloved Shabbat will not be a difficulty. No one will question my limiting my days of activities. But the atmosphere, the synagogue, the prayers.... Similarly, to abstain from bread during the Passover will not be difficult. But how will I manage without community?

---

[39] It is striking that we find the terms "inside" and "outside" here, referring to behavior and language within the Jewish home or group and outside of it, with non-Jews. Herman Wouk used the same term 350 years or so later, with his novel *Inside—Outside* (Random House, New York, 1958).

I conclude with this prayer: May the above be found in time to come, enlighten its finders and eventual readers, and anticipate some of the queries they may have.

Let me add a warning to those generations. Though we are told that "by stratagems shalt thou make war," prevarication and dissembling should be avoided, for this is evil.[40] It is prohibited behavior, dangerous to the soul itself. But, beyond this, life is the greatest gift we have, and we may, nay we must preserve and prolong it, up to the limit of — Heaven forbid — idolatry, incest or adultery, and the spilling of blood. These we must never do, on pain of death itself.

---

[40] Proverbs 24:6.

CHAPTER THE SIXTH

With the help of Heaven

The days that followed were packed with every possible emotion that novelty brings. Our faces were set for the fertile Plain of Messara, where the Duke's properties lie.

My retainers from Messara had been summoned by a swift courier to lead us on our way. (How speedily one becomes accustomed to lordship and possessiveness.) They came with a bodyguard of fierce-looking swarthy horsemen, eight in number, armed with gigantic mustachios, swords, daggers, and muskets. Bandoliers with bulging pouches of gunpowder and musketry balls criss-crossed over their black handsomely embroidered Cretan vests, contrasting with their baggy white trousers. The Duke of Candia sent along another eight heavily armed men, wearing the armor and bearing the sword, dagger, musket, and livery of the Venetian soldiery, under the command of an Italian junior officer. Thus we formed a heavy party, mostly on horseback, with muleteers leading their pack animals laden with the food and supplies we would be bringing to our new home.

The entire trip was about only twenty-five miglii, perhaps even thirty, as measured by the milia passuum of the Romans.[41] But being so heavily laden and climbing on mule tracks, up mountain and down dale, with stops at villages that received us royally, it took three days. From time to time, I was

---

[41] A thousand Roman paces, somewhat shorter than the British mile. In all, 25 Roman miles would be about 22 miles or some 35 kilometers.

taken to holy Christian sites as well as ruins of ancient pagan temples and villas near our road.

The route to Messara took us out of Hania Gate into a lush valley in which olive-green groves in the lower, warm areas, alternated with carefully tended vineyards through the Malevisi area. The young officer — by accent and speech obviously well educated — spoke with pride of the local wine.

"Excellency," he said. I almost turned about to find whom he was addressing. "Excellency, this area is world-famed. The wine from these grapes of Malevisi naturally is called malvasia, and is well liked throughout Europe, reaching even the distant shores of the British peoples.[42] They, however, call it 'malmsey,'" he said with a dismissive laugh. "Their rough tongues must mangle words as much as the barbaric Teutons." His source for this information was the wine-exporters, he told me, and I marked it well, to see whether we might not use this grape in our region, in Messara, were it not yet there.

We were traversing one of the several long narrow parallel valleys, separated by hills and low mountains. Anxious to show his military knowledge, young Severus (for so I gave him a semi-mocking cognomen) explained the strategic implications of these ridges running from the north to the south of the island.

As we mounted the hills, the Sea of Crete sparkled in its azure beauty, stretching off to the horizon into the Mediterranean. Perhaps the white-crested wave I saw would eventually caress the shores of the Holy Land. The poems of Rabbi Yehuda Ha-Levy the Spaniard echoed through my head. The wave might very well touch land at Jaffa or Caesarea, leading me again to ask myself the recurrent question, "What am I doing here, rather than there?" Crete, after all, is not the

---

[42] See Chapter the 5th, note 9.

reaches of the uttermost West, where the poet had been, but just—even in rough seas—a few days' sailing to our Land.[43]

Once again I was distracted by the beauty of this terrain. Unlike the barren wastes of the Holy Land, watered more by tears than rain, the abundant Cretan winter rainfall had left the hillsides sparkling with flowers: anemones, narcissus, and daffodils were the few I knew personally. As a doctor, I was better at recognizing the herbs I saw growing along the wayside and into the valleys: foxglove and sage, rosemary and thyme. My escorts from Messara identified for me a plant they called alabdna, from which we can extract ladunum.[44] Their scents perfumed the valley, and bees could be heard in a bass accompaniment to the higher octaves of chattering birds, some en route to Europe, and others—the nightingales especially— indigenous. So Severus told me, at any rate. I also learned that the peasants boil sage tea, which they call the brew of health, to strengthen their constitution and stamina. They dry the plants in large pillowcases hanging from a ceiling beam or doorway, so even indoors the air is fragrant and refreshing. The sage tea seems to do good, judging by the industry and diligence of the strong countrymen and women.

Agios Mironos, a village where we slept the second night, is named for an early Bishop of Knossos, both a slayer of dragons and a martyr. We continued on past smaller villages, setting our face for Agia (Santa) Varvara, as the local populace pronounced Barbara. Agia Barbara/Varvara also was a martyr. Christianity seems to like having martyrs.... I wondered how far I, as a non-Jew, could discuss religious matters theoretically

---

[43] Yehuda HaLevy (often referred to as ha-Sefaradi—the Spaniard), about 1075–1141, was an important medieval Jewish philosopher and the great beloved poet of the love of Zion. These poems were canonized and appear in the most solemn days' prayer books. The reference here is the poem, "My heart is the East, while I am in the uttermost West."
[44] Foxglove is digitalis purpurea, whose leaves are used as a powerful medicine, both as a sedative and diuretic. Ladanam, or closer to the original Greek, labdanum, is a gum resin gathered from cistus plants (rockroses) and used in perfumes and plasters.

in my new capacity. Thus I attempted to draw out my intelligent "fellow Gentile."

"Young Severus, what do you think? Do we not have an abundance of martyrs in our sacred tradition?" I asked. "I wonder whether people really choose to become revered as martyrs, or whether they would not prefer to live ordinary lives."

Severus stared at me, startled, perhaps shocked. "Excellency, we are taught...."

"Of course, we are taught that our Holy Saints rejoiced in the opportunity to martyr themselves, but I—for one—have never really wanted to be a martyr. Have you?"

The young officer checked his horse's pace, and in a quiet voice admitted, "Well, when I was educated in the lives of the Saints, I often thought I would prefer to go to a ball, or attend a theater, or drink with my friends. But we who are born to the nobility must uphold the ways of the Church and of our own city. We leave these issues to philosophers."

I remained silent for some time. Finally, I said, "Have you read 'The Prince,' a short treatise by Nicolo Machiavelli, the Florentine?"

"Yes, Excellency, I have."

"You will know then how, as he describes it, power is wielded by the secular rulers."

Severus nodded. A spark of light flashed in his brown eyes. He thought a while, and then said, "Yes, I see. Power is power, secular and sacred. But the ultimate power is that of forgiving sins and promising Paradise."

"This indeed gives the clergy great power." I said no more; I was afraid that to do so might be dangerous. Severus was a thinking man. He would yet go far.

God, gods, faith, reality…. There, off to the right, we saw the cruel and desolate Psiloritis mountain range. Rising above them were the twin peaks of the fabled Mount Ida, where little Zeus, later to be chief of their gods, was hidden by Rhea, his mother. It beggars understanding how the ancients could have truly believed that Zeus was hidden by his mother on distant Mount Ida to prevent his dread father Kronos from finding and devouring him.

We continued through Agia Varvara, once again simultaneously suffering and enjoying the hospitality of the elders. Did it just seem to me that along with the courteous reception by the leaders and Greek priests, there were glances of anger and perhaps hatred towards us? I asked Severus.

"Sir, I am here but one year and have little direct knowledge of the island's villages. My fellow officers say the Cretans are fierce fighters, with long memories; perhaps their old animosity to us, invaders with a different language, culture, and religion, still smolders. And maybe as well, it is due to the taxes we take, the soldiers or galley-rowers we press into service."

Given my own background, from outside their religious struggle, I wondered whether the Lion of Saint Mark of Venice did not symbolize for them the Catholic "heresy," for compared to differences among different kinds of Jews, the hatred of Christian for Christian is unparalleled. The European Crusaders, the so-called Latins, en route to liberate the Holy Land and its sites from the "infidel" Muslims, detoured to sack and pillage Greek Orthodox Constantinople, Byzantium.[45]

[45] Crusaders pillaged the city in 1204, and controlled Byzantium until it was retaken from the Latins in 1261. The gallantry attributed to the Crusaders in folklore and literature bears little relationship to venal reality. The Crusades stamped Jewish history into a martyrology, and surrounded Ashkenazi Jewish history with a permanent wall of lamentation, tears, and sense of powerlessness. The historian, Salo W. Baron has called this the "lachrymose" school of Jewish historians. A martyrology is still recited each week at the Sabbath prayer following Torah reading in Orthodox Jewish Ashk services and on days of mourning and fasting.

Church treasures were stolen or wantonly damaged — by Christians — priceless icons destroyed and innocent women — even nuns! — raped, abolishing possibly forever any hope of tolerance between the Eastern Greek Church and the Western Roman Church. And I, the impostor, though Italian and seeming Latin, but nonetheless a crypto-Jew, might become the butt of this long-standing and deeply rooted prejudice. Neither side may remember why, but all carry on the hate from generation to generation. We sons of Jacob know it so well, for the Crusaders, en route to their holy mission, martyred entire communities. In the name of God, the rulers canceled their debts to us and their sins to man and God by killing women and children. Vae victis et victoribus vae erat.[46]

At first, my attention had been distracted by the beauty of the route, and the novelty of meeting the local inhabitants. Now, as if to emphasize my new perceptions, I could see that not all was well between the mainlanders and their regular soldiers and the islanders in my escort. They rode separately; they barely exchanged more than perfunctory greetings.

We headed along a winding difficult road, and the peaceful, rich Plain of Messara, my new charge and home, came into sight. Sheltered by the rough Asteriousia Mountains from the hostile dry Libyan winds, the rich plain has known cultivation from ancient times. It stretches from the Gulf of Messara across many miglii. Tender green fields of sprouting grains — wheat, barley, rye, and spelt — yielded to the olive trees and vines, while near the scattered villages and small clusters of houses, vegetable gardens abounded. This is a land of milk and honey. Its mountainous surroundings provide protection from invaders as well as excessive exposure to the elements, and its sun-bathed valleys give forth rich crops.

---

[46] The author paraphrases the Latin "Woe unto the vanquished, woe unto the victors," by adding the word that turns it into a curse, "and may woe betide the victors."

We passed Gortyna, the ancient Gortys, capital of Crete in olden times. Doubtless, Jews lived here even earlier, or at least in the port cities, for I recall mention of this in some documents possibly as far back at the Maccabean era. But the only recollection I have of a specific source is Yosef ben Mattityahu, the historian, known to the Gentiles as Josephus Flavius. He mentioned Crete as the place where a Jewish impostor sought to be recognized as King Herod's son Alexander.[47]

Gortina of old was supposed to have had imposing buildings, and one can see that it was at once large and prosperous. The ancient structures themselves have been raided for their building stones and bricks, but nonetheless one sees an amphitheater as befits the ancient lovers of drama, and nearby they say there was a stone bearing a mysterious code of laws that was written and promulgated there as far back as two thousand years ago. It was a code that dealt with the same issues of family law, slaves, and property rights that Moses and our later sages similarly had to consider and adjudicate.[48]

This part of the world, which produced such great civilizations that were so close physically — Egypt and Sinai, Israel and Judea, Greece and Rome — this basin in the Eastern part of the sea, which more nations than Rome saw as mare nostrum — gave forth codified laws at about the same time. The thought struck me overwhelmingly in this blessed valley. Perhaps that is what brought some of our forefathers here. Law and safety, peace and prosperity.

---

[47] Josephus Flavius had been commander of the Galilee during the Jewish War (whose rising up against Rome began in 66 of the Christian Era). He evaded a suicide pact he had initiated in the fortified and besieged Yotfata, when the defense against the Romans was hopeless, and defected to Rome, where he became a noted historian. He married a Jewish woman from Crete (!) whose family had moved to Rome. The actual reference is in Antiquities17:12.

[48] The Gortys Law Code was discovered in 1884. It is written in an old Doric dialect of Greek, dated the first half of the 5th century before the Christian Era, therefore about 2,000 years before our narrator's period.

This is not a travel book, like that of the illustrious Benjamin of Tudela, so I will not go into further details.[49] I will just remark that the Basilica of St. Titus is nearby — in Greek he is called Agios Titos. He was supposedly sent to Crete to convert the inhabitants to Christianity while his namesake mounted the siege of Jerusalem.[50] I thought once again that perhaps this is the way of the world, that it is a scale or balance: when one side goes down, the other goes up. The Cretans celebrate their Titus with memory and buildings; we Jews will not walk through boastful Rome's Arch of the other Titus, Commander of the Legions in Palestine and later Emperor, symbol and reminder of Judea's capture and desecration, a painful memory ever to be borne. A pang of envy passed through me toward these people rooted in their land since before time was counted.

The lush lands of the Messara Plain were indeed a "breadbasket," as it is called. In the past, Messara had grown field crops — wheat, barley, oats. But with the prices that olive oil and malmsey wine command in the West, as well as in some Eastern ports, here too olive trees and vineyards were planted during recent decades. The Messarans are good farmers; I saw that the vines had been planted on slanting hillsides, and the olives on hardier and rocker soil, saving the flat lands for grain.

The donkey and mule trains leave for Heraklion and for Hania regularly, bearing sacks of grain, and large earthenware jugs filled with the rich wine and the viscous olive oil, virgin green and pungent. The jugs lack the ancient beauty and

[49] Benjamin of Tudela (Tudela is a town in Spain; Benjamin died in 1173) was a noted traveler who covered the main regions of Spain, France, and Italy. His book is an account of his travels—using every means then available—into today's Iraq and Persia, Arabia and Palestine, returning via Egypt and Sicily. To this very day, geographers and historians recognize the debt they owe him for his concise and illuminating notes.

[50] Titus, according to Acts of the Apostles, was commissioned by Paul to restore peace among contending Christian groups. According to legend, he died at Gortys at age 94. During the 4th century, he was beatified and declared the patron saint of Crete.

delicate design of the amphorae preserved in the collections of
the mighty and the rich on the mainland. I also saw some green
citrus trees bearing a fruit that may indeed have been the etrog
of the Talmud, the Bible's lemon-like fruit of beauty.[51] They
immediately added a note of familiarity, almost homecoming;
come the harvest feast of Tabernacles, I will at least be able to
finger one and make the blessing silently, with none the wiser.

A large company of armed Cretans came riding out
toward us, a veritable troop of Esau come to receive Jacob.
Unlike our forefather, I had no reason to fear. They were led
by the chief retainer, Stavros, who welcomed me in a short
address. He rode at my right side, and offered simple and
direct explanations of the view in Greek-flavored Italian.
The rest of our welcome was generally warm, and though I
could see both frank and less frank stares of evaluation. Their
hospitality was stronger than their suspicion, or at least they
were willing to suspend suspicion until they could take my
measure. After all, I was the Lord Lieutenant of the Duke of
Mantua in this place, and my decisions would affect their daily
lives and their prosperity. In truth, they would want to know
if I would treat them with respect, and protect them from
confiscation of crops and forced recruitment to the Venetian
regiments to which they had all too often been subject. Even
worse, as they told me when they felt comfortable enough to
speak more freely, sea captains pressed poor simple peasants
into slave labor to row their galleys. In brief, their glances said,
"Will he be like mild Mantua, or like venal Venice?"

[51] Leviticus 23:40. ". . . the fruit of the hadar tree," or in a more poetic translation "of the
beauteous tree," or just plain "citrus-tree," as in modern Hebrew. The etrog is used on
Sukkot, the harvest Festival of Tabernacles..

The center of our area was in a small village officially called Gonzaga, but its Greek name was Betadas.[52] The locals always called it Betadas, but in reports home we referred to it as Gonzaga da Messara....

The festivities lasted almost a week. One dinner at the home Stavros, chief retainer, steward of my affairs, and therefore, indeed, of the Duke's. Then I was the honored guest at the table of the local priest, Michaelis; the local village headman, Ioannis; and the schoolmaster of the church school and the most literate man in the village, Danielos. The final dinner was mine, in the fine stone "mansion" provided to me as the Duke's Deputy or Lieutenant as I was called (Il Tenente del' Doge). In our lands, the title *Doge* referred to the Duke of Mantua; the Venetian Duke, who was elected rather than born to his rank, was known as Il Doge Veneziano.

The festivities very nearly came to a bloody end. The troop of "Venetians" had been invited to stay and enjoy a few days of our hospitality. It was almost evening, and a table had been set for them, and for the younger men and older boys curious to meet the soldiers. Suddenly I heard a commotion, a clamor, shouts, and women's screams. The troop stood in a semi-circle, swords drawn, ready to defend themselves, while perhaps twenty or twenty-five villagers advanced toward them with drawn poignards and swords. Some ran to get their muskets.

Stavros stood between the two groups, which were loudly cursing one another in language I could understand only from tone and gesture. Suddenly a village lad threw himself at a soldier and, in his rush, felled the man. The other soldiers were about to use the flats of their swords on the

[52] Careful review of the literature of the period, and consultations with specialists in Cretan history and geography show no record of these names. For reasons known to de' Pomi, and which we shall see hinted at later in his text, the writer may have wished to preserve the secret of the exact location.

young villager, when the sergeant of the troop uttered a loud command in Italian. "Cease and hold your arms!" Stavros turned to the villagers and hurled a few angry words at them in Greek, and they too stood transfixed. Both sides remained frozen, while the soldier and the village boy wrestled in the dust.

I strode out, unarmed, with my head uncovered, and stopped next to Stavros. In uncontrolled rage, I lifted my hands to the skies and shouted, at first, unwittingly, in Hebrew "Dai! Dai!" and then "Basta! Basta!" Arms still raised, like Moses, I stood and commanded the sergeant, "Control your man!" I turned to Stavros, and tilted my head toward the village lad. The two senior men pulled the younger men apart. They stood abashed and ashamed.

I asked Stavros to bring me a chair and heard their case on the spot. There were two elements to it. First, the soldier had seen a village girl walking by and had made a crude remark. The girl's brother rose to protest the insult. He knew the soldier had been pressed into duty from a captured Turkish ship, and must originally have been a Muslim. As I have already noted, there was no love lost anyway between the locals and the Venetian soldiers.

"Mohammed is a pig and so are you," the lad had cursed the soldier. It was a double insult to a man striving to fit in with rest of the troop, all Christians. An insult to one of their cohorts became an insult to all the soldiers, out of solidarity with their fellow.

"Your mother is a whore and your father a Jew!" The return taunt was not long in coming.

I heard the evidence, in a clamor of variegated and strange Italian accents and ordered the sergeant to report the incident to Severus, who was out hunting. My recommendation was ten canes on the shoulders and confinement to prison, unless the soldier did not immediately apologize fully to both the lad and his sister in front of all. The sergeant was advised to announce that he would send two goats as a settlement (which later I would privately repay, to save face all round), and then called the lad over. I asked Stavros to tell the indignant young brother that Jesus forgave sinners, and that the soldier wished to make a contrite apology and the troop would make a settlement to salve the lass's honor. He had no choice but to practice Christian charity. So the blood-letting was averted this time. Just barely.

The curses, though, resounded in my head for many a day. "Mohammed, pig, whore, Jew!" It was a refrain. "Mohammed, pig, whore, Jew." A cloud on my week's festivities. A warning, perhaps.

In the end, as the Bible says, "From strength came forth sweetness," another way of saying all's well that ends well.[53] The villagers and the inhabitants of our estate learned that I have strength, that I am not a coward, and that I will defend their interests. The Venetians saw I was neither fearful, nor unfair. Thus my name and that of my master gained in reputation. A sad comment: our good names are built on others' weaknesses.

---

[53] "From the strong, etc." Judges 14:14.

CHAPTER THE SEVENTH

Stavros had seen to it that the "mansion" was sparkling. Sage and rosemary were drying in each room to add sweetness to the clear air, protected by the mountains from the cruel dry Libyan winds. By standards of terra firma or even of Candia, this would be an ordinary solid and respectable house for a good citizen, banker, or merchant of medium standing. (And incomparably better than the houses of Jews in Venice, which tend to be cramped together in order to have proximity to one another, to the purveyors of kasher food, to the ritual bath and the synagogue.) Here in Messara, comparison must be made to the small stone houses of the more prosperous villagers, and to the even smaller and simpler houses of those of lesser rank.

Stavros had staffed my house with an old retired retainer, a kind of country butler, and a Bosnian serving-girl. Nikos, the "butler," spoke both Italian and Greek, and could look after my requests and translate to the locals as needed. He could also cook simple fare when I ate at home — finer meals came from the table of Stavros himself.

Now, in regard to the servant-girl, dear reader (and dear descendant, if God wills that these writings fall into your hands generations hence), "my sins will I recall today."[54] It is not against the Jewish way for a person to respond to the needs of the flesh, but, "from the Torah," he is to refrain from

---

[54] This is a reference to Genesis 41:9, and became a cliché in the hands of writers and preachers.

adultery or incest, and, "from the Rabbis," he is also to abstain from profligate behavior.[55] Having been without my dear Gentilla who mothered all my children and stood by me in the vagaries of life for some thirty years until she was summoned to the Court on High, I have from time to time assuaged my bodily needs in accordance with the advice of our Sages. That is, I have not behaved in profligate fashion, nor — of course — compromised my relations with my patients, beautiful as some were, and among whom romantic dalliance is part of the culture. (If I may digress, the knowledge that the act of confession brings forgiveness, and that indulgences are readily available — often for a price — from priest and even Pope, made this dalliance, or even outright adultery, a "sin" not to be taken seriously.[56] The example of senior prelates and ordinary priests having mistresses and bastards certainly provided an example easier to follow than that of the dour new Christian exponents of reform: Luther, Calvin, and Knox.)

The basic problem was that the Christians forbid us to have carnal knowledge of non-Jewish women. Though not unknown, it is very dangerous. I thus found Jewesses who had strayed into evil ways. Twice, in different places in my wanderings, did I rescue these fallen souls from further servitude in the "houses" where I found them. Twice did I pay a heavy redemption cost to release them from their bondage. Twice did they find discreet places where they could live an honest life, but for the several hours a week they devoted to

[55] These are translations of the Aramaic Talmudic expressions for mide-oraita and mide-rabbanan: the first usually dealing with specifically prohibited or sanctioned behavior in the first five books, (the Pentateuch or Written Law), and the latter covers behavior proscribed by the masters of the Mishna and Gemara (Oral Law or Talmud) in the approximate period of 300 BCE to 500 CE.

[56] Indulgences supposedly lessened the sinner's time in Purgatory. Their sale, castigated by Luther, was outlawed at the Council of Trent in 1545.

me. Without my doctor's robes and hat, in the swirling fog, or in the rain of a misty night, or sometimes even in my robes in broad daylight, as though visiting a patient, did I find solace in their grateful attentions.

The dowry I gave one of these transformed fallen woman provided the basis for a marriage that lasted and brought fine children into the world, children who will never know their mother's past, for she moved to the land of the Magyars, where her husband dealt in furs and pelts. I will not pretend that I did this purely for the sake of heaven, but I hope my finding comfort in this will not be accounted a fault or sin, but a natural act, ending well for all. The other, poor soul, contracted the lung disease, and all my potions and medicines could do naught for her until she was brought and reconciled to her old mother, and now they lie side by side in the Hebrew cemetery in....(Even in this memoir, I will not cast suspicion on anyone.)

Of course the situation here is simpler. I was no longer limited by the prohibition of lying with Gentile women. To the contrary, while I was in the home of the Monsignor, and in Candia, in the ducal palace, the maidservants made it clear that they would be willing to provide every feminine kindness.

My Bosnian servant-girl was among a group of Muslims who had been abducted by Christians, and sold to pirates who brought her to Crete some years ago. Her beauty and form commanded a goodly price at the slave market in Hania. Stavros had bought her along with several able-bodied men, and the local priest had converted them to the Greek Church. She spoke both Italian and Greek and had been given the name Sophia, meaning "enlightenment" or "wisdom," symbolizing her transition from Islam to the "true faith" of the locals. It could as well have been a symbol of reconverting the Mosque of Agia Sophia in Constantinople into the church it had been under Byzantium.

She was perhaps in her early twenties—she was tall and full-breasted. She seemed spotlessly clean, and, of an evening, would sometimes put a sprig of green or a flower above her right ear, though it was mostly Cretan men who had this prerogative. Her eyes were somewhat aslant, pale blue verging on gray; her hair, bundled into a string coif veered from dark blond to reddish brown or chestnut; her cheeks were wide with high bones, and she moved with a rhythmic flow. At first glance she captured my interest, as she lowered clever eyes to my frank gaze.

In brief, as the days—and nights—passed, she entered my bedroom freely, and then my bed, and swiftly went from being like David's Shunammite to my own Hagar.[57] I called her this in the privacy of my bosom, and sometimes also Ketura.[58] She had been ill-used by men in the past, so it seemed from her fears and lassitude, but kindness and patience brought her in short shrift to enjoy the fruits with which the Creator has blessed us, for "male and female did He create them."[59]

Clever Sophia, having grown up a Muslim, certainly knew that her kinsmen were circumcised, and that Christians were not. I had to think of some way to explain the sign of the covenant on my member. Dear reader, we are taught that white lies are permitted to preserve peace, and certainly to promote safety of life and limb. Thus, falling back upon my medical standing, I told her that in an epidemic that had struck men in Ferrara, the doctors observed that Jews had survived better than the Christians. As a result, many Christian men were circumcised by Jewish mohalim, specialists in circumcision.

[57] Avishag the Shunamite (i.e., from Shunam) was the "young virgin" brought to warm the bed of King David in his latter days, "and the King did not know her" (I Kings 1:1–4). Hagar was Sarah's handmaiden given to Abraham the Patriarch by his wife to bear children for her barren mistress, and was mother of Ishmael (Genesis 16:1–3). Perhaps choosing the name Hagar had meaning both because of the narrator's first name, or perhaps to hint at Sophia's Muslim origins.

[58] Ketura was Abraham's mistress or concubine after Sarah's death (Genesis 25:1).

[59] Genesis 5:2.

This explanation passed without a problem, probably due to her great intelligence. I found a further indication of this that occasioned me much pleasure.

One day, as I entered the parlor of my home, I saw her trying to stuff something behind a pillow strewn on the divan. A blush suffused her pretty face as I gazed at her, the unspoken question in my glance. She asked my permission to leave. I gently asked her to sit down, and then she answered my unspoken question directly. "I have kept this secret from you, master, because I have gained something precious, and awaited the correct moment to tell you of it. But I was afraid you might not approve."

"Have no fear, sweet Sophia, and tell me."

She brought forth a "Libro delle Ore," the same Book of Hours I had seen on the reading tables of the patrician ladies whom I had treated on the mainland. I leafed through the beautifully illuminated pages, filled with prayers, psalms, and martyrologies to while away the hours of ladies of leisure, languidly leafing through the pages. The book was designed for the ladies of the rich, the powerful, the aristocrats.[60] Doubtless one of my predecessors had left it behind. Now, here was a poor woman, a slave, no less, able to read. More than that, this was in contradistinction to most of the men here, and all of the women. Sophia/Hagar/Ketura had learned to read by begging occasional help from Danielos, and then assiduously struggling on her own to form words, sentences.

The problem was to find books for her, and to hide her knowledge from the curious who might tell the priest, who had cast an eye on her for himself. This man of God had a fear of learning, which I later discovered was not a private

---

[60] The Book—originally handwritten and illustrated manuscripts that began their evolution in the 13th century, when lay people wished to emulate the prayer cycles in the breviary used by monks and nuns. From this eventually came the *Book of Hours*, later, of course, printed, but hand-illuminated.

predilection. In effect, it was more or less inculcated by the
Church, for the Eastern rite despises the Western, inter alia,
because of the latter's pride in intellectualism and learning
amidst the prevalent clerical vices I have earlier recounted.

Sophia "belonged" to Stavros, but in truth, the Cretans
did not agree with slavery and treated her well—somewhere
between an indentured servant and a poor dependent relative.
I resolved to buy her from him, and give her manumission. She
deserved better from life than to live in fear of discovery of her
crime: literacy!

The time soon came for Stavros to sit down with me and
induct me into the affairs I needed to master in order to carry
out my responsibilities to the Duke. In a careful and unhurried
way, Stavros reported to me at great length about our holdings,
that covered many dozen square miglii—had they indeed been
square—and on which hundreds of villagers lived in smaller
and larger hamlets.

"Are we required to levy troops?" I asked him.

"Because of the Duke of Mantua's treaty with Venice, our
men are exempt from impressment or service in the galleys...."
He paused. "But when the Turk attempts to conquer us," he
said, in a cold grim voice, "we raise four hundred foot muskets,
and all the mules needed to bear their supplies, as well as a
troop of fifty horsemen."

So rich were the lands of our Duke, I thought to myself.
"What a blessing that it has not been necessary," I added out
loud.

Again the steely determination, the controlled anger
changed the lines of his face. Even his large mustachios seemed
to quiver, and his jaws clenched. "The Turk will never stop
trying. For them, we are infidels, and our land, they claim 'once

Muslim, is forever Muslim.' Every treaty we make is honored only as long as we can fight them off. They know our strength and constantly probe our weakness. Excellency, you are new here. Remember the Turk is never to be trusted. They kill, they rape, they pillage, they burn...."

"But Stavros, peace has reigned for a long time here."

"We will not forget what they did to us. One day, we will pray again in Agia Sophia in Constantinople, and our Church will again live in freedom on both sides of the Greek isles. Even the Frankish crusaders, with respect, sir, need to be shown that Agia Sophia and the true Christianity will be restored to the great city."

"Please God," I replied piously, and changed the subject. But his face clouded over again at my next question, "What about within our lands, dear Stavros? Do the villagers live in peace among themselves? Will I be called upon often to adjudicate among them?"

"There are occasional arguments, sometimes some bloodshed in fist-fights, or with mattocks. Naturally these fights are over the exact boundaries between holdings. But these are unusual and the bad reputation of the transgressors spreads quickly, so they bear the brunt of our judgments. But...."

"But," I encouraged him.

"But we have a number of ugly vendette, which in some cases have been going on for generations. Sometimes they have decimated families, often for reasons that are all but lost in the mists of memory. He sighed. "We Cretans value pride and manliness. We have a rich sense of virtus, he added, using the Latin word. "Insult arouses blood-lust, and killing calls for revenge."

Yes, I thought, revenge plays its role today, just as it did when Moses our Teacher wisely set aside six towns of refuge to protect the accidental killer from the avenging family's rage.[61]

Stavros continued. "You saw the other day how a word or a look can kindle fire." He paused, searching for the right phrase, since he was not a man given to smooth speech. "If I may say, Excellency, your firm intervention and wise decision have made a very good impression. We are always careful when new representatives come from Mantua — actually, sir, anyone from the mainland — for affairs are not always seen eye-to-eye by the Greeks and the Latins. Your decision reassured our men, and the word will reach far and wide."

I tried to hide a smile of pleasure, and nodded my thanks. We returned to our estate's reports. The financial books and lists were meticulous, written in a careful Italian hand by Danielos: quantities of grain grown, or kept for planting or provisions, and amounts sold. Vineyards (more and more of which were being planted for the good prices brought by wine) and olive groves were in a separate report. They also showed quantities sent to the mainland in kind, for sale by the Duke's factors in Venice as well as those sold here or in Hania or Candia for gold or other currency. In all, the report seemed as solid and factual as Stavros himself. As a token of my respect and trust, I invited him to take lunch with me that day.

The next few weeks were busy and enjoyable. I wished to spend four days each week on inspection tours of our villages, hamlets, and fields. We rode out every Monday, with a small band of retainers, and on Stavros's advice, I brought gifts for the various headmen: purses of coins and a collection of spices or other expensive delicacies — also some for the village elders. Often we halted at a roadside icon or a small country church,

---

[61] Numbers 11:13, and especially Numbers 35:6 ff.

and though not every hamlet had its priest, there was always a simple place of worship. Some had primitive mosaics set in their walls, others paintings by some local unskilled but devout soul. Though not as gracious as the soaring bell tower of Mantua or the brooding beautiful churches of Venice looking at themselves in the waters of the Canale Grande, their simplicity embodied a touching manifestation of faith. This in itself was a beauty consonant with the land itself.

In these simple places of worship I joined Stavros and his men in silent devotion, removing my hat, and bowing my head as they crossed themselves the Greek way and sometimes kissed the icons. I knew that the theologians argued that these were not idols, but rather material representations of the spiritual idea, but nonetheless wondered what the unschooled and unsophisticated peasant really felt. This after all was not Alexandria or Byzantium. Here, some priests were barely literate. But literacy is not always a test of knowledge and certainly not of wisdom; perhaps these honest and brave men understand this without reading, or an elder at home or church has explained it. Nonetheless, I am uncomfortable before any figure or representation of the divine. As Maimonides teaches, I could more readily pray in a mosque where all images are forbidden, than in a church, whether Roman or Greek. God forbid my charges here could read my mind, considering how they hate the Turk.

These people impress me as being honest and brave. I base this on my evaluation of Stavros and of our retinue, who have a steady gaze as well, and show signs of toil and effort and satisfaction; they put me in mind of what is written in Psalms: "When thou eatest the fruits of thy toil, happy art thou and it is well for thee."[62]

---

[62] Psalms 128:2

In one hamlet, in which lived perhaps some eight or ten
families, I did feel a difference, something I could not put my
finger upon. Here there had been a bitter vendetta between
the ancestors of the residents of this hamlet, called Galuta, and
the people of Betadas or Gonzaga, my home village, where
they had originally lived. Stavros did not know the reason for
the vendetta: hatred often continues without recollection. He
thought perhaps Danielos might know: either both his parents
or certainly his mother came from here. Since young Danielos
had shown signs of a quick mind while he was very young,
they had moved to Betadas, so that he could learn to read and
write under the old long-dead schoolmaster.

We slept, invariably, in the headman's house — that
is, I did, and sometimes Stavros, too, if space permitted; the
residents moved out to make room for us. The other men
quartered among the villagers and, if not, in the sheds of the
fields where sometimes watchmen slept during harvest. Word
had spread of my healing prowess, enhanced by gossip as it
had passed from Candia to Betadas, and often the lame or the
halt, the weak of eye or strained of heart or lungs would come
to consult me, begging for my time and attention. In keeping
with my physician's oath, and in the best interests of the Duke,
I faithfully received them. As everywhere, some could be aided
more than others, but a kind word and willing ear cannot be
bought for gold. I also learned that some of the seemingly
ancient women — hesitant, black-clad widows for the most
part — possessed a wide knowledge of herbs and barks. They
taught me about some of the local plants, for not every plant
that is found here grows in Italy, or it may take a different
form. Thus I increased my knowledge and added to my
pharmacopoeia, and kept some of my old skills intact as well.

The people of Galuta looked similar to the rest, but I felt
a reserve and guardedness. It was difficult for me to converse,

since I was just learning the spoken Greek dialect, and my proficiency and vocabulary were rudimentary. I marked well in my memory to discover more about this place—and about Danielos—once back at my "home," as I had begun to think of it.

Friday, Saturday, and Sunday I had chosen as days of rest and restoration from the rigors and responsibility of the visits, for to ride for hours, and go from one place to another every two days was arduous in the extreme. This also gave me the opportunity for abstaining from desecration of the Shabbat. I could then pray in privacy, reflect on my new life, and review mentally the tomes I had all but committed to memory in the days of my youth. Shabbat, whose warmth and familiarity I missed, whose familiar odors and tastes and customs I longed for, and whose prayers in synagogue were a memory sometimes bringing a private tear. It was the time of reflected pictures of the past—of my childhood, of that of my children, and, sadly but sweetly, of the early healthy years with my late wife. Sometimes I asked myself whether in saving my life from the Pope's assassins, I had lost its very essence.

I found new meaning in the essence of Shabbat. It is a proclamation of the ultimate freedom and integrity of man and beast. If only one day a week, but now and forever, man and beast—all of God's creations—cannot be told what to do, cannot be burdened. Slave and draught animal, as well as their owners, are on that day equal and free. What magnificent tidings this must bring all mankind. Oddly, though, this thought made me long even more for the learned discourses with my fellow scholars, and for the give and take of the House of Learning.

This was exacerbated even more when Passover came. It was no problem for me to instruct my butler/cook and Sophia that in my family, we did not eat bread one special week during Lent. Since the Orthodox Easter fell so close to Passover, that was easy.... But what about the Seder, the singing, the four cups, the joy of Exodus to our own land.... How hard those festive days have become, how bleak!

Sadness, though, and black moods are dangerous, as I know, having experienced so much loss in my own life: the premature death of the woman I loved so well. It was a marriage arranged by my parents with a fine family, but as the wedding date approached, Regina fell ill. I had come with my older brother to arrange details of the wedding, and help with the arrangements, only to see her waste away before my eyes, as her fine face became drawn and her delicate facial skin roughened and took on pallor beneath the stylish pallor then in the mode. Her magnificent head of red-blond hair lost luster, and under the blankets her body became shrunken and small. The coughing and other symptoms I prefer not to mention—for it still grieves me—worsened, and I felt that not *I* would be her bridegroom, but though I pitted hope against hope and prayer against prayer, the Angel of Death himself would wed her first.

All this time we had longed for one another, but very properly; out of respect for her and for our custom, we had no more than exchanged glances. And perhaps—just barely, perhaps, for I am not entirely sure—the merest brushing of our hands when I brought her a drink of lemonade or sweetened boiled water. Then, on what turned out to be her last day, Regina called me to her bedside.

"I know this seems brazen," she said softly, "but the one God knows that over this entire year of engagement we have not touched at all. Now death grants us permission. I shall not be blessed with being your wife. What can I do, so heaven has decreed?" And then, only then, did she finally embrace me and kiss me.

Gathering her last energies, she made the final confession
of sins, and asked her parents for their blessing before leaving
us forever; her memory stays with me even now. Only years
later did I marry — and the pen almost wrote "remarry," for so
close had I felt toward her.[63]

When I finally found the courage, I searched for and
found another wonderful woman, for that has been my
blessing, but Gentilla too passed away even before the first of
our three surviving children had reached the marriage canopy.
My first love, and then my second — my beloved wife — and
then three of my children could not be saved for all the medical
knowledge of my greatest colleagues and myself. There is
much we do not know: perhaps something carried in the air
and invisible, or in the water, that brings dysentery and disease
upon us. Thus my accumulated knowledge has been tempered
by pain and loss, and I have witnessed much suffering.

Why do the righteous suffer, and the evil so often
prosper?

"Thou shalt call the Sabbath a delight...."[64] To turn
my mind from sadness and the black bitterness, as we say in
Hebrew, I began to recite unto myself the Sabbath prayers, and
silently found comfort once more in the words of Psalms, and
the fixed formulations that contain so much hope and faith.[65]
Prayer is like walking down a beloved path, discovering each

---

[63] It seems that this story totally parallels that of Rabbi Leone da Modena. (See his
chapter entitled "Engagement, Marriage, Children" in his memoirs, the section in "The
Life of Yehuda," in Collected Writings of Rabbi Yehuda Arieh of Modena [Hebrew],
edited with introduction by Penina Naveh, Jerusalem, Bialik Institute, 1968, pp. 34–35.
One wonders who borrowed from whom, but the pain expressed is real and moving.)
"Confession" is recited aloud on the deathbed by the individual or another person (not
necessarily a rabbi), and is the wording used by the community in the Yom Kippur
service, beginning Ashamnu, "we have sinned...."
[64] Isaiah 58:13.
[65] "Black bitterness" is an interesting translation for marah shehorah. Marah is bile, and
the ancients located "melancholy" there, as they attributed various qualities to other parts
of the body.

time anew a flower, a bird, a shadow, the play of light.... It restored my soul....

It was on the Sabbath days that I began my talks with Danielos. He read Homer with me, and then Xenophon. The words of the ancient poet, who they say lived at the time of Isaiah, offered a fascinating look at a different world, a world I had known from the Latin. The original, though, is always more authentic. I asked him to begin making lists of words we encountered, so that I could repeat them. How well I knew from my own early studies that repetition keeps the memory green. As my reading improved, Xenophon's histories of the Persian Wars caught my attention. It amused me to think that they were "more recent" than Homer — only about two thousand years old! Who knows, perhaps they are contemporary with Mordecai and Esther, also Persian?

Thus my world expanded beyond the plains of Messara, and the ancient Greek I had studied enriched the constantly growing proficiency I was developing in the spoken language. Danielos gained as well: his Italian accent and pronunciation was also improving. Over wine and nuts we sat and chatted after our lessons until he was quite at ease with me. I saw in him a dependent, like a son in terms of sharing pleasures of mind and intellect; he was curious and as eager to learn as I had been. I began to teach him some medicine, since the area could use more skill to fill out the work of the healers, the women who had learned the secret herbs, and the men and women who could cast off spells. These latter healers seemed to exist alongside of the priest, but not in conflict with him. Possibly the priest himself would go to them to invoke their timeless incantations against the evil eye or the melancholy spirit.

At long last, when Danielos felt more relaxed with me, I slowly began to piece together the history underlying the estrangement between the inhabitants of the larger Betadas and the outlying Galuta. This, then, is Danielos's tale. I will tell it in his words, or rather reconstitute it, after days and weeks of pondering and reflection.

"Somewhere in the misty years of early history, perhaps before the time of the Nazarene, sea-faring people came from the East. They came in swift light ships, single-sailed craft. Among them were traders and merchants, and others were farmers and tillers of the soil. They came from Phoenicia, from Tyre or Sidon, whose names we know from the Bible, and from Jonah's home port of Jaffa. They spoke a language different from the Cretan Greeks, and they worshipped in strange ways. They would not bow down to the local gods nor consult the oracles, and refrained from work one day a week. To me," Danielos explained, "reading the Bible, and comparing their behavior to the rules in the Books of Moses, it seems that perhaps they were Hebrews fleeing from war, or simply seeking a different fate and fortune. When I once said this to my parents, they told me that God forbid that any of our forebears could be among the killers of our Savior, and washed my mouth with harsh soap. This made a lasting impression on my young mind, for if they had not punished me, I should not have recalled the matter. Because they did, my thoughts turned to the matter again and again, but I said nothing about them... until this very day.

"Sir, he implored, pray do not feel I am uttering words that you should not hear, and pray I am not shocking you with this revelation. Yet, in many ways, they reminded me of the sons of Jacob at Shechem. In a moment I will explain why.

"The newcomers settled in Gortys, which we call
Gortyna, and then, drawn together by a mysterious magnetism,
they moved to Betadas, a name they gave that we think was
part of their lost and secret language. There, they built strong
homes and became prosperous farmers. Their daughters were
not permitted to wed men from outside their village, and their
men, who could marry outside women if they so pleased, had
to pay high bridal prices. This was both to compensate the
bride's parents and ease the understanding that they might
visit their daughter but once a year. Outside the village, they
built a special guesthouse for these visitors. They say that in
the early days there were seventy heads of households; others
say they were six hundred, but we do not, of course, know. No
written records have been found, whether in Greek or in their
own tongue.

"After many centuries, the people of Betadas became
Christians. Some say that was at the time of Agios Titos, some
say later. When the Saracens came, Betadas suffered because
of the Christian devotion of its inhabitants.[66] Then Byzantium
returned, and there was a rift within the community of Betadas,
and some families, my ancestors among them, went into the
countryside and built their own village. Over the generations,
we lost the knowledge that the ancients carried, and we do not
know why they left."

It took Danielos many, many meetings with me to tell
me this tale, and press as I could, I did not find out much about
their customs. Here are some of things I could piece together
as I listened to his words. "We observe certain customs, known
only to us, which we must not reveal to outsiders on pain of
death." Once, after drinking wine with him, I praised him
greatly as a teacher, for indeed I had made much progress with

---

[66] The Arab conquest, mounted from Egypt, began in 823 CE, and continued until 961.

both the Iliad and the Anabasis, seeing the differences between the Greek of Homer and that of Xenophon. Even my spoken Greek had improved.

"Tell me something of these customs," I urged, "and I swear on all that is holy that I will not betray you to your people in Galuta, or ever bring harm to you in any way." Danielos looked steadily at me. He then cast a sidelong glance — perhaps longingly, perhaps cautiously — at Sophia, visible in the forechamber, sewing. I suggested to Sophia that she should retire, as Danielos and I would continue reading together. He remained silent. I did not want to break the spell of the moment, for confidences have their own time of birthing and of dying. We both quaffed deeply of the wine. Then in a strangled whisper, he spoke.

"On entering church, when we cross the threshold, and before we bless ourselves, we close our eyes and whisper a secret word."

I dared not ask what the word was. My silence encouraged him. He paused and went on.

"On Fridays, we wash our bodies prior to our evening meal, and before we break bread we raise our glass to one another and say Sabatyini. This is also secret, but less so, because we make this toast even when we have guests. We tell them that this was the name of the first winemaker in Galuta, whose memory we recall and bless in this way. Indeed, some of us believe that this is so, that there was such a man, but the elder who whispered the secrets to me told me this was not true, but a story for the uninitiated. So be it.

"I have broken an oath," Danielos closed, "but you have given me oath for oath, as God is our witness."

"As God is our witness," I said, and clasped him to my heart.

CHAPTER THE EIGHTH

With the help of Heaven

I was duty bound to inspect my lord's lands, and to preserve and enhance the human and material wealth at his disposal. Happily, I discovered that I took pleasure in it. Nonetheless, my essential training was in the field of learning: the realm of thought and spirit. In that realm, I am able to record two conversations.

The first was with Michaelis, the priest. I attended the church service on Sundays, since to do otherwise would be to scandalize my retinue and tenants. Naturally, being in their eyes a "Latin," and not knowing Greek, let alone Church Greek, I was not expected to be able to "perform" satisfactorily. And quite naturally, Danielos sat next to me, and Ioannis, the headman or mayor of the village, sat on the other side with his family. On occasion, Michaelis glanced over at me as he officiated at the service, possibly to see if I were a true believer; that is, Greek Orthodox.

Now in Candia, Greeks and Latins often worshipped together, more usually in the Latin rite since that was the language of those in power, but frequently Latins attended Greek services for their special and colorful holy days. Over hundreds of years, the Greeks had learned that the Venetians did not take religion as seriously as they did trade and profits, while the clerics sent out from terra firma did not engage in disputations and encourage public hair-splitting theological debates. We heard that there were struggles between the Jesuits

and the Greeks in the barbarian lands of the North as far as
Poland, Russia, and the Baltic countries. I had also heard that
now the Reformers, followers of Luther, were beginning to
spread their word there, too. But this isle has seen conquerors
and religions come and go, and — for the most part — the
inhabitants maintain their own ways without too much visible
rancor. Of course, below the surface, there may be a volcano
brewing, but I am too new here to know.

The priest was reputed to be a fine man. He had spent
a few years in the famous monastery of Mt. Athos island, but
the monastic life had not appealed to him. Nevertheless, he
had remained in the priesthood and — since he was no longer
a monk — was allowed to marry and father a family. Once
admitted to a monastery, it was not, so I was told, so easy to
leave, but his patent honesty had convinced the bishop. Richer
spiritually, but perhaps poorer in prestige, he had returned to
Betadas. Here he had found a young and pretty daughter of a
cousin, who was honored to wed a man of God. So the people
said. I had seen him cast a covetous eye on Sophia, but for that
who could blame him?

They also said that the priest was a Hesychast, meaning
that he was one who had mastered ways of praying from the
heart, and that the Jesus prayer poured out of him whenever
he was not officiating at services.[67] "We are lucky to have such
a pious and learned priest," everyone said. From the praise
I understood the obverse side: not every priest was pious, or

---

[67] Hesychast, from hesychia, inner stillness, refers to "a prayer of silence;" that is, a
prayer stripped of all images, words, and discursive thinking. It is an ancient way of
praying with the entire being, and can be attained only with long exercise. As far back as
the 5th century, Church fathers recommended "the constant repetition or remembrance
of the name Jesus." This became crystallized into a short sentence, the Jesus prayer:
Lord Jesus Christ, Son of God, have mercy on me. Then, centuries later, special posture,
focusing the eyes on the heart, and special breathing forms developed as well. See
Timothy Ware, *The Orthodox Church*, Penguin, London, 1993, especially pp. 64–65 ff.
Ware is a Greek Orthodox Bishop, having taken the name Bishop Kallistos of Diokleia.

learned. Now I wished to hear from Michaelis himself, and
ask him to help a poor benighted Latin understand the Greek
Orthodox way.

It was a memorable conversation. I had had such a talk
with the powerful Bishop in Candia, when I was just newly a
"Christian." Now it was with an Orthodox priest who lived
on land I governed. Simply put, I would be able to speak to
Michaelis, as it were, goy to goy. In spite of that, I still needed
to watch my words. Doubly: once, because I was a foreigner,
not Greek Orthodox, but Latin, and once because I was
actually, albeit unbeknownst to him, a Jew and a poseur. I took
care not to offend the priest, since he might be able to influence
the behavior and attitudes of his flock towards me.

What was the basis of the Greek Orthodox faith, and
what made it different from Latin Christianity? This is what
I wished to learn from my serious-faced, somewhat ascetic-
looking visitor. "From all my teachers have I learned."[68]

"The most important possession we have," the priest told
me in an accented but understandable Venetian-Italian, "above
all else, and above anyone else, is the true Tradition."

Every religion and every faith claims the same, I thought,
but held my silence. He sensed my questioning, and continued.

"Ours is an unbroken chain since the Apostles. It is a
direct line from those who were present — who saw with their
own eyes — when our Lord was betrayed to the Jews, tried,
crucified, and then rose again. The Greek islands and mainland
were among the first stops of St. Paul. The Church Fathers
continued to develop and discuss our tradition in the language
of the Bible." He meant of course the "New" Testament in
Greek, but again I held my tongue.

He spoke with deep conviction, with warmth, even
passion. This was not a catechism, a set of parroted phrases.

---

[68] Ethics of the Fathers, Chapter IV, Mishna 1, quoting Psalms 119:99.

This came from his heart. I nodded encouragingly.

Michaelis explained that the tradition embraces the totality of the Church's history and credo. The teaching of the Church fathers was amplified and strengthened by various Councils held across the centuries, but I cannot recall them in any order. "The Canon Law, the prayers, the icons, everything that goes into an individual service and an individual church— all these form an unbroken chain back to Jesus, and to the original Church."

He referred to the Roman Church as Latin—eyes averted out of respect. He could barely disguise his contempt for the Roman Church. "In our kyriakon, the man of enlightenment is the man suffused with the spirit of God.[69] In Rome, book learning is more important than Divine inspiration." Beyond this, Rome was heretical in its definition of the Holy Spirit. Michaelis patiently explained to me wherein the Greek doctrine of the Trinity—the Father, the Son and the Holy Spirit—differs from the Latin doctrine. Apparently the Roman Catholic believe that the Creator, the Father, and his human expression, the Son, both—if I can clumsily write what I barely understood—gave forth a third persona: the Holy Spirit. That is in Latin thought. In the true Church, he said, the Son's role in the forming of the Holy Spirit is much more limited.[70]

At this point, I lost interest because I have never been open to any deviation from monotheism. To attribute three

[69] There are two words for "church:" kyriakon, belonging to the Lord, and ekklesia, the body of Christian society. See Victoria Clark's *Why Angels Fall (A Journey through Orthodox Europe from Byzantium to Kosovo)*, London, 2000, p. 196, which I have paraphrased, and p. 260. I have heard the same thoughts in Crete today.
[70] Translator's note: These points are certainly too arcane for me. I resorted to Timothy Ware, *The Orthodox Church*, Penguin, London, 1993, pp. 196–218, especially the discussion of Filioque, pp. 215–218 to enable me somehow make sense of Avraham de' Pomi's words. Ware, a Greek Orthodox Bishop, quotes church writers who argue that this has led to "subordination of the Holy Spirit [to the Son — SA] and over-emphasis of the unity of God — have helped bring about a distortion in the Roman Catholic doctrine of the Church, p. 216.

personae to one God, and to make one of them human, I find
contradictory to all I believe. Perhaps my mind is too blunted
by age — or even some measure of prejudice — to follow the
niceties of such a complicated theology. I, in all humility, am
a devoted follower of the great Maimonides. We cannot really
"attribute" qualities to God. He is the unknowable Creator,
indivisible. Thus, the babble of the Kabbalists, who "attribute"
ten "emanations" to God, and male and female aspects, and
other irrational elements of their path, can only lead to a
nonsensical Jewishness, and eventually deification of some
human being. My friend Leone da Modena is wont to say,
"Why ten, why not three, and embrace Christianity?" His sharp
words against the mystics echoed my own thoughts.[71]

The priest gave me much to think about. His description
of the Church and people and his description of Canon Law
and interpretation of the Bible all were familiar to me. We
were the first to use the unbroken chain argument, running
uninterrupted from Sinai until today. Now I have heard the
argument in a Christian context and hierarchy of authority. I
shall have to reflect on this as we travel.

Having traversed "my" lands sufficiently, the time had
come to visit Hania. I must now write out of the chronological
order, however, for I fell ill for several weeks, and was unable
to write again until well after the tiring trip home.

In Hania I faced a great test. Here I search a way again to
be in the midst of a Jewish community, even if only for a day,
an hour. How I have longed for our hallowed rhythm of life
these many months. This longing was strongest about a week
after our arrival.

---

[71] Only in 1638 did Rabbi Leone publish his thesis castigating the Kabbalah and its
followers. Therefore, we must assume that his thoughts were known to Avraham through
sermons and discussions. See Yehuda Arieh of *Modena Selected Writings*, [Hebrew]
annotated by Peninah Naveh, Jerusalem, Bialik Institute, 1968, especially section "Ari
Nohem" (The Lion Roars), p. 201 ff.

It began the day before the day of mourning, the Ninth
of Av. Since earliest childhood, I recall the heavy impact of this
day, the Black Fast.[72] Dark clothes replaced the flounced and
colorful striped silk or brocade that men wore, in spite of the
rules and Christian regulations forbidding opulent dress. By
ancient custom, that day we wore black suits, plain hats, no
leather, but instead felt or cloth slippers, belts of felt or twisted
flex or strands of wool, and for the poor, twine.

The bright candelabra of the synagogue were dimmed
for the evening prayer, and then extinguished, one by one.
Darkness. Pitch-black in our House of Prayers. Then the
quavering voice of our senior elder, coming from the podium
in front of the Holy Ark in a strained voice and choked with
sadness announced:

"Our brethren, sons of Israel, woe unto us! One thousand,
six hundred and so many years have passed since our Holy
Temple was destroyed and we were exiled from our Land.
Woe unto us...."

The candles flickered and scrolls of the Lamentations
opened; all the men sat on the bare planks of the floor,
mourning. The reader chanted in the haunting cantillation of
Jeremiah, "How doth she sit alone, that City once thronged
with people hath become a widow...."[73] Tears and lamentation,
foreheads tinged with ash in the hot summer night. The Black
Fast.

And now, here I was on this great isle, and now it was
the morning of the Eighth of Av, a day before the Fast. And
here I was—it could be thousands of miles and hundreds of

---

[72] The Black Fast is the Day of Mourning for the destruction of the Temple (by tradition
in the year 70 of the Christian era) which is marked on the ninth day of the Hebrew
summer month of Av: Tish'ah be-Av. The White Fast is Yom Kippur, when white is worn
as a token of purity.
[73] Lamentations 1:1.

years away from all I have known all my life, all that is, it
seems, imprinted in my blood. Today I will finally cross the
line for the first time. I do not think that the others — Christian
or Muslim — believe I am not what I pretend to be; tonight it
will be the Jews whose scrutiny I shall have to withstand.

How did this all come about? "By ruses shalt thou
wage war."[74] It was not by accident we were in Hania right
then. Since it is the other major city on the island, and a major
shipping center, it was not difficult for me to ensure that we
were there on that date.

This morning I have asked to visit an owner of ships
and farms, the chief Jew of this place, the Rosh Ha-Kahal. He
must also be a learned pious man if he be like his kinsmen, the
Delmedigos.[75] His great-uncle, the Rabbi and Doctor Elijah,
was one of the masters of Talmud and Jewish lore, Bible, and
the Holy Tongue, and at the same time, a famed philosopher,
teacher, and professor.

The Jews are major exporters of our Messaran wine,
olives, and cheeses, and major importers of spices, cloth, gold,
and silver from both East and West. What would be more
natural than a courtesy visit by the bailo of the Mantuan court,
whose exports are often carried by these merchants and their
merchantmen?

Delmedigo was dressed in clothes of a Venetian
gentleman, perhaps not as vibrant in color, and with his Jew
hat and colored patch in place. He is not tall, and his light
eyes and skin, as well as the reddish brown of his hair betray
the northern origins of the family: German Jews en route to
the Holy Land, who stayed on here instead. Well, we are a
wandering people. After all, German Jewish communities rose
around immigrating Italian Jews, beginning with Colonymus

[74] Proverbs 24:6.
[75] The Hebrew words mean "Head of the Community." The name Delmedigo (i.e., Del
Medigo), means, literally, "of the Doctor," or of the Doctor family.

of Lucca who reached Mainz centuries ago; ever since there has been contact back and forth with Italy.

Here stood Delmedigo, medium height, stocky, intelligent, his light eyes wary. Wary eyes, Jewish eyes. Captain Caponegro had already remarked on that. We exchange pleasantries in Italian. I had to crush my instinct to speak Hebrew or our own Judeo-Italian. All in good time, should the good time ever come.

"I have had the honor of meeting a member of your distinguished family. The great Elijah is famous in our universities and academies. Philosophers and linguists cherish his name."

Delmedigo bowed in acknowledgment. "It is not usual, honored bailo, for one in your role to be so well versed in the arenas and halls of philosophy."

A reversal of roles, a polite insinuation, a conversational ploy. Perhaps this is one of the artful gambits of language that make the goyim not care for us, to put it mildly. He, in all, just a merchant—speaks to me—a farm manager and factor for the Duke of Mantua in a superior tone. It implies, of course, that Jews are scholars, thinkers, and that non-Jews are not. Yet I decided not to take umbrage. Let me first learn what manner is the man. After all, "…a soft tongue breaks bones."[76]

"Indeed. I however had the good fortune to be a distant kinsman of milord, the Duke of Mantua. Thus was I chosen from the original family village—Gonzaga—to be elevated, educated, and was sent to the great seats of learning in Padua and Bologna."

"Did you—were you so lucky—as well, to meet the master doctor and scholar Davide de' Pomi, honored Sir?"

Well, that struck too close to home—of course Davide was my uncle and in many ways my model. I responded

---

[76] Proverbs 25:15.

gravely, "I'm sure I must have met Doctor de' Pomi more than once."

We discussed trade, the predatory attacks on shipping and trade centers by the corsairs, of whom the Maltese, the Greek Islanders from the Dodecanese Sea, and the Scots were probably the worst, and the high cost of shipping as a result.

I proposed a new way to increase income for the Duke, perhaps with less work for me, which would bring Delmedigo profit as well. "Would you undertake to purchase our crops in advance, and in return you use your vessels for shipping them?"

He kept a steady and non-committal gaze on me. I added, "In that case, using your ships, I would be prepared to share in the losses should my cargo be taken by pirates. Since you would have other cargo as well, with respect I suggest that you might thus be able to increase the number of vessels in your fleet. Then you could spread your own cargo onto more ships, thus lessening the risk to you (and to us, I may say) should one of the ships be lost."

Delmedigo seemed quite interested. Our talk went well, and concluded with refreshments. In addition to tasty Venetian delicacies, he served me a delicious malmsey, served in a fine blown-glass decanter and glasses. He poured himself another drink, though, with mint and sliced lemons. "I beg you, esteemed Sir," he said, "to permit me to conclude our arrangement with a toast, but ask you as well to defer the actual conclusion of it for two days. I then shall be able to toast you just as well with wine, but for today, I am bound to a lighter drink."

Feigning ignorance, I pretended to be astounded, and almost offended. To assuage me, he explained further. "There is, Sir, in my request, not only respect for you, which I owe you both as a honored representative of the lofty Duke, may his glory increase, but also to my own principles of faith. You see these are the sad days of mourning, which conclude this evening with a twenty-four-hour fast. We mourn our destroyed Temple and the devastation of Jerusalem, and the loss of our freedom as a people. Thus we shortly will have our concluding meal before the fast. I would not dare, Sir, invite you to a repast of sadness, but if you would join us in two days' time, we shall celebrate as is your due and my pleasure."

He spoke with great dignity and respect. I held my silence for a moment. Then, I bowed slightly, and thanked him profusely for the invitation, asked if I might bring my steward as well, to discuss details, at a convenient time before the meal. This did not yet satisfy my desire to attend the service that evening.

"Signore Delmedigo," I said, "your distinguished uncle, in a discussion I once attended at the university, made a remarkable statement, which is etched in my memory." Delmedigo arched his eyebrows into a question, and cocked his head to one side. "He said, 'A people which remembers can never be destroyed. A people which only remembers cannot be revived. A people which, defeated, both remembers and hopes for the future will reach that future.'"

He stood silent, frozen, and deeply moved.

I continued. "I have seen much of your people, and many of its members, especially the de' Piatelli, Norsa and Colorni families of Mantua. I recall hearing distinguished preachers like the great Rabbi Leone, whom princes flock to hear when they visit Venice. Tonight you begin your day of mourning. As an occasional student of the Bible, I would like to know more—"

He held up his hand, and invited me, with great courtesy and utmost dignity, to join them at a fixed hour, and proceed to the Delmedigo synagogue, close to the port. As the archisynagogos, which he explained was the old Greek title for "synagogue elder," he would be on the elevated reader's platform, but he would commission his first-born son to sit next to me and explain the service.

Thus, a ruse brought me to the happy-sad day when briefly, though hidden from their eyes in strange garb and in strange pose and forcing myself to sit dry-eyed and unmoving, I was again among my people and within my familiar and beloved tradition. It was followed by other good days, if few, in Hania.

Before taking leave of Mantua I visited Delmedigo again. I handed him a letter sealed with the Mantuan emblem in red wax.

"Is it true that Jewish practice does not permit the opening of another person's letters?"

"Of course," he said. "For five hundred years it has been a strict prohibition by our great Rabbenu Gershon."[77] I nodded as if in gratitude for his confirmation.

"I have a somewhat different request, but ask that you treat it similarly. This letter is for you, but it is not to be opened until a messenger comes to you from me. He will say to you words that will free you from my request, and I would be grateful if you open the letter then. Only then."

"I understand," he said gravely. He extended his hand toward me with solemnity, perhaps even with understanding. Silently, we shook hands, and silently we parted.

---

[77] Rabbenu Gershon, known as the Light of the Exile (960–1030) lived mainly in Mainz (Germany) and was the major figure of his era in the Franco-German (Ashkenazi) Talmudic tradition.

CHAPTER THE NINTH

With the help of Heaven

Two days later, Stavros and I and one other armed retainer, Nikos, were riding out of Hania, to meet an olive grower nearby. Suddenly six or eight well-armed men came galloping out of a stand of trees, next to a stony dry stream bed where they had lain in wait. Before we could even utter a sound or draw weapons, they were holding us at gunpoint. Two of them bound Stavros and Nikos's hands behind their backs, and wrapped dark strips of cloth around their heads. Two men stayed with the retainers. The others removed my sword and musket.

They promised that no harm would befall any of us, and quickly forced my horse into their midst and dashed up into the hills along the coastal road. They spoke Italian with an accent that seemed familiar, and their Greek even more reminded me of someone.

We rode for three days—I think—at a pace much too hard for a man of my age and stage of life, through mountain tracks and around villages. Once we were well away, I saw them pause, and dismount, face southeast, and fall on their faces in prayer. I had never seen this, but heard it described by my Levantine brothers in Venice. Muslims! What were followers of Mohammed doing in this Christian land? This, endlessly, I kept turning over in my mind. They prayed five times a day.

Three days on horseback. My captors had hard goat's cheese and flatbread, honey and yogurt. We did not starve, but barely had time to swallow our food and again we were on our way. At night, we slept in caves, or in hidden clefts in the mountains. They knew their route, and a young, handsome, and somehow familiar-looking young man was their guide. Among themselves, they spoke in a murmur, but the sounds that reached me were not in a language known to me. The young man consulted a fierce-looking older man who looked much like a Cretan warrior, but he was not Cretan. It was usually this older man, with a lined sun-bitten face, full-flowing mustache and straggly beard, who spoke to me, and who, it seemed, was the leader.

Now, after these three hard days, I have been left alone in the cave. Two men stand alternating watches — one always alert and awake, one resting or dealing with the food. They permit me to go outside the cave and into a small stony depression to look after my animal needs. I had neither washed, nor changed my linen, and my bones felt shattered. Thus one falls so quickly, "thy glory, O Israel, slain on its high places."[78] Even now, though, I must be grateful for the luck or prescience or the good stars that guided me to keep my scribblings with me in my saddlebags. Originally, I feared leaving them at my house lest they be seen by curious eyes, but the suspicion has led to an auspicious result. I am able to continue to write, to commune with myself, and save something of this tangled tale for posterity.

These lines, like the last preceding ones, will be hard to read, and perhaps muddled. Woe is me, at my age to be at the mercy of a gang of kidnappers, armed highwaymen, people of brute force.[79] But now is the time to be strong. I must admit

---

[78] 2 Samuel, 1:19 the lament of David for Saul and Jonathan, continuing, "how are the mighty fallen."

[79] Translators' note: The writer uses Talmudic expressions, such as listim mezuyanim, "armed robbers," and I have sought the English equivalents without relying on such anachronisms as "gangsters." — SA

these armed men have treated me with respect; however, I do suffer from exhaustion. My mind is numb from the fatigue of riding, not knowing where I was going, surrounded by silent armed riders dashing through the coastal road and into the Mountains of Darkness, to this cave somewhere on the other side of the Sambatyon.[80]

I have borne myself with as much dignity as possible, as befits a man representing power. Truth to tell, I had my natural dignity as a member of the Hebrew race, descendant of kings, priests, and scholars. Further, I could call on my heritage as a de' Pomi, of one of the four founding families of Jewish Rome at the time of the Maccabees.

I had at first feared for my life. After all, why had I been waylaid and taken into the hills? I could not fathom who would wish to kill me. It does not seem reasonable that my person is important enough for the Pope to send assassins from terra firma. And Muslim brigands to boot! These brigands cannot be Papal murderers.

The cave was dark, and I was able to sleep. The guards awakened me in the dead of night. I silently recited the Confession. I was sure that my time had come. In my waking hours and in the twilight between sleep and awareness, I have been reviewing my life. It has been fortunate and blessed; tragedy has not crushed me. Now it would come to an end, but I would try to face that end bravely.

The younger man, the one who has been the scout, joined the two guards. In the dim light, I wondered for a moment of whose visage he reminded me...but the idea was so farfetched that I dismissed it. Then fear crowded in on me and left no room for anything else. The men gestured for me to be silent. The younger man and one of the guards placed themselves

---

[80] Sambatyon is a mythological river that casts up stones to protect those Jews living in a mythical Jewish land, to prevent invasion. On the Sabbath (Sambat??), it rests. It lies "beyond the Mountains of Darkness."

one in front of me, and one behind. They moved me forward. I
understood that this was my path to death.

Shem'a Yisrael....[81]

~

The Holy One seems to have given me a reprieve, which
is, in the final analysis, merely a postponement. Let it be so. I
am alive, in a labyrinthine cave on the outskirts of the valley
of Slavokampos. They must have made a number of feints and
circles and backtracked because it turns out we were not that
far from Messara. Now begins an even stranger tale than mine,
and I shall attempt to recount it briefly.

In the cave, the young familiar-looking man began to
speak to me kindly. His name was Ayub. I have said that he
looked like someone — but had dismissed the similarity out
of hand. However, he was indeed Sophia's brother. We spent
a few days together in the cave and he unrolled these events
before me. Simply, I asked him, "Why have you come here?
And what do you want with me?"

"It is a long tale, sir, but I shall tell you all, from the
beginning." His story was told with pauses and breaks, as
his other duties required, but I shall set it down as I heard it,
without my prodding questions.

Ayub's Tale

"We had been living a comfortable and peaceful life in a
lush Bosnian valley filled with cattle and with corn, wheat
and flax fields. My father was a wealthy landowner, and the
family had been Muslim since the Turkish conquest some
two hundred years before.[82] In our home, the father was

---

[81] The Credo: Hear, O Israel, the Lord our God, the Lord is One. Deuteronomy 6:4.
[82] Either Ayub was misinformed or our author misremembered. The Turks actually
conquered Bosnia in 1463, that is, 137 years before their meeting. Nonetheless, that is
still six or seven generations.

the lord, and the many children, slaves, and serfs respected him mightily. My father had a first cousin, whom he called 'brother,' who lived across a ridge of the Dinaric Alps, and the cousins had pledged their children in marriage to one another."

On the fateful day that set off this strange chain of events, Ayub's family had been celebrating the nuptials of his sister — whom I will continue to call Sophia — in their home village with a festival that lasted for days, if not weeks. When the festivities were over, the bridegroom, his family, and a small armed party had then set out, with Sophia and her two brothers, to escort her to her husband's family, where she would live.

"As we made our way along the mountain ridge, our pacific joy was torn into tiny pieces. A band of Serbian brigands, Orthodox Christians who hate Islam and us, swept down out of the hills and fell on the caravanserai where the wedding party was sleeping. They killed some of the men, including the groom and his father, and took the survivors into captivity, to be sold as slaves. I alone escaped. I ran into the forest while the Christians swooped through the rooms, killing, plundering men and women. The innkeeper's children were left for dead, bleeding and tossed in a heap. Their pitiful cries had shielded my flight out of the inn through a window, into the obscurity of the night and the trees."

Ayub's face changed as he told this story. His eyes dimmed and his voice cracked. His return home was indeed an echo of the story of Job, his biblical namesake.[83] Overnight his

[83] Ayub in Arabic = Iyov/Iyob in Hebrew, in English, Job.

father had lost two sons and a daughter, four escorting riders,
a new son-in-law, his cousin, and his cousin's wife, mother
of the groom, and certainly least, but enough to be remarked
upon, munificent gifts of cloth, silver, and gold that had been
given the new couple. Shocked beyond recognition, Ayub's
father was beset with deep melancholy and, inconsolable,
began to waste away. Only in his forties, old age fell upon him.
During the days of mourning, the imam tried to comfort him
that such was the will of Allah, from Whom all things come.
Ayub's father knew better though: he knew it was the Serbians
and their priests, Christian hatred of the Muslims, and greed.
Who knows how long they had waited? Probably they had
heard from the innkeeper that the groom's party had passed
that way, that two rich cousins were celebrating the further
close union of their families and wealth. They had lain in wait,
silently, patiently. Now they would sell his close ones and his
retainers as slaves. Traders from Illyria would carry them in
small ships to the Greek isles, to Crete, to Malta, and even to
Egypt and Libya, where light-colored slaves brought the best
prices.

That had been four years ago.

His father, who had fallen into a slough of black moods,
constantly called for revenge: burn a church, sack a village,
kill the inhabitants! Revenge, revenge! Ayub's mother, with
womanly wisdom that so often surpasses the manly, argued
that it would be better to find the living and free them than to
add to the dead. Besides, she added sagely, the Christian God
was already dead and hanging, what good would burning his
house do? The mother emerged from behind the once powerful
paterfamilias, who now lay powerless, slack-mouthed and
dull-eyed, on the divan, day after day.

"I began to make my plan," continued Ayub. "I am the fourth son; my remaining older brother would become the man of the family, responsible for the farms and the livestock. I would leave and search. I would find and free those left living. If they were dead, I would kill the raiders, their abductors.

"I found a small Christian village on the road between and the Illyrian coast, and near it a monastery where lived the holy man Vassileos, named after the Saint known as Basil in the Roman rite. The monastery was a site of pilgrimage; when I entered the men inside immediately made as if to stop me, perhaps to kill me. In my limited language, I explained that I wished to learn about Christos and about the Ekklesia.

So was it that Ayub the Muslim became Paul, named after that Paul who had seen the vision, and then the light. "Let it be so."[84]

Ayub settled in the Dalmatian town we call Spalato, which he called Split. He found employment in the Orthodox monastery nearby, an island of Byzantium in the midst of Roman Catholicism. In secret he was a Muslim, in public he was an Orthodox Serb Christian surrounded by Italianate Dalmatians practicing the Roman rite. I could barely hide a smile — we were indeed brothers in misfortune and circumstances. But he was the braver. He had been willing to do all this to find and rescue his kidnapped sister. I was merely running to save my life. As Satan said to God, "Skin for skin."[85]

Ayub stayed in the monastery long enough to become familiar with the Italianate people and those who worked around the port. Finally, he felt ready, and found a coastal

---

[84] The Hebrew is dismissive. Not a prayer but a shrug and wave of the hand.

[85] Job 2:4. Satan and, self-mockingly, de' Pomi both meant that people will do anything to save their skin.

boat that would take him to Hania. All these preparations —
"conversion" to Christianity, service in the monastery, spying
out Split and its ports, and working on the vessel — took up
over two years. "Why, then, did you decide on Crete? How did
you know to come here?"

"During those two years, my family had sent out
feelers via travelers, itinerant preachers, and family who were
scattered across Bosnia to connections in Turkey and the
islands. In the end, word came back that a beautiful Bosnian
girl had been sold with a group of Bosnian and other slaves
to Maltese slavers, who had then taken them to Crete. At this
point, the stars or Divine Providence once again intervened. I
encountered Hisham.

"Hisham had been among the riders escorting the bridal
party and then had fallen into captivity as well. He is a brave
and strong man, very intelligent, and with a great facility for
languages. Though he was by then already approaching fifty,
when most men are already old, he had a strong constitution. It
was said that all his ancestors died over the age of eighty, with
all their teeth in place.

"Hisham had been brought to Heraklion, and was
purchased by a young man from Slavokampos to tend his
ailing father. He had the opportunity to learn Greek and Italian,
and, in turn, to read to his old master, who never ceased asking
questions about Bosnia. Their conversations often turned
as well to religion. The old man had seen the venality and
depravity of some of the priests and monks. Jesus Christ had
seemed to him to be a simpler man, and the Son of God did not
need — surely — so much statuary, paint, and gilding.

"Hisham was emboldened to admit that his faith
tolerated no images, that God was one, and Mohammed was —
like Jesus — 'just' a prophet and messenger of God.

"All this transpired in the first year of Hisham's captivity, and through the second year, the friendship deepened. It seemed, if such be possible, that what was happening was almost a cry of 'blood to blood,' that somehow, almost animal-like, each saw similarities and resemblances in the other. Originally, after all, centuries before, Slavokampos had been settled by Slavs — Bosnians....

"During the second year, Hisham told his benefactor about the dreadful night of the Serbian raid and the kidnapping. He sought ten days' leave to search for Sophia. Hisham's owner had no difficulty granting his request. He merely asked that, should he require more time for the search, he send a messenger to bring the news so that the old man would know that he was well. As far as he was concerned, Hisham's word as an honest and God-fearing man was sufficient to guarantee his return. He also gave Hisham food for the start of his journey, a fair purse to keep him in food and shelter, and a mule on which to ride. Hence, Ayub said, the stars or Providence must have kept a protective hand over Hisham, and he had felt encouraged to believe firmly that he would find Sophia and eventually free her and return her to her family.

"It was not as difficult as it would seem: he began at the slave market in Hania, where he learned from the hangers-on which dealer had bought her. He found the dealer, who was as venal as might be expected from one in his trade, and approached him with a tale that would appeal to the man's greed. Hisham said he was looking for a lost sister, since his master, a good man, had agreed to buy her from her present owner, in order to reunite sister and brother. He was authorized to give the dealer a generous consideration should the present owner agree.

"The slave dealer saw an opportunity for further profit from a transaction long past, in other words, pure profit. Therefore he entrusted Hisham with a message to Stavros. He set off then for 'my' valley, ostensibly to deliver the message. When he arrived at Stavros's house, he saw Sophia at work. He did not make himself known to her, nor did she recognize him, dressed as a Greek.

"Hisham returned to his employer, whose health continued to deteriorate. The friendship between the two men was such that the day of the old man's death brought sorrow and weeping to Hisham, and he mourned as one of the family. At the end of the allotted mourning period, he approached his young master and asked if he could redeem himself with money and have full manumission and the right to leave guaranteed in writing. The young master took his word that he would return within the year with the gold, but asked for only half the price originally paid.

"'You tended my father as if he were your own; indeed no Christian could have given him better support you did. Bring the money when you can. And if you do not return, or send it, I will know that only God's will prevented you from doing so. And I will deed you some land which we have not used for decades, so you may indeed be free.' His master then fetched him a goodly purse, a mule, a donkey laden with food, and the deed to a distant valley that was too far away for the family to tend properly, and sent him on his way with a caravan heading for Hania.

"When Hisham reached Trieste, he headed down the coast homeward, making inquiries wherever he went, but still not yet revealing himself as a Muslim. And then Providence led him to Split on market-day, where he recognized me, 'Christian' though I seemed…. Again, the hand of Providence.

"Yes, Hisham recognized me. That was great luck—
thank Allah—because I would never have recognized him,
so much had he changed. We rode to our home village, took
a band of six young men, as well as money and horses, and,
in the guise of Turkish traders came to the shores of Crete.
Both of us knew how to pose as Christians. Thus, in the
mountains, we assumed our new clothing and new identities.
We reconnoitered until we found these caves. Some Cretans
are afraid to come here because of the pagan Gods who they
believe once dwelt here."

And thus they had established their base, and proceeded
to take me captive.

"But why me?" I asked. "Why did you simply not
capture Sophia and free her?"

There was a sudden alarm. "Later, later," Ayub shouted.
He ran out in great haste. I heard hoof beats and then they
faded. The guard returned as though to warn me that he was
still there.

CHAPTER THE TENTH

With the help of Heaven

Living in a cave has its own rhythm, logic, and fears. And — in spite of my rational beliefs — in this cave I sense spirits of the dead. We find human bones from time to time. The series of caves has been carefully excavated, and sometimes even timbered for support, hewn from the rock in ancient times to provide limestone. The souls of overworked slaves are all around us; the place is impure because of the body parts strewn hither and thither. In spite of the impurity, I chant a silent Kaddish every morning and evening for those who died here: doubtless there were Jews among them, captured in raids, swept off ships, or maybe even driven off by the Roman conquerors of Jerusalem and brought here to be worked to death. I pray as well for the poor and innocent young Gentile slaves, made old before their time, living in the dirt and dust and never seeing the light of day, starved, wet, and cold. O Lord, is there no end to human cruelty?

I must note what alarm Ayub heard.... The people I was with (I no longer call them my captors) included a shepherd, positioned nearby to warn of strangers approaching. When he needed to sound an alert he played a certain Cretan air on his Pan's pipes, a lament of a black-eyed maiden for her fallen warrior. It was reassuring to learn this: it shows a subtle irony not consistent with the behavior of ruffians, rapists, and robbers.

Indeed, I have said I do not refer to these men as my captors, for I now have discovered why I am so well treated.

The cave was a temporary post, from which they could conduct careful surveillance of the movements of the other person they wished to kidnap. They, of course, did not use the word "kidnap," but rather "save from captivity." Once his sister had been freed from captivity, she would be brought here. Then, stealthily and by night, we shall make our way westward, through the mountains to a deserted village that sits at a high altitude.

There we shall settle, for Ayub deems it too dangerous at this time to return to the land of the Bosnians and Serbs. They will establish a new home here, and since it is in the hills overlooking a Christian holy site, they will continue their pretense, and every major Orthodox holiday will walk to the nearest Church, which is a few hours away. Their new village is nestled in a valley surrounded by hills. It is supposedly cursed by the plague, which has time after time devastated its settlers; it will not attract casual visitors. They can live as they wish, with only one sentry posted high on the mountain — the shepherd.

But why have I been stolen, and like Joseph, held in a pit, though my new friends have been kinder by far than Joseph's very own brethren? Why? The book of Psalms says, "The Lord guards fools," and if so, perhaps even learned fools. Ayub's troop needs assurance that the plague will not return once more to the village, and for this they put their trust in Allah! But they also — wisely — believe that another blessing would be to have a doctor with them, and one who can train others, one person in particular. One who has already begun to study with him....

That night, after midnight, we heard the approach of shod animals. There she stood, bundled into man's clothing, alternately sighing and smiling, crying and laughing.

It was indeed Sophia....

Now comes an even greater surprise, for Providence hides in it mysteries that, when revealed, blind the eye of the beholder. Sophia is in great discomfort, and I am asked to examine her immediately. There are signs of bleeding, and clearly she is with child. I made her some herbal tea, blended to give her strength and assuage her pain, and commanded that she be put in a dry and warmer part of the cave, to be watched day and night, night and day, until she recovers, if this be His will. For such a rough trip, accompanied by fear, difficult trails, hill, dale, mountain, and valley — well, I need not say more. She is in danger, and requires the mercy of God to surmount and overcome her hardships and safely bear a healthy child.

A child of whom I am the father.

For three days Sophia lay there, while the men rode out to steal or buy hens and bread so we could feed her, cooking broth by night in the furthermost smoke-filled cave, lest smoke be seen by day and reveal our hiding place. Slowly, the color returned to her pallid cheeks and her slate-gray eyes began to shine again with intelligence and restored health. We decided — for now I was included in all consultations — that the main body of men would go ahead to our village. We — three armed riders and Sophia and I — would remain here for a few more days to ensure that all is well with her and the unborn within her. The men would stand watch in turn. We had decided that were we to be discovered by "my" men — that is, by Stavros and his retinue or soldiers of the city garrisons who would be searching widely for me, out of respect to my master the Duke of Mantua — the men would run, and we would permit ourselves to be "liberated," never to reveal the truth!

For the first time since captivity, I began to ponder my moral dilemma. Am I honor-bound to seek to free myself and

return to the Duke, to whom I owe so much? Does my fealty to
the House of Gonzaga not bind me yet? Can I—dare I—requite
evil for good, for the immeasurable grace they extended to
me by saving my limb and probably life from the hands of
Inquisitorial prelates? While we tended Sophia, bringing her
water, broth, morsels of well-cooked chicken and chunks of
softened bread, I had time to ponder and weigh my conflicting
obligations. Perhaps my role is to guide new life into this
world, for all of us in this small band have felt the weight of
persecution and exile.

~

On the third day, a further surprise: straggling into our
cave, at the end of a dagger held by one of our fierce guards,
came young Danielos.

"Sophia is safe. Thank God!" he said.

"Why is she lying down? Sophia, Sophi, I am here. I am
here! You are safe."

She looked up at him, smiled, and then turned her head
away.

"What happened, Danielos?" I asked him. "Why are
you here?" He looked so bedraggled, haggard, and he seemed
confused.

"Is Sophia sick? What's wrong?"

"Danielos, she is well, but she is with child. We are
letting her rest, to ensure her health and that of the child."

He too looked away from me. He was about to faint.

"Water, water!" I shouted to our guard.

Danielos drank as though there were not enough water
in the world to slake his thirst. "Let us first feed you. Then you
will tell me everything." I had a sense of foreboding.

He drank and ate ravenously and immediately fell into
a deep sleep. Many hours later, restored as only young people
can be so speedily, he was prepared for my questions.

What a world we live in — full of surprises, upheavals, and demolition of accepted truths. How powerful and harsh truth can be.

Danielos had seen the men take Sophia and had followed — at a distance — hoping to save her from what fate he knew not.

"Maestro, I cannot face you. I have to make a confession to you. I have sinned. I have repaid your trust with betrayal. My life is yours to take."

"Speak."

With a full measure of pauses and hesitations, euphemisms and circumlocution, cloaked in shame and embarrassment, his confession amounted to one simple fact. Corni, Danielos has pinned horns to my head. Danielos had indeed entered a den, the den I thought had solely been mine. He loves Sophia, fell in love with her with glances exchanged and furtive brushes of the hand while she learned to read. When I was away on my rounds, they consummated their love. More than once.

I sat humbled, stunned, and angry. Only Danielo's palpable pain, and red-faced mixture of fear and abasement, combined to restrain me. I motioned weakly for him to leave me, and sat with closed eyes....

In the space of a few days...too much, too much had transpired. From fear of being killed or enslaved to reassurance. From reassurance to the joy of making new life, of fatherhood. And then the fall, from new-found paternity to cuckoldhood.

I slept. Sleep soothes the wounded soul and spreads healing balm on aching hearts. I sat with my head bowed on my breast in a dark corner of the cave. The thoughts, dear children, that strayed into my teeming brain were swift and contradictory. The story is after all not unique. Adultery is an ancient crime. Torah, Talmud, literature—all tell such tales. The great Poet described almost exactly the same incident, in his Canto describing Francesca da Rimini and her illicit love:

> Noi leggiavamo un giorno per diletto
> di Lancialotto come amor lo strinse
> soli eravamo e sanza alcun sospetto
> Per piu fiate le occhi chi sospinse
> quella lettura, e scolorocci il viso....[86]

But, in our case, Sophia is not my wife. After all, I had no exclusive right to her. We had never sanctified a marriage, by any law of God or man. In truth, of course, I could not marry her, a captive, since I had not followed the laws of Deuteronomy.[87] Even though carnal congress can consummate a marriage, it requires advance intent of both partners to be married. In our case, there had been no intention of marriage between Sophia and me. Nor could there be with a woman of a different religion. Thus I had no claim on her, except perhaps the normal expectations of fidelity....

Hours passed. Her defending angel spoke out to me.

What fidelity may a man of my age expect from a slave lass, free in practice, chosen for my house and bed, undoubtedly ravished by previous captors, humbled and

---

[86] The great Poet was of course Dante Alighieri, and in Canto V he sees the beautiful Francesca da Rimini and her brother-in law Paolo, expiating their adultery in the first ring of the *Inferno*. The lines he quoted are 127–131, and he did not need to cite the entire passage, for every learned Italian knew them by heart. In brief, the couple was reading of Launcelot's great love, and exchanged blushing glances, until the moment when the book spoke of Lancelot's kissing Guinevere. Unable to contain themselves, they kissed as well. *Quel giorno più non vi leggemmo avante* — "that day we read no further." Dante Gabriel Rossetti painted a romantic triptych of the doomed lovers.

[87] See Deuteronomy 21:10–14. The passage endows the woman taken captive in war with wife-like rights and privileges following a process of separation from her past life and mourning for her family.

degraded? Then under my roof she recovers her human face —
her divine image. A handsome and young man opens the
world of books and learning for her, a man close in age who
loves her. The two qualities of youth and young love I had
never shared, nor could I ever share with her....

I sat long in silence, head on breast, and then the words
of the sage Fathers rang in my mind: "Be not a single Judge."[88]
And in the same text, they warned: "Do not judge your fellow
man unless you have been in his place. Give him the benefit of
the doubt, and weigh the scales in favor of innocence."[89]

Longer yet did I sit and through my tired head let
reverberate these thoughts, verses I had recited from age three
or four every summer Shabbat afternoon. So many changes,
and I am not as young as I was when I could slough through
rain, snow, sleet, and mud, and face the next day with renewed
vigor and restored strength. Now I needed time, time to
absorb, time to react, time to judge fairly, to give the benefit
of the doubt, and not to play the lone judge. I prayed for my
blessed father and grandfather, long dead, to sit in judgment
alongside of me, a tribunal of three.

Thus I heard the arguments of Danielos and Sophia,
separately, in my mind, and consulting my ancestors, and
relying in particular on Rabbenu Tam's practicality in applying
the Law, I reached a ruling.[90] Danielos has every possibility
of being a good father and, one assumes, a longer-lived father
than I. Life should determine in all matters.

I called Danielos and Sophia into my presence, and
as they helped me rise from the cold hard stone floor, I felt

[88] Ethics of the Fathers, Chapter 4, Mishnah 10.
[89] Ibid., Chapter 2, Mishnah 5 and Chapter 1, Mishnah 6, paraphrased.
[90] Rabbi Jacob Tam; born in Ramerupt, on the Seine, in 1100; died at Troyes 1171. He
was a grandson of Rashi, and considered the greatest tosafist of the French school, and
to have turned Halachic interpretation into new modes. See Avraham (Rami) Reiner,
*Rabbenu Tam and his contemporaries: Relationships, influences and methods of
interpretation of the Talmud*, doctoral thesis, The Hebrew University of Jerusalem, 2002.

taller than all men. I rose on tiptoe, held my hands together
outstretched and slightly trembling over their bowed heads.
I closed my eyes and in Hebrew whispered, and then in full
voice recited in Latin the priestly blessing with which the Rabbi
or father of the groom sometimes blesses the marrying couple.
"Benedicat tibi Dominus et custodiat te. Ostendat Dominus
faciem suam tibi et misereatur tui. Convertat Dominus vultum
suum ad te et det tibi pacem."[91]

Though each of differing faiths and language, the
couple understood clearly and radiantly my intent. Overcome,
tears falling, Danielos pulled me to his heart. A moment
of compassion and grace illuminated our dark and dank
cavernous hiding place.

[91] "May the Lord bless you and keep you. May the Lord make His face shine upon you
and be gracious unto you. May the Lord lift His countenance upon you, and give you
peace." Numbers 6: 24–26. Latin from the Vulgate.

CHAPTER THE ELEVENTH

With the help of Heaven

We rested yet one more day, and then set out at night, following a circuitous route, finding caves and once even a deserted house. By day we slept. As dawn broke following the second night, we found the main body of our group, already in terrified conjecture about our fate, and all the while busy establishing their new life. Our new life.

This then is the shape of our life-to-be, if it so be granted by Heaven. We number the original group of eight, plus Sophia, Danielos, and me, eleven in all. In planning their flight from Bosnia and their resettlement in Crete, Hisham had told them of the valley he had inherited. It was surrounded by hills, hours by foot from the nearest village, in virgin land, watered by both rain runoff and a spring, which he now owned. Thus they had used the valley as their main base while they explored the terrain and routes for freeing Sophia.

They knew that I had been instructing Sophia in the ways of healing, in the use of herbs, and setting of bones. They planned to bring young Muslim women from Bosnia to wed and build families, and would be happy to have a doctor among them. An old man such as I could do no harm, but could transmit to Sophia his accumulated knowledge. They also never said it explicitly, but I assume they would use me as a bargaining card in case they were in danger. However, with dignity and wisdom they treated me with great respect.

In the months of preparation and waiting, they had built a few stone cottages, cut wood to dry for cooking, and Hisham had bought sheep and goats that they had herded back to the valley. Geese and chickens were bought from closer by and dragged in wooden containers thrown together as best they could. Wild fruit grew in abundance; they had planted a small orchard and vegetable garden. Wheat flour and olive oil they brought from Kastelli. To my regret, they did not drink wine.

The first days were spent making sure Sophia was being restored to health. Then began the days of peripatetic teaching, walking through the wild-goat and ibex trails as we collected medicinal herbs for drinking and for making potions. A week or so later, the youngest member of the group cut deeply into his leg with an axe, giving me the opportunity of teaching Sophia, and others who crowded about, how to make a tourniquet, bathe the wound with fresh flowing water, and then apply a potion of sage and myrtle liquid, somewhat fermented, which I had found prevented evil humors from infecting wounds. We set the broken limb of a little lamb that had stumbled down the slope, and thus I could show how to set a bone, fixing it with splints, a firm bandage and twine.

We ate simple food, drank pure water, sheep's milk, goat and sheep cheese, rough bread, and, on Muslim feast days, of which they kept careful count, they broiled a lamb or sheep on a spit. I was asked to serve as slaughterer, and thus could see that the animals were killed in the humane manner prescribed by Halachah. This suited their ways of kashrut, which they call halal, and one of them recited the ritual name of Allah as I did my part. Our common ancestry shows in these everyday matters, and sometimes I wonder whether we do not exaggerate our differences to our mutual detriment.

Two occurrences broke the steady rhythm of night and day: walks and air, sun, wind, and rain. First, Danielos and Sophia were wed. In preparation for the wedding, Danielos

agreed to become a Muslim. He uttered the Shahadah,
giving testimony of his faith in Allah as the only God, with
Mohammed his messenger. Somewhat wickedly, for a moment
I wondered whether circumcision, a Muslim practice too, is
not required for conversion, as it is with us. I held back my
questions, lest I impinge on the joy. And so it was, amidst the
dancing and singing that echoed through our valley from the
surrounding cupping hills, he and Sophia were led through the
ceremony by Hisham, the oldest and most versed in Muslim
lore. Again, I understood another similarity, when Sophia
explained to Danielos in Greek that she had foregone any
demand for mahr, or as we call it, mohar, the bridal payment
made by the groom. Though with us, it is the bride's family
which pays the dowry.

The human mind is indeed a wondrous feat of the
Creator, for Danielos went from one form of monotheism to a
purer or simpler form; to be fair, Islam does accept Jesus as a
prophet, so he did not exactly abjure his previous faith, at least
in that sense. From what Danielos told me later, this was less of
a problem than I thought. And the other wondrous working of
the mind was my own delight at their being wed. Thus, even
though I lost my claim on a young and warm-hearted and kind
lover, I see her future as more assured; obviously my days are
more limited than Danielos's.

Therefore, with a full heart and no misgivings, I
slaughtered a sheep and the men set to cleaning and browning
it on a spit over the wood fire, while others cooked soup and
prepared salads from the bounty that the land had already
provided. The men danced wild dances, and I knew not
whether I was seeing Muslim fervor or the ways of the Balkans
and Slavs, but there was joy and release in the dance. As the
meat and bread were put onto the rough-hewn tables, Ayub

rose to his feet. His words led me to solve the problem that had been lingering in mind since my first days in Messara.

Sophia's brother, speaking in conversational tones (translated by Sophia), announced that Hisham and he had decided that they would call their village Novo-Dom. I assumed novo was the cognate of "new" in Latin languages. Sophia explained to me that the word meant house or home: Novo-Dom — New Home.

His announcement set my thoughts on fire again, stirring up brands that had flared up and fallen into quiescent embers....

That evening, as the others slept, the bride and groom in their own small newly built one-room stone house, I returned to the restoked embers, reflecting on the name. Novo-Dom means new home, new house. New house is in Hebrew bayit hadash. What had I written at the time of my conversation with Danielos, when first I beheld glimmerings of the idea that now seized me? I leafed through my written pages by the flickering light of the dying fire, long after the others slept. And I found Danielos's words:

"Somewhere in the misty years of early history, perhaps before the time of the Nazarene, seafaring people came from the East. They came in swift light ships, single-sailed craft. Among them were traders and merchants, and others were farmers and tillers of the soil. They came from Phoenicia, from Tyre or Sidon, whose names we know from the Bible, and from Jonah's home port of Jaffa. They spoke a language different from the Cretan Greeks, and they worshipped in strange ways. They would not bow down to the local gods nor consult the oracles, and they would refrain from work one day a week.

"To me, reading the Bible, and comparing their behavior to the rules in the Books of Moses, it seems that perhaps they

were Hebrews fleeing from war, or simply seeking a different
fate and fortune. When I once said this to my parents, they told
me that God forbid that any of our forebears would be among
the killers of our Savior, and washed my mouth with harsh
soap. This made a lasting impression on my young mind, for
if they had not punished me, I should not have recalled the
matter. Because they did, my thoughts turned to the matter
again and again, but I said nothing about them until this very
day....

"They settled in Gortys, which we call Gortyna, and
then, drawn together by a mysterious magnetism, they moved
to Betadas, a name which we think was part of their lost and
secret language. There, they built strong homes and became
prosperous farmers. Their daughters would not wed men from
outside their village, and their men, who could marry outside
women if they so pleased, had to pay high bridal prices. This
was both to compensate the bride's parents and ease their
understanding that they might visit their daughter but once a
year. Outside the village, they built a special guest house for
these visitors. They say in the early days there were seventy
heads of household; others say they were six hundred, but
we, of course, do not know. There have been found no written
records, whether in Greek or in their own tongue.

"After many centuries, the people of Betadas became
Christians. Some say that was at the time of Agios Titos; some
say later. When the Arabs came, Betadas suffered because
of the Christian devotion of its inhabitants. Then Byzantium
returned, and there was a rift within the community of Betadas,
and some families, my ancestors among them, went into the
countryside and built their own village. Over the generations,
we lost the knowledge that the ancients carried, and we do not
know why they left....

"On entering Church, when we cross the threshold, and before we bless ourselves, we close our eyes and whisper a secret word....

"On Fridays, we wash our bodies prior to our evening meal and before we break bread we raise our glass to one another and say 'Sabtyini.' This is also secret, but less so, because we make this toast even when we have guests. We tell them that this was the name of the first winemaker in Galuta, whose memory we recall and bless in this way. Indeed, some of us believe that this is so, that there was such a man, but the elder who whispered all these secrets to me told me this was not true, but a story for the uninitiated. So be it. I have broken an oath, but you have given me oath for oath, as God is our witness."

This then was the second break in the rhythm of our bucolic life. I was now able to understand the reality, the truth behind Danielos's account. With the Phoenicians came the Hebrews, their cousins and allies, and settled in Gortys. Possibly they were part of the northern Ten Tribes of Israel. Thus, I cannot even call them Jews, but rather Hebrews or Israelites.

After some time, to preserve their unity, they moved to a new village — their Novo-Dom, or Bayit Hadash — Beit Adas — Betadas. They kept the Shabbat. Their daughters could only marry their own kind, but the men could marry outside women. These were then initiated into their new families. Their parents and siblings of outside wives could only see them once a year.

Over the centuries more and more of their language and lore were lost, more and more their lives resembled their neighbors. Even their village assimilated its name to the Greek pronunciation: there is no "sh" sound — this Bayit Hadash — Beitadas....

Some centuries later, we know that observant Jews, that is, people from Judea, settled in Gortys. These newcomers maintained contact with Jewry and followed rabbinic practice. It was easy for Agios Titos to convert some of the separate crypto-Hebrew or crypto-Israelites of Beitadas to Christianity, just as some of the Judeans must have converted. Beitadas became Christian and eventually lost its separate identity. Those who did not accept the new teaching of Agios Titos, who rejected Christianity, broke away — a tiny group of more stubborn people. They called their new small village Galuta: Exile.

Over the fifteen centuries that elapsed only some traces of the Shabbat remained: Shabbat-yeini, or even Sabbat-oini. The Hebrew or Greek words for wine are similar (yayin and oinos): this was their toast and sanctification of the day.[92] Over the centuries, they too became Christians, but memories of the old practices continued, so that they said a special word or words when they entered the Church. The crypto-Jews from Spain and Portugal, the "forced ones," did something similar on entering the Christian house of prayer. Shem'a Yisrael![93]

The very name Galuta, Exile, reverberates with the sound of their first flight and exile from their home in the Land of Israel, a memory they lost. Perhaps it was these closed qualities and hidden memories that I had sensed the day of my very first visit there, mere months ago.

Then I slept for twelve hours, and the others left me undisturbed. It was a clear and healing sleep, as though my body was rewarding my mind for its success, and

---

[92] De' Pomi referred to the word for wine in Hebrew (ancient and modern): yayin, and in ancient Greek, oinos. For sanctification of the day he used the Hebrew word Kiddush, as it was and is known in Judaism then and now.

[93] These words are the first two of the central statement of Judaism "Hear, O Israel, the Lord our God, the Lord is One," taken from Deuteronomy 6:4, and recited morning and evening at all Jewish services to this day.

compensating for the effort I have made carrying parts of these secrets in my being.

Thus months passed, at a steady pace, while Sophia's belly swelled. Her head seemed to grow older as she learned some of my medical terms and explanations. She will be more than a village healer, and less than a doctor, since I cannot read with her the basic medical canon that we study in Bologna and Padua. What I have been able to recall from memory I explain, but the books, those pleasant tomes in Latin, and my own private collection in Hebrew are in far-off Mantua. We have also bought a few Greek books, which Danielos and Sophia read.

Danielos also has found a new role, which gives him renewed pride. Ayub and Hisham see him as a gift from above, for he filled a need that they had not clearly thought through. They must have some contact with villagers and with the small town of Kastelli on the shore: to buy staples, to sell excess produce, and to alleviate suspicions and the spreading of rumors. It is known in the few villages within four hours' walk that we are here on land sold to Hisham, whose Greek is passable and appearance reassuring. Now Danielos has been instructing the men to make responses in Greek at the services they must attend from time to time on feast days, to show them how to cross themselves, kiss the icons, and carry on their pretense of being of the Orthodox faith.

In this way, Danielos has become an additional and unexpected asset. He will be the public face of Novo-Dom, its link, however limited, with the land and with the Church. In exchange, though, he has been instructed orally in the daily prayers of Islam, and has been taught some of the rules.

Hisham is scheduled to go back to Bosnia with one of the younger men, to bring back brides for the others. He hopes to be able also to bring back seeds and saplings and try to grow some of their home vegetation here. He will also bring the Koran in its original and a Greek-Arabic dictionary, so that Danielos and Ayub can read together, and then read for the others. I cautioned Hisham to buy an old edition, and wrap it in silk, so that if they are searched by Christians they can claim they have bought the book as an investment to offer for sale to a library.

Hisham will be leaving soon, for winter is approaching — we feel the colder winds and the whipping rain. Our village is high enough to have snow here as well. My private count of the Hebrew months coincide with the lunar count of my new "family"; Rosh Hashanah and Yom Kippur and Sukkoth are long gone and soon Hanukah will be here. Snow, perhaps, and winter, and then spring and the birth of the first child in Novo-Dom.

There is one more matter I should record before concluding this chapter: Danielos's reaction when he heard of his true origins. The moment for the two of us to be alone was hard to find. Both of us had our allotted tasks, and he naturally wished to be with Sophia as much as possible. One day, though, it rained heavily, and I took shelter under an overhang on the hillside as the rain beat on all sides. Danielos stumbled into the same refuge, a few logs under his heavy winter cape. The rain seemed to have no end. He stacked the logs and built a fire, beginning with shavings and his flint and stone. Slowly the flames took and I saw we were actually in the mouth of a cave. Gently I said, "Your childhood intuition was right."

He looked back at me blankly, raised his thick eyebrows and opened his eyes wide.

"I do believe that your ancestors in Beitadas and Galuta were Hebrews."

A look I could not decipher crossed his bearded features, and his eyes flickered with a light that only the intellect pours into our clay bodies. Much as I set forth above, so did I explain to him the meaning of the names of the villages, and my conjectures, which I believe to be firm truths. I also told him at greater length about the similarities between the customs he described with those of our oppressed brothers, the "forced ones," called Marranos by the enemies of Israel.

He sat silently, and wrapped his arms about himself, rocking slowly back and forth, and began to weep, as a patient whose pain has been alleviated does sometimes weep tears of relief, and possibly also tears of joy.

We sat together in silence as the flames of the growing fire mounted. Then he said, "Maestro, I must confess — to my shame — an act that will, I hope, not sunder us." He paused, searching for the words. "But, perhaps, they will bring us closer together." Eyes lowered, abashed, he spoke slowly, switching from our usual familiar ti to the formal Lei. Flashes of lightning and rolls of thunder punctuated the rain that was the background to his narration.

"One day, when you were visiting the lands with Stavros, and I was…to be teaching Sophia…" again a pause a slow dull red flush mounted from his neck to the roots of his hair, "…she said she wanted to show me something, something of the Master's, to see if I could explain it.…" Danielos held his peace for a few more breaths. "That morning, you had left unlocked the wooden box on your bedside table, one that she would dust daily, and had noticed that it was always locked. She thought it might have been either money or letters from our Lord the Duke of Mantua. In replacing it, however, the top slipped open, and she saw therein items that she could not identify.…"

Again, silence. He breathed deeply, eyes still downcast, shame on his features.

"I did not think to pry into the Master's affairs. Only to slake the curiosity of—of the woman I felt love for." Another pause. "Perhaps, Maestro, I wished to impress her…. I do not rightly know."

At this point I said directly, but with kindness, "Enough self reproof. That matter closed with your marriage. Now, I think I know what you saw."

"I saw a fringed garment, with stripes on it, and a strange lettering on its collar. I knew it was a prayer shawl because I had seen similar ones on the Catholic priest in the Latin Church, but I knew the writing was not Latin. And then the fringes. I knew it belonged to the Jews, but dared not tell Sophia, lest she change her ways toward you.

"I pretended that it was a valuable copy of the early Christian martyr's shawls, since it was too new in appearance to pass for a garment so aged. I told her that as a scholar and devoted believer, you probably put it on when you prayed privately, to link yourself to the beginnings of your faith."

"It was a good answer, Danielos," I said deliberately, "and you did the right thing."

The stiffness went out of his body, and the tears again came back.

In a strangled whisper, he said, "Maestro, we are of one blood-line, and our veins carry memories of our joint fathers."

I rose to my feet, bade him rise as well. As once before when we shared secrets, I pressed him to my bosom.

CHAPTER THE TWELFTH

With the help of Heaven

For Thy salvation do I hope, O Lord?[94] The weeks have passed uneventfully, and thus I have had no need to write, but now I must, for who knows what tomorrow will bring? Danger threatens our lives as winter tightens its cold grip on our bodies.

Hisham and Danielos have returned through swirling snow and heavy winds, laden with supplies for the winter, lest Novo-Dom be cut off. We had hoped to pass the cruel winter months snuggled in this valley, protected by the very hills that may become impassable if the snow becomes ice. They bore bad news, however: the Plague has visited Kastelli.

Plague. How often and in how many places have I fought you, and with what little success? I find this report strange, though, because usually the Plague does not strike in winter. It seems to hibernate then, to revive in the spring.[95] Perhaps this is not the Plague, but some other illness; nonetheless, we cannot rest quiescent. The village has turned to me, and I assume my medical mantle. I see fear in everyone's eyes. Like me, they know how powerful a killer this may be.

First, like Jacob our Father, I put my mind to the children. In our case, a yet unborn child, but one day a soul who could carry on the flame of life that is so holy. I go directly to Sophia

---

[94] From Jacob's blessing to his sons, Genesis.
[95] Plague, the Black Plague, the Black Death, or bubonic plague swept through Europe and killed one-third of its population in the mid-14th century, and then recurred from time to time across the next few centuries. It is a disease carried by rodents, spread by their flea ectoparasites.

and Danielos's house, and have Sophia move — immediately — with the baby still safe in her womb — to my quarters. I will share their room with Danielos and let a week go by, to see if the danger passes.

I charged Danielos to gather all the men and make a large fire. They were to boil water, and throw wood ash, animal fat, and lye into the boiling pot. Into the fire itself Danielos and Hisham were to throw the clothes they had worn in Kastelli and the clothes they now wore. The others were to give them some of their own clean clothing — we must share since we have so little.

Meanwhile evening fell. With the cold air purpling their bodies, Hisham and Danielos stood naked and shivering as I scrubbed them with the strong simple soap boiling over the fire. They then dressed in clean clothing. I recalled the words of the Torah regarding the Red Heifer: we are warned that the man who performs the cleansing becomes defiled by the illness. This I washed myself carefully as well, the raw soap stinging everywhere.[96] I burnt the clothes I had been wearing as well. And then, freshly dressed and warmer, Danielos and I scoured the walls and floors of his house with the remains of the evil-smelling brew we had cooked up. May its evil smell be in inverse proportion to the good it does. Amen.

Above all, we are all now more than ever in need of Heavenly mercy. I well know, no matter how hard I have done battle against this persistent enemy, Plague, ultimately "who shall live and who shall die" is not in our hands.[97]

For Thy salvation do I hope, O Lord! Amen!

~

[96] Numbers 19.
[97] From the prayer U-netaneh tokef of the Additional Service on the High Holy Days, the traditional time of judgment for the year to come. It was used in the Ashkenazi rite, and would have been known to a scholar like de' Pomi.

It may be difficult now to make out my writing. For two days I have had a high fever, vomiting, and diarrhea. I need the salvation that I have prayed for. The potions and medicines Danielos has brought me have not helped. Sophia has wanted to nurse me, but I have forbidden her from approaching me. I am very weak, and drink only sage tea and thin gruel. Everything is an effort, even writing.

~

Εγώ Δανιέλος.... [98]

I, Danielos, now write at the behest of my lord who is so very ill and weak, and needs the mercy of the gods—Allah, the Lord, Jesus, Zeus, whichever or whoever is Lord of Creation—send him healing. If Zeus still has some jurisdiction in Greece, may his messenger Hermes bring him healing or may Apollo be his Healer. Amen.

I now write verbatim at the bidding of my lord:

"I believe that I have reached my last days. I do not question God's decision, for there must be a reason why He sent me to Crete, and why He chose this place for me to meet my eternity. Faithful Danielos will wield the pen for me, in the hope that one day these words shall see the light of day.

"Sophia is now large with child, the almond trees have begun to blossom, the birds begin their time of returning, singing, from southern climes. I will die

[98] The translation that follows was made by Avraham Ben Hayim. I assume he had the translation made by or through Ariadne because of its arcane language. On checking it, even though I could read the original Greek, I consulted with experts at Hebrew University for help with specific Cretan and/or medieval or Renaissance vocabulary.

knowing that that life, that holiest gift we have, that which I have long striven to save and prolong in others, goes on. Danielos and Sophia have offered to name the child Abraham/Ibrahim or Sarah, but I asked that if the child is a girl, she be called Grazia/ Hannah, after my mother, who lived long good years; my wife of blessed memory, Regina/Malkah died so young and that would not be a wise choice.

"Now, this third night of my burning fever, Danielos has come to me in the dead of night to tell me what he has overheard, which I asked him to write it down in his own language—in brief, but with the words of the speakers."

I, Danielos, now write at the command of my lord to relate exactly what I have heard, I do so, knowing that my pen is untried. I was walking in the pitch dark, before the moon rose, from the sheep pen lower in the valley back to nurse the Maestro. I passed the house of Hisham, who was left alone in the house he had shared with Ayub, for fear of illness. Ayub stood outside the door, and I could hear their voices. I do not follow their language perfectly, but God has blessed me with a quick facility to learn, and these are the words they spoke.

Ayub said, "At home, when there was terrible sickness, plague, or danger of attacks upon us, we slaughtered a sheep or goat, poured out its blood as a sacrifice, and made special prayers to be saved from pestilence."

Hisham said, "Why tell me this? Of course we should do that. It is good that you reminded me. I have been away too long."

Ayub said, "No, no, that is not what I wanted to tell you, that is the beginning.... After you were taken captive, and the Christians came sweeping down so often, and sickness and disease spread, some of the old villagers said that they remembered their grandparents whispering by the fireplace. They spoke with secrecy and in hints, but I understood: in times of great troubles woe and misery, they would abduct a Christian and...." Here his voice dropped and I could not hear the rest of what he said.

Then Hisham shouted, "Pagan idolatry. This is against the Holy Quran. And how can we requite evil for good? Sophia told us how the Mantuan treated her, and let her rise from slavery to freedom. He has taught her healing herbs and potions and how to set broken limbs. Now he is very ill, perhaps—probably—dying. This we do not do to an old, weak, good person who has worked with us faithfully, has healed us and helped as best he could. Christian or Moslem, we do not kill people as a sacrifice. This is pagan. Idolatry!"

My blood ran cold. This is not how I too had understood my new religion. As I stood frozen in my place, I heard Ayub again. "He is old. He will die soon anyway. He is a Christian, and perhaps because we have accepted him in our midst, after all they did to us, perhaps because of him we are being punished."

Hisham said nothing. And then Ayub continued. "Christians believe that God became a man to let himself be a sacrifice and that the young Prophet Iss died to save mankind.[99] Now let an old Christian die to save our village. Perhaps it will make him happy to know that he is giving his life to save ours."

[99] The Arabic for Jesus.

Hisham said, "No man wishes to die before his time. We are not judges or in place of Allah the great Judge to decide to take life."

Ayub replied, "We shall sacrifice a sheep tonight. If that does not stop the illnesses, we shall ask the entire brotherhood what they say. Their lives are at stake as well."

Hisham remained silent. I rushed to the bedside of my lord and told him of this conversation.

He too remained silent. I gave him some cold sage tea, and a spoonful of honey, and I could see on his face and in his eyes that he was weighing everything he heard. He is the most intelligent, most learned man I have ever met. He signaled to me that he would now sleep, and I left his bedside. But the night for me was full of dread.…

Finally I fell asleep on my cot, and awoke with a start as the morning star was rising. I made tea for both of us, and he spoke. His skin was pallid, his eyes sunken, his cheeks fallen; his eyes, burning with intelligence, seemed to fill half of his pitiful face. His voice came rasping, each breath an effort.

"Write down these words." These are his exact words:

"This first part is just for you, Danielos. When I die, wash my body with water and bury me on my back, hands outstretched by my sides, wrapped in a clean simple cloth, if there is one, and my feet pointing to the east.

"After that, if and when you think that it is not too dangerous for you, go to the Head of the Jews in Hania, Yosef Delmedigo, and tell him as follows:

"The representative of the Duke of Mantua who spent the Black Fast with you sends messages of peace and blessings from his deathbed. He bids you open the envelope he left with you. After you read it, pray act in accordance to misericordia da verità.[100]

"Say to him then: "If you believe there will be no danger to the holy community in Hania, and no danger to the bearer of this message, please arrange to have my bones brought to proper burial, as you can safely do it. Whether you are able to do so, and bury me with all the rites, or whether you are unable so to do, please have *Kaddish* said for me regularly, in keeping with our laws."

The word "Kaddish" he repeated to ensure that I had written it correctly.

His breathing worsened, his breath was bad, sweat stood on his waxen face. He lay there breathing with an effort. When he gathered what little strength he had left, he continued:

"Now write this down as I say it: Gather the men of Novo-Dom together, four paces from this doorway, and as the sun sets, read them what I now say.

"I, representative of the Duke of Mantua and Governor of Messara da Gonzaga and responsible for all the Duke's lands.…'"

With gasps and pauses, weakening with each breath, he forced himself to finish what I was to tell them. I feared he would die then and there. I brought him another spoonful of honey, gave him water, and sponged his pallid fallen features.

---

[100] The Hebrew term hesed shel emet, the loving kindness of truth, refers to the requirement to bring each Jew to burial in consecrated ground and in accordance with tradition. De' Pomi used the Italian equivalent for obvious reasons.

~

The sun set, the hilltops around us shone, while
here, in the shade the flames of the fire on which the
sacrificial sheep was roasting flickered on the black
stone houses. The men stood in a semi-circle around
Hisham and Ayub, four paces from the doorway. I stood
in front of the lintel, the paper in my hand shaking,
and read without difficulty, for though it was darkening, the words were stamped into my mind, and rolled
off my tongue. Nonetheless, my voice also shook and
I read slowly in Italian, translating as best I could
into Bosnian.

"My lord, our healer, who was Governor of Messara,
commands me to say this to you, for he is too weak to
speak to you himself. These are his words:

"I, representative of the Duke of Mantua and Governor of Messara da Gonzaga and responsible for all
the Duke's lands, was born a Jew, Avraham de' Pomi by
name, doctor and rabbi. I was born a Jew and I shall
die a Jew. Circumstances forced me to pretend to be
a Christian, and I was blessed with the favor of the
duke who sent me to Candia.

"Some of you wish to take my life before its
time. Both Christians and Muslims say that their
teaching supplanted the teaching of the Torah, but
they both accept this foundation: of everything created, the holiest is Life. It is a gift, given and
taken without our will. This is the cycle of Creation.
No man dare place himself in the role of Taker of
Life.

"I shall die within the next two days; my science tells me this. From a deep sleep I shall pass from life to death. You have the power to take my life before that. Choose now, whether you want my blood on your hands and on your heads. Our Holy Book says, 'Choose life.'

"Whatever you choose, Peace be upon you."

As soon as I finished I felt drained of all energy, and fell into a faint.

I awakened on the lintel of the house. Wisely, the men had not approached me—fear of plague kept them away. Nor had they stepped over me to the bedside of my lord. I heard his rasping, uneven breathing. Again I entered, and gave him drink and bathed his face. He whispered words of thanks, and asked me to help him sit up. With great effort, I propped him against the pillows. He bade me bring water and help him wash his hands.

Then with shaking hand and rasping breath he wrote some words in his language on a fresh sheet of paper. "Now I shall make my final confession." He said words I did not understand. It took no more than a minute. Then he said in a loud voice words that sounded like those I had learned to say on crossing the threshold of a church.

"Sema Isral."[101]

---

[101] Shem'a Yisrael… Hear O Israel, the Lord our God, the Lord is One. The central prayer of Judaism, from Deuteronomy 6: 4.

My lord, who was so good to me and to Sophia closed his eyes, lay on his back and, exhausted, fell into a deep sleep.

Night fell and dawn came, and now I, Danielos, write again. I feel I too am in the grip of fever. I do not know what awaits us all.

We all require the mercy of heaven.…

SHEM'A YISRAEL

שמע ישראל

[THIS IS THE END OF THE MANUSCRIPT
FOUND IN MELIA]

CHAPTER 5

As I read Avraham de' Pomi's last words, Mozart's *Requiem* played in the background. Truth can sometimes be an awful cliché.

And so Avraham de' Pomi's account, stranger than fiction, ended. I wanted to know what had happened to everyone in Novo-Dom. We are all children when it comes to stories: "So what happened then?" I assume that de' Pomi died, probably as he foresaw, within the next day or two. He would not have lived much longer anyway, given the average life expectancy four hundred years ago. But did Danielos die of the plague? And Sophia, did she survive? Did she bear her first child? Did she have more children? Was it their descendants who were wiped out in Melia 150 years ago? Or did they leave, and move to another village?

After sitting for so long, I had to walk. The sun was beginning its return run behind the western hills. I walked along a goat path toward a point where I could see its golden path streaming across the green-blue sea, leading to the stony fishing port to the east of the town six kilometers away. Rock-like cliffs framed the fishing vessels as they bobbed at anchor in the calmer evening waters.

During the day and night it had taken me to read the manuscript, I had been lost in the Renaissance world of de' Pomi, forgetting everything else, including the cell phone. When it rang, I jumped.

"Where are you?" The voice was Yosef's.

"Never mind where I am. Just stop calling me. I didn't even know I still had the phone on me. Better that no one knows where I am and what I plan."

Silence. Then slowly, slowly. "Okay, you're a free man, not under any discipline. No one can give you orders. But I found out something that I can't talk about on the phone. Tell me how I can give a message to the young lady you were with. Soon. I won't be staying in Heraklion too long."

I called Ariadne and asked whether there was a safe place they could meet. After a moment, she chuckled. "I need to pay an overdue speeding fine. Tell him to meet me at the traffic police station tomorrow at eleven."

I had to laugh. I've always believed women are smarter than men. Even Yosef laughed when I called him back.

Ariadne drove up the next day. A hug and a kiss on both cheeks and a clouded forehead. "He said it's urgent to tell you this." He had asked her to commit his exact words to memory: "'When you got picked up on the bus and taken to the safe house, I did it as a favor for Manny. I used some new boys who are doing field training with me. Then I got a call that Manny was coming to Crete. My boss said, Remember, he's retired. He's out. Out. Keep it that way.' Yosef said to tell you these words, which I wrote down. She read them out loud. *Hu ba-hutz… ba-hutz.*" She looked at me with lifted eyebrows.

I said, "That means he's totally *out* of the loop. Now he's an outsider, not just a retiree. The system, the establishment won't cover for him. Looks like they don't trust him." I was trying to process this.

Ariadne continued, "Then Yosef said, 'I decided to let you go, and get the trainees out of there before Manny arrived. I've filed a full written report, and ignored Manny's phone calls. I've spoken to some of my pals back home, and they all said Manny's gone sour. They didn't know more, or didn't want to talk about it.'"

I sighed. "Or maybe they couldn't!"

Okay, now we knew. Or did we? I had to watch my back from every direction. I even started to wonder whether Yosef's message was on the up-and-up. This was not my world. I was new at this game of duplicity. Triplicity.

Ariadne watched me closely, and when I seemed calmer, she added, "He said, very quietly but emphatically, 'Just tell him to go. To keep changing identities and go. Don't trust anyone. Anyone. He said that word twice and then said it in Greek—anyone."

Now it was my turn to lift my eyebrows.

She had a hurt look on her face. "He meant me, didn't he?"

"No, that doesn't make sense. If he meant you, why would he ask you to bring me the message? Why would he have you meet him? If he didn't trust you—if he thought you'd make trouble for him, he'd never agree to talk to you at all."

She seemed placated.

"Do you have a map of Crete in the car?" I asked what she thought of Kissamou, a small town at the far northwestern end of the island. Kissamou-Kastelli is its full name. De' Pomi's chronicle mentioned Kastelli as the place where they bought supplies, and from which they had imported the plague. Today, ferries run from there to Kythira, to the Peloponnesus and on to Piraeus.

I asked Ariadne if someone in the village could drive her car, wearing her head-scarf and sweater. That night Marco, the baker's son who was mooncalf in love with Ariadne, drove off in her car. She drove his van. She had brought her CD player, and we listened to Savina Yannatou's *Songs of the Mediterranean*. A waxing moon had risen and whenever the National Road veered along the coast, streaks of silver illuminated the black waters of the nighttime sea; mountains hugging the bays stood in stark silhouette against the luminous star-pocked skies. The fierce music of the Mediterranean—Sicilian, Turkish, Arab, Sardinian, Hebrew—resonated with the elemental culture that washed the littoral lands of the great inland sea.

The Sicilian mourning song of a mother for her child, sung deep-voiced from visceral pain, cut through us both, "*O murte, murte tradittur....*"

We drove to a touristy beach-side hotel just outside Kissamou. I made a face at the ugly concrete spread, but Ariadne drove another fifty meters to (another!) Giorgio's restaurant. Above the name of the restaurant, his few rooms were advertised with a crudely hand-lettered sign—*Zimmer Camere Chambres Rooms.*

It was a brief night; we had to be on the road by seven to make the ferry to Kythira. Ariadne dropped a folded poem into my shirt pocket. "It's by Tom Waits. Keep it until you've slept a bit. Then read it." She played me the song on the CD player: a gravelly voice came at me in a violent style that I usually avoid. I listened, and then she played another song that ended with the lines "I watched you as you disappeared."

She drove onto the stone jetty where the ferryboat was waiting. I leaned across the seat, and she leaned into me. I held my cheek to hers. Wet cheeks. She kissed me lightly on the lips and then I walked away, my bag held loosely, and stumbled by the waiting cars, supply trucks, and vans. I joined the line of passengers straggling into the large cargo hold and car park, gestured onward and up a flight of stairs by the white-uniformed ship's crew. Into the belly of the whale. I fell onto my cabin's bed and slept.

Last night I dreamed that I was dreaming of you
And from a window across the lawn I watched you undress
Wearing your sunset of purple tightly woven around your hair
... Moving in a yellow bedroom light
The air is wet with sound
... And the ground is drinking a slow faucet leak
... I hear your champagne laugh
You wear two lavender orchids
One in your hair and one on your hip

. . .

And you dance into the shadow of a black poplar tree
And I watched you as you disappeared

I watched you as you disappeared
I watched you as you disappeared....

As I heard the words, I was once more sitting in the car, again stealing glimpses of the damp cheeks. I woke up in the sterile cabin bed, clenched cheek muscles aching.

I went up onto the main deck and stood at the rail watching the foam the ship left in its wake. Two excited young men stood close to me—one tapped my shoulder. I jumped, but they smiled and pointed across the sea. Spouts of water rose, and sparkling forms darted up in graceful arcs. "Dolphins?" "*Nei nei, dhelfini, dhelfini.*" Their delight was so very Greek, or was it Cretan? These people are still close to nature. For a long moment, the sadness at leaving Ariadne, my fears and worries for the future, the need to plan—all were banished as the dolphins gamboled beside the ship, escorting it out of their waters.

I decided not to open the note she had given me. I headed to the main deck, where a large bar filled most of the forward part of the boat. The bar was crowded with groups of families and friends drinking Greek coffee, ouzo, or *raki*, children running with small bags of potato chips in their hands, ducking behind the padded armchairs, loveseats, and sofas.

A slim white-haired man took a fiddle out of a battered case and began playing a Cretan folk song with a strong Middle Eastern beat. Three heavyset middle-aged women began dancing, while the others pushed their chairs back to make a small dance floor. This was not Hollywood—these were no lissome beauties. They bore the heads high and backs straight, the bearing of villagers aware that the dance restored them to youth, to high spirits.

The women looked off into space, much as I remember my gray-haired mother dancing polkas with her sister at family weddings. Their feet moved lightly, and more and more women joined the circle until eight or ten of them were whirling and dancing with great dignity. The fiddler got to his feet and changed to a wilder tune; his wife, sitting next to him, rose, clapping her hands and gracefully wheeling into the middle of the dancers as she had done at her wedding decades ago.

I took a paper napkin and wrote "a pilgrimage to beauty, light, color, vitality." Back in the cabin, I found what Cretan Nikos Kazantzakis had written in his *Report to Greco*.*

"There is a kind of flame in Crete—let us call it "soul"—something more powerful than either life or death. There is pride, obstinacy, valor, and together with these there is something else inexpressible and imponderable, something which makes you rejoice that you are a human being and at the same time tremble."

The ferry took four hours to reach Kythira. By the time I arrived there, the sun was setting softly, illuminating the Hora of Kythira—a small village capped by a Venetian fortress—and settling into the sea a few kilometers away. The breathtaking beauty saved me from self-pity, the trap of the fugitive.

My route took me by ferry to Gythio in the Peloponnesus, by bus first to Sparta, and then to Napfoli, by yet another ferry to Thessaloniki, and finally by plane to Corfu. I was still using Yosef's passport. That worried me, too. Who knows who tells what to whom?

I needed to be more careful with money now. I spoke to Vi every few days, and our longing for one another was tinged with worry and unspoken fear. As Crete faded, and the time to plunge back into life approached, my mood swung sharply between paranoia and euphoria, and always an abiding sense of being alone. I was increasingly afraid of speaking to strangers in case I revealed too much.

But in Kyrkira, Corfu's main town, I found not only a room, but both intellectual and comic relief. I had blundered into a magnificent bookshop on the main street, just beyond the Bank of Greece. Thanks to a magnificent publisher, Denise Harvey, I was able to find some excellent anthologies of modern Greek poets in translation, as well as Robert Graves's *Greek Mythology*, and a pocket Greek-English dictionary. The bookshop carried Gerald Durrell's *My Family and Other*

---

* See Faber and Faber, London 1973 p. 82.

Animals, and this reminded me that the Durrell family had lived here for a few years. I had days to kill until Vi and I would be able to rendezvous, as she had just set off on her own series of false-trail travels. The family antics of the eccentric Durrells and the poems would help time move.

Laden with my new book purchases, I continued my walking tour of Kyrkira and, on a little side street, I came upon a beautiful little synagogue, which the next-door Jewish storekeeper opened for me. Everywhere the tradition goes with us. I silently recited the *Kaddish* prayer for Avraham de' Pomi, and the full *Shem'a Yisrael* to the end, and hurried to leave, honoring the frantic gestures of the volunteer beadle, who had to rush back to his store that he had left untended. At the bottom of the dead-end lane stood a police car, and next to it, two young armed policemen were smoking. Here, too, in this distant island, as in other European cities, the synagogue needed a police presence!

I kept walking, moving back and forth in history, until I found myself in a small undistinguished square, where the sight of an utterly unexpected statue, a group of three nudes—a mother, father, and child—stopped me in my tracks. Their pose was silently supplicating. Here, too? Did the manic search to destroy Jews not stop anywhere? A small plaque at the base of the statue read *To the memory of Corfu's Jews exiled and killed by the Nazis 1940–1945.*

Continuity, danger, death. Continuity, danger, life.

The brain is blessed with the ability to forget. I forged on, hungry, until I reached a small storefront restaurant named Chrysomallis that stood closer to the port and promenade. I chose a table that was folded into an alcove formed by the window and the door. Behind a U-shaped counter stood a middle-aged man and woman—his wife, I assumed—busily preparing food. I was pleased that I'd found the kind of papa-mama place I prefer. I sat drinking red wine and consuming immense quantities of *salata horiatiki*, which we call "Greek salad" and they call "village salad." An old woman, a wizened villager dressed in black, sat by herself across the room. I wondered whether she was the mother or mother-in-law of the proprietors. She ordered her food with commanding aplomb and a high voice that betrayed her advanced years. If she wasn't family, what was a village woman, old and alone, doing in a restaurant? I wished I could speak Greek and join her and find out.

I took out the Durrell and lost myself in the undoubtedly exaggerated antics of his teachers, the servants, the peasants, written in his engaging hyperbole until I heard someone laughing out loud. It was me! Just then, the waiter asked in hesitating English what I was reading. "Durrell," I said. He asked to see the cover, and said, *"Nei nei, Doo-rel, Doo-rel.* TV, TV too," making a rectangular screen with hand gestures. He took the book from me, ran three paces back to the counter, and shouted, *"Pappas, pappas, Doo-rell, Doo-rell."* The father came round the counter, wiping his hands on a tired old towel, and hovered over my table with total camaraderie.

"This table, this table here where you sit, Durrell come every day, every day, sit there, drink, drink, drink, write, write, write, every day, every day, drink-write, drink-write. Then they made film, film, TV, TV!" I understood. It was Lawrence who had sat here, the oldest brother, not the youngster Gerald, whose writing about the family's shenanigans were making the entire restaurant ring with reflected pride. Here the great Durrell had sat, here he had written, inspired by the bottle and a fecund imagination and immaculate style. Here I sat laughing, distracted by his brother's writing.

The old lady in black came over, tiny, bent, wizened, and demanded an explanation from the owner. Gently he explained, as he wiped his hands on the apron. He brought over a bottle of *raki* and poured drinks for her, me, his son the waiter, and himself. We drank a toast to Durrell, and another to me for bringing back memories from early adolescence. Durrell. The lady smiled and greeted me in polite language, *Yassas* flowing in all directions. She scuttled back across the floor and took her seat at the table against the wall, her face ringed in oniony concentric lines, her eyes shining with brightness, and her toothless grin flashing at me for bringing a moment of excitement to her lonely life and her lonely table.

I shrugged my head toward her and said to the owner, "Your mother?"

He laughed. "*Ohi, ohi*, no no, she is from a small village. She has had many husbands, and they had much land. When she became old, *Kyria Dhelfina* took her money and rented a room in town. She is alone and so she eats here every day. Every day." He winked at me. "Many husbands." What lay under that somber black garb, you never know, his eyes told me. "*Yassas*," another *raki*. I paid for my meal, shook hands all round, and walked somewhat unsteadily along the main *corso* to the Cavalieri. Finally I was ready to see what Ariadne had put in my pocket.

More Tom Waits. This time it was "The Fish and the Bird":

> *They bought a round for the sailor*
> *And they heard his tale*
> *Of a world that was so far away*
> *And a song that we'd never heard*
> *A song of a little bird*
> *That fell in love with a whale.*
> *He said: you cannot live in the ocean*
> *And she said to him:*
> *You never can live in the sky*
> *But the ocean is filled with tears*
> *And the sea turns into a mirror*
> *And there's a whale in the moon when it's clear*
> *And a bird on the tide....*

Sitting there on the porch, back at my room, I was consumed by a wave of melancholy and aloneness. I nodded off and dreamt of Ariadne, in her black modern dress. Suddenly her features became shrunken and wizened, and the dress turned into the black mourning garb and a black kerchief of old village women was on her head. Then her face became that of Manny, poised over me, a knife in his hand.

There was a knock on the door. I pulled on a pair of pants over my pajamas. It was the old-looking stooped man with the lined face, always with cigarette ash on his jacket, who was the night manager, accountant, receptionist, porter, and whatever else. I lifted my eyebrows, and—without a word—he signaled for me to go back into my room. He followed and closed the door quietly behind him. I motioned for him to sit. I stood, defensive and watchful.

He pulled a single sheet of A4 paper out of his jacket pocket. It was an official-looking document, written in Greek, with a picture of me without my beard and change in hair color, and three other variants of my face—one with clean-shaven head, one with a small beard, and one with a full-blown *hasid's*, or artist's, flowing beard. All the pictures were in black and white. I saw my name and the name I'd used in Heraklion written in Latin letters.

CHAPTER 6

For the first time I looked carefully at him. Sad, dark face, slightly hooked nose, stubble under the chin and jaw-line, quick mournful eyes, creases of worry, and smoker's hatch lines across his rather noble features.

"Mr. Dickson, if that is your name, I did not come to make trouble for you."

"Why should you make trouble for me?"

He looked at me coldly for a moment, his mouth set into harsh lines. "Just listen to me for a few minutes and all will be clear."

I nodded, and sat down as well.

"This paper is signed by a very high-ranking policeman. It is a circular that has been faxed to every hotel and guesthouse in Greece via the local police. Anyone seeing you is requested to contact Brigadier-General Limnos.

"I hate the bastard. I knew him once very well. He is cruel and very corrupt, and terribly smart. Anything he touches stinks. So I came to warn you. Get out of Greece immediately. This paper came during my shift. No one will see it. You can take it and destroy it. But the port police probably have it as well. And the police have ambitious, bright young men.

"I will help you—I will tell you what to do, how you can get away, on the ferry to Bari."

I sat motionless. When in doubt, say nothing.

He read my reaction. "Alright," he said. He heaved a deep sigh. My mother would have said *a yiddisher krekhtz*, a Jewish sigh.

"When I was very young, an uncle who had fought in the nationalist underground against the Germans helped me get a job. There was great unemployment, and he knew people who had been his leaders, right-wing fighters who became important in the army and police and government. One of them got me a place with the police. After training, I was recruited into a special unit. It was the time of the Government of the Colonels. It was a harsh dictatorship. My unit was commanded by Lieutenant Limnos. The same man. Thirty years ago.

"We picked up what they called 'dissidents.' We put them into secret places and did bad things to them—very bad—to make them confess, and then we shot them. Limnos worked with a few higher-ups. They would then buy up their homes and businesses for a little nothing. He got rich, he got promoted....

"What did I get? I got a nervous breakdown, and a health discharge from the police." He sat silently for a moment, re-tasting his anger.

"We are cousins to the Arbitraki family of Corfu; my grandmother came from here. My cousin got me got the job in this hotel. For twenty-five years I have been the night manager, bookkeeper, night porter, night everything. Every day, every night, I thank God I am far from Limnos, and far from the special unit. I live in peace with myself. No wife, no children. I live. And when I do not sleep, I walk to the little port, and I cast a line into the water, and look at the Venetian fortress and the mountains....

"I am clean of the bad."

I sat still, thinking, saying nothing.

Finally, he broke the silence. "I will get you out of here. I will not let Limnos find you. This evening there is a ferry. I am a lay cantor in the Church. The priest is my friend. I will borrow an old cassock and *kalimafki* from him."

I did not know the word.

"It is the round hat with the brim on top that our priests wear. On the ship, there is a first officer whose sister owns the house in which I live. I will tell him you are on a mission to the Greek-speaking villages in the southern tip of Italy."

"I didn't know there were such villages.... "

He cut me off brusquely. "But there are. Greater Hellas. Once there was a Greek-speaking empire with settlements and cities in all our neighboring countries. Some speak a Greek dialect until today."

"I don't speak Greek."

"Yes. I have a solution. You will wear a scarf around your throat, and I will tell him you are getting over laryngitis. I will give him some money to have hot tea and some food brought to you. Tomorrow you will be in Italy. In the south there are *Mafiosi*. You will be able to get a new passport."

"What passport can I use to get into Italy? If Limnos is covering Greece, they may have the same arrangement in Italy."

"I will give you my EU Greek passport. While I am gone you will need to trim your beard and shave. The *kalimafki* will cover your hair. I will have the barber come to your room. Do not speak to him; you have laryngitis."

I took out two hundred euro. He looked offended. "Give some to the priest or the Church for his kindness and for his clothing. The rest is for the barber, the fare for the cabin, and any other expenses. When you come back, please bring my bill for the hotel so I can pay it when I leave."

He nodded. "That is good. An hour before embarkation, I will come for you with a car, and drive you to the boat. It is not far. In the car you can put on the robe and hat."

"You have thought of everything."

In his Greek matter-of-fact way, he nodded. "Yes. Yes. Finally I get back at that bastard."

"I am grateful to you."

"Okay, okay." We shook hands, clasped hands really, and he left. He was shorter than I. Perhaps the cassock would cover any differences. I had nothing to lose.

I remembered once when Levi Eshkol, then Minister of Finance, was negotiating with the Canadians to buy jet aircraft. I was in his suite in the King Edward Hotel in Toronto. Over the phone, in his *basso profundo* voice, he said to the ambassador in Ottawa, "Tell them they are twenty-four wings of peace." At the time, I marveled at the felicity of the phrase, just as I wince at its Slavic *schmaltz* today. How innocent were those days. And then, to my staggered mind, he took off his shoes, stretched out on the chesterfield, and said, "Now, a nap...."

And I thought: Imagine! A dozen modern jets are in the balance. The Czechs—really the Russians—are selling MiGs to the Egyptians, wholesale Russian MiGs. And he can sleep?

He could sleep.

I took off my trousers and shirt, drew the curtains, and got back under the covers. Bless your memory, Eshkol. I slept.

Everything went according to plan. In truth, I was shaking as we boarded the tall, clumsy ferryboat. Only when we entered the tiny private cabin, tired from walking with a stoop—my beard, a loyal companion now trimmed—with my face muffled, did I allow my breath to escape. My ally from the hotel had trotted along my side, carrying my small case in subservient respect to a priest on an important mission.

I sank down on the only chair in the cabin, removed the *kalimafki*, and waited until my pulse quieted. Then I rose and pulled him into a strong embrace. Only then, so intent had I been, did I realize what I had forgotten.

"What is your name?"

"Michaelis. Michael in English."

I smiled. "He did double duty today, as your guardian angel and mine."

"Travel safely. Do not contact me. It is not safe. I have left you a post-card addressed to me, in Greek. Mail it to me when you are in Bari. After that, you will find your way. And, oh, yes," he stammered somewhat. "I wish to remind you that as long as you wear the cassock, people look upon you as a priest."

I nodded. We clasped hand earnestly, and he moved now erect and, I thought, prouder. He closed the cabin door.

I looked down at my old worn cassock, looked at myself in the mirror over the tiny dressing table, and started to laugh. I was reminded of the funny tragic tale Yehuda Bauer told in his book *Flight and Rescue: Brichah*. A group of World War Two survivors were being smuggled across a European border on fake Greek passports. One of them wrote a doggerel poem, which ended with a line like, *Un yetst bin ikh a Grikh*: "And now I'm a Greek!"

I was a Greek, and not just a Greek, but a Greek Orthodox priest. My grandfather—had he come back to life and seen me garbed in the robes of what he would recognize as *Pravaslav* (Russian Orthodox)— would have given one look and died again of shock. Maybe of shame. But if he knew the reasons, he'd say, in our Polish Yiddish accent, "*Avroom, git getiyen.*" Well done!

I arrived safe and sound. I disembarked in "uniform," and whispered my replies to the immigration officer in Italian, pointing to my muffled throat. Duly saluted, as a man of cloth deserves even though not of quite the right religion, I was in Italy. The question then was how to get out of my priest's garb while avoiding the loyal Greek-speakers from the villages of Apulia/Puglia. And how was I going to get a new passport?

The change of dress proved to be easy. I bought a backpack, found the busiest hotel in town, walked into the men's room, put the costume into the backpack, and walked out a different man. I went down Via Roma, on a whim walking toward Via Dante Alleghieri, and bought a knock-off Borsolino—nothing too fancy—to cover my head, and a large pair of sunglasses.

I was tired, drained, but managed to find a small hotel near the railway station. Just after midnight, when surveillance would be less rigorous, I took the train out of Bari Centrale. I dozed off and on, wolfed down sandwiches, drank coffee, and guzzled liters of bottled water before staggering off the train in Reggio di Calabria. By then it was close to noon. Forcing myself onward, I walked to the port and caught the ferry to Messina. So far, no passport was needed. In a neat three-star hotel near the straits, I slept until the next morning.

At this point, I decided that I would have a better chance of finding a passport in a bigger city. Using a Greek passport might be a trap, if I ever met a fellow Greek. *Un yetst bin ikh a Grikh!* I took the train to Palermo—a schlep, but I'd been schlepping for a few days now.

Palermo has a bad reputation; friends of mine were pick-pocketed there, twice on the same trip. I made sure Michaelis's Greek ID and my money were hidden in a stomach-hugging money-belt. I avoided the scruffy area near the railway station, and ended up in the once-grand Primo Albergo, a hotel now fallen on poorer times, with scuffed furniture and a gigantic bathroom. I was beginning to see the end of the money I had taken with me from Jerusalem, and would have to arrange for Vi to get some untraceable funds via relatives or friends.

But for the moment, dressed in fresh and jaunty Italian clothes, I began to relax. I walked, saw the rich Greco-Roman museum collections and the ancient theater, and had a quiet meal in a neighborhood restaurant. Lulled by my anonymity, by the sightseeing, the wine, and the grappa, I almost forgot why I was there. Except that the loneliness kept hitting me in the face. In the hotel bar, a magnificent turn-of-the-century area full of glass and dark wood that gleamed in a hall off the lobby, I drank another grappa and walked the three flights to my room.

That evening, another uninvited visitor. It was beginning to be habitual. The knock was peremptory.

"Open, please!"

I peered through the eyehole and saw a distorted figure in light brown uniform, a Sam Browne belt, a pistol in a shining leather case, and badges of rank on the shoulders.

I opened the door.

"Thank you. I am Captain Virgilio Armerino, *Guardia di Finanza.*"

"You are the economic police, then. What can I do for you? Please sit down." We sat facing one another.

"I always wanted to know how one says *Guardia di Finanza* in Greek." He stared at me and I lowered my eyes.

"Alright, Signore who calls himself by a Greek name, and has a Greek document, clearly you do not know."

I just looked at him, dumb. Stupefied. What now?

"*Guarda, Signore*—look, you should know that this city is a major contact point for various international criminals. Our informants tipped us off: a Greek citizen who speaks only unaccented English. We have watched you. So far you have had no contact with anyone. That increases our suspicion... perhaps you are a patient and clever man."

I sighed. I was never patient, and being caught so easily is proof that I'm also not clever. Still, I remained silent.

"On the other hand, you have so far committed only one crime: illegal entry into Italy with a false document. I do not want to waste time on a fruitless surveillance.

"I wish to make a suggestion to you. If you have something to confess, and if you are part of a conspiracy, cooperate with us, and we will help you. We can overlook the entry business."

I went to the mini-bar, took out water, soda, and wine. "Captain, let me think. Meanwhile, please help yourself."

He is disarmingly polite. He is street-smarter than I, and he will see through any cock-and-bull story I invent. If I were even able to invent one under such pressure. I felt my pulse quicken and reached for a glass of water.

"Captain, do you have fifteen minutes to hear a fantastic story—fantastic but absolutely true?"

"I've heard many fantastic stories. How do I know it's true?"

"When you hear it, you will understand that I am putting my life in the hands of an unknown police officer in a country not always noted for the probity of its public servants, on an island that has... a certain reputation."

"One to you, so-called Mr. Michaelis. *Vederamo*."

I was sweating slightly, but was able to tell him my story in just the allotted time. Israel. Threats. Flight. A bent Mossad agent, or ex-

Mossad more precisely. My travels. The Greek police circular. The only lie I told was that I had "found" Michaelis's passport. I could see an almost-shrug when I passed this obvious piece of prevarication.

"If you check this story with the Israeli police—they know nothing about it," I concluded. "But there are two ways I can prove that part of my story is true, so you can believe the rest."

"*Dica me.*"

"If you look for my real name on the Internet, you will find references to me in the Israeli press, and maybe even articles and books I have written. Then, once I have given you my name, I am entirely defenseless." I took a piece of paper and my hand shook. Could I trust this man? Did I have a choice?

"What is the second?"

"I have found a four-hundred-year-old manuscript in Crete, written in Hebrew by an Italian rabbi. I have it with me. I can show it to you, and I can show you the translation in my computer, which at least shows that I know Hebrew."

"It could also show that you are a smuggler of old manuscripts."

"It could. But the manuscript and what you will find on Internet should convince you that I am exactly what I say."

"I am very disappointed, my Israeli friend."

I just looked at him, lack of comprehension mingled with the question not asked.

"If you are telling the truth, Israel is becoming corrupt. How could you do it so soon? We have had over two thousand years of experience. Your state is barely a half-century old."

"Well, Captain, in human history, beginning with the story of Adam and Eve, whether you believe it literally or as an allegory, corruption began as soon as there were three characters on earth."

For the first time, the trim police officer smiled.

"Show me the manuscript, *Signore*, and the computer."

It took him a minute to glance at the Hebrew, while I turned on the laptop. Another few minutes to scroll down the translation. "The translation is much longer than the original."

"Yes. Hebrew is a very concise and compact language, with conjugations and declensions combined into the same word."

"I see. Like in Latin. And in Italian, we never use one word if three will do. Okay, Mr. Avraham, I buy half of your story. Maybe. And maybe you deal in shady provenance manuscripts. I will check the other half tomorrow morning on the Internet. Please give me your Greek document now, and do not leave the hotel until I call you tomorrow morning. I have my ways of knowing if you do."

The captain phoned the following morning. "You are free to go out, but stay close to the hotel. Do normal tourist things. Meet me at 9:30 p.m. Between Piazza Marina and Piazza San Francesco, there is a small restaurant, you'll see the sign, Pizzeria Ristorante Il Fornito. Go through the restaurant to a back room. I will be there with another person. We'll be dressed in normal clothes."

What could I say? To hell with all this mummery? Bugger off? Hardly. I repeated the name of the meeting place. That afternoon I visited the Teatro Massimo, Cattedrale, Palazzo dei Normanni, and called it quits. Too bad I wouldn't be able to take in an opera at the Teatro, a grand old building where the greats had been appearing for more than a century. I checked out location of the Il Fornito, had a quick bite at a wine bar around the corner, and took a nap.

At 9:29 p.m. I walked into Il Fornito, past the knowing eyes of the barman, through the aisle separating the tables in the long narrow room, and crossed a dark corridor flanked by the *Uomini* and *Dame*, and through a heavy door that stood welcomingly ajar. The captain and an older man were sitting at a table set with a tablecloth, napkins, a tureen steaming with a rich minestrone, and the usual bread, *grissini*, olive oil, vinegar, and a bottle of Mt. Aetna dark red wine. The condemned man, et cetera, et cetera.

The point is, after very little politesse, while they consumed quantities of food I couldn't stomach, they offered me a deal. The captain did all the talking. The older man said nothing. He had theatrical gray hair and the faint scent of cologne that was the mark of the higher-up. But he watched very carefully. I was being given an offer that I truly could not refuse. It might be a trap. It might be a way out. "Let my soul perish with the Philistines!" I'd had enough. I wasn't sure that I could lose any more by going along. But if it did turn out to be a trap, Vi might never know. I was forbidden to use a phone or the Internet, or to write letters. I was sure I'd be under surveillance. I probably had been all day.

The bottom line—how much nicer it sounds in Yiddish, *untershte shureh*, half Germanic, half Hebrew—is that they wanted me to take a small suitcase from Cefalu to Lipari island. The upside was that the captain promised to get me a clean passport, any nationality I wanted, any name I chose, on completion of the operation, which should take only two days.

But I wasn't really sure what the downside was. Was I a drug courier? Was I part of a sting operation? Was I being set up to improve someone's arrest record? Was I dealing with the police or a combination of the police and the Mafia, or was I dealing with the good old Cosa Nostra, plain and simple? Was the gray-haired higher-up a *colonnello* or a *consigliere*? Would I be killed en route? Or at the end?

They pointed to a door at the back end of the room. Outside, I found two dark cars. I had been told to get into the second. Two heavies were sitting in the first car and a third man loitered nearby, wearing a loose car coat large enough to cover a machine-pistol.

I settled down into the second black Alfa Romeo. The driver pulled away quickly. When we had looped around enough streets, we made a quick run up back roads to Monreale, and back down to the main coastal highway. We moved forward smoothly and then the driver veered onto the road, still marked A19, toward Enna. Once again, I tried to remember our route. It's not as though I had anything better to do. I saw the lights of Enna winking high up on a hill and hoped that's where we were heading. But before we got there, the driver turned onto a smaller road and drew up in front of a small hotel on the outskirts of Piazza Armerina.

The driver said, "The Captain's family owns this hotel. It is safe here. We have brought your case from the hotel in Palermo, and settled your bill there. Tomorrow a commercial tourist company private car will take you to Villa Romana. You will just act like an ordinary tourist, and will join a busload of German tourists on a visit to the Roman villa there. Continue with them to the Hotel Mediterraneo in Cefalu. We have bought you a used camera, new walking shoes that we have scuffed, a fresh change of clothing, and your Greek travel document. You also have two guidebooks in English and a map. You will sleep tomorrow night in Cefalu, and in the morning, a used suitcase with wheels, small and easy to carry, will be delivered to your room. In the outside flap there will be further instructions.

"If all goes well, you will be finished the day after that, and someone will come to meet you. In the meantime, you will be watched constantly. And make sure always, always to wear the belt we have left you in your case, and the shoes we have bought you. Don't worry. They are your size. Both will enable us to monitor your movements. There are two tracking devices, in case one fails."

"Why German?"

"That's what we have here now. I hope you understand their language." He didn't wait for an answer. "If anyone talks to you, reply in English. If you don't understand the language, use the guidebook and ask the tour leader some questions, so you will seem *bona fide*."

He saw me to an adequate room, clean and warm, but decorated in horrible taste. I leafed through the guidebook for a little while and then went to bed. It was late.

The condemned man enjoyed Villa Romana. How could anyone not? Hundreds of square meters of mosaic: vibrant hunting scenes and mythological gods, the colored stones almost as bright as they were seventeen hundred years ago, when a very rich patrician built the large villa. Maybe he too was called Armerinus....

Of course, like every other dumbstruck tourist, I could not get over the absolute modernity of the women's dress in the exercise room. Bikinis! How backward the Victorians were!

After the villa, the bus drove on for close to two hours and finally rolled into Cefalu, and stopped in the main square, with its magnificent

Norman cathedral showing Byzantine and Arab influences. Towering behind it were the jagged heights of a seemingly perpendicular mountain face, La Rocca.

I consoled myself with the thought that if I was going to end up in jail for this Sicilian venture, or get killed, at least it had been diverting so far. I found a small restaurant on the winding main street. Suddenly it all came together. Cefalu. No wonder I felt as though I had been there before. That's where *Cinema Paradiso* was filmed. I looked at the narrow lanes, the laundry hanging across the street in places, and the glint of the sea at the end. In the restaurant, everyone seemed local. Good food, good wine. I returned to the hotel, and, as promised, I found two bags; one was mine. I opened the front flap of the strange one. In it were train and ferry tickets, and one simple instruction:

YOU WILL BE ENDANGERING YOURSELF IF YOU TRY TO OPEN THIS BAG.

The following morning, after a night of tossing and turning, the train ride to Milazzo passed uneventfully. I had dreamt that I was carrying a bomb. It was designed to explode and kill many people in a place like a railway station. Maybe a port? Maybe it was the ugly little town of Milazzo, mostly just a port, with the Aeolian Islands standing smudged on a cloudy horizon. At dock there was a somewhat rusty and crusty battered Syrian-registered freighter. Now what, I thought, am I going to be the target of abduction?

Rather than waiting for the slower heavier ferry, I got onto the smaller hydrofoil. An hour later we slowly entered Lipari harbor, where the Venetian castle and the rise of hills cradled a jewel of a port, and a fine old town. I decided that I was a travelwriter *manqué*—visiting all these magnificent Greco-Roman towns, touring, eating, walking, driving, and getting paid for it all.

Instead, I had spent most of my life meeting the mighty and the self-important whose superb manipulative abilities, with few exceptions, disguised unredeemable mediocrity. Now I had become a forced traveler, looking over my shoulder, snatching moments of peace and tranquility and beauty, just as the sun sometimes bursts through leaden skies onto a scene of breathtaking if illusive peace. And that was exactly what happened as the hydrofoil slowly and carefully docked.

Carrying the two bags, I almost stopped in the middle of the short gangplank to look in delight at the Mediterranean light shading the waters black and a livid blue. The houses stood out on the hillside like beautifully set pieces in an early Impressionist landscape.

"Signore Michaelis?" a voice said. I nodded. "We have your room ready." A rough-and-tough type, who only came up to my shoulder and looked like a retired sailor, took my bags and set off up the hill. Twenty paces along was a small bed and breakfast. Inside, he gave me a key and kept walking out into a small yard, to a separate neat studio room with a small well-equipped kitchen. "Please rest. Your friends will be here in one hour. There is fruit and cheese on the table, and crackers. Soft drinks and beer in the fridge. Have a pleasant stay."

My friends? I locked the door of the quiet shaded room, dropped onto the hard bed, and slept. Tension is more tiring than hard work.

A knock on the door. Two men dressed in civilian clothes came in.

"Questa?" I walked to the bags, took mine and pointed to the other. "Quella. Non aprire." This one. Don't open it.

They graced me with a look of disdain and walked out, the second one carrying the case.

What now?

The first one came back. "Per Lei!" He handed me an envelope containing another brief note:

TOMORROW MORNING ON THE FIRST FERRY SOMEONE WILL BRING YOU WHAT WE PROMISED. BE HERE.

I shrugged and took a small pamphlet with a map of Lipari from the chest of drawers. I walked up a steep road to the citadel, found the Church, and stumbled across a small but fascinating museum. The volcanic dust had preserved miraculous finds, some of which were thousands of years old. Terra cotta theater masks and perfectly sculpted figurines that had long outlived the mortals whom they were to accompany to the underworld. The treacherous winds and rough seas had sunk shiploads of amphorae throughout the millennial history of the region.

I strolled along the ramparts of the protective walls surrounding the castle/fortress. The blue waters and soft twilit sky deepened as night fell. In the distance I could make out Volcano Island, thin streaks of steam rising from fissures in its rounded hilltop.

Vi and I must come back here. If Cefalu was *Cinema Paradiso*, this was *Paradiso*.

I made a wide circle back to the other side of the town, and sauntered down the main street.

No one followed me back to the bed and breakfast. At least no one that I could see.

I bought a small bottle of grappa in a convenience store that was still open, and turned off the street to my room. I still couldn't see anyone behind me. For a change, no one was waiting for me either. Tomorrow is the reality test.

CHAPTER 7

I passed the test. I was safe—at least for the moment. They had kept their word, whoever "they" were. The passport had come as promised.

As the time for meeting Vi drew closer, I became as impatient as a new bridegroom. I often saw her face before me, and, when I closed my eyes on the ferryboat to Naples, floating images of Violetta lying uncovered, expectantly, on our freshly made bed, her arm bent at the elbow flung across her face.

I had another few days until she could join me. I decided to go to Mantua/Mantova! Checking in at the hotel near the historic center (*centro storico* has such a more exciting ring), my new "legal" Canadian passport merited only a cursory glance. I had chosen a French-Canadian pseudonym. There were echoes of high-school humor in my choice of name: Guy Avecq Longtemps.

The room was old-fashioned, large, warm, and with a large bathroom. I soaked in the hot tub, enjoying the expensive luxury after days of constant movement. Ferry, train, foot. At my age, I need time to recover, though fortunately when the adrenaline flows, the stamina makes me better than ever. The toll is paid later.

At 10 a.m., a leisurely Italian breakfast, and quiet. Blessed quiet. I felt my vigor flowing back, but decided to prolong the process. I asked the receptionist to book me for another night.

I walked out onto the street, and saw the street sign: *Via Scuola Grande*. The word *scuola* literally means a school or a schoolhouse, and among the Italian Jews the term was used for *Bet HaMidrash*, House of

Learning, since in all synagogues, classes for the adults and for children would be held in the building. The name for *scuola* among Eastern European Jews was *shul*.

This is where the Great Synagogue stood. I could recall the words of Avraham de' Pomi almost by heart:

> *The two men… led me quickly through the long street lined mainly with Jewish homes, past the Chief Rabbi's four-story home with its beautiful wrought-iron balconies. The streets were quiet on this damp night, though as we came closer to the Ducal Palace, the noises of revelers and gamblers came out of the tawdry taverns. In minutes we had passed the Rotonda da San Lorenzo, and the Tower of Santa Andrea, and made our way through the pungent Piazzetta dell' Olio. The church buildings lining the Via della Dottrina Cristiana reminded me of the dangers I sensed lay ahead. A few streetwalkers forlornly sought custom in the damp, shuddering under the eaves of the Palazzi along the remaining short route.*

> *The escorts exchanged some murmured words with the Duke's armed bodyguard, and we entered the precincts of the labyrinthine Palazzo Ducale, and continued on to a small section of the long house on the edge of the sumptuous central part of the main palace. The fog and moisture steaming off the road and the walls of heated buildings, mingled with the smoke emitting from the dozens of fires—two chimneys to a room— and made my head spin and my vision unclear. We entered the simple house, simple indeed by those sumptuous standards, yet furnished in good taste. A fire had been laid and lit, and in front of the flickering red-and-yellow flames stood G.*

> *Madama Gloria, reputed mistress of the good Duke Vincenzo, daughter of my friend and kinsman, Jacopo da Pisa. Gloria was justly named; indeed she was full of glory, beautiful of limb, and fair of face.*

Using the map I took from the hotel desk, I traced de' Pomi's route. Step by step, step by step. I cannot say what I felt was déjà vu; it was more than that. I felt I was hovering above the *centro historico* on Leonardo-da-Vinci-like wings, and below I could see two Avrahams become one, and remain two, walking—one with trepidation, hand on hidden sword—one with mingled, tingling anticipation and a sense of return, clutching the map and a pen. Suddenly, an ancient phrase crossed our minds: The book and the sword intertwined descended from Heaven.

In this chronicle, I will not go beyond this. What more can I add? Perhaps one day I shall write the tale of Mantuan Jewry, for what could be more moving than to speak to members of the Norsa family, whose ancestors' medieval bankers are held to shame in the great painting on the wall of the Church of San Andrea, dating back hundreds of years? That very evening I had met three members of the family, attending visitors to the Norsa synagogue, where I stood trembling. It is no stretch of my storytelling to add that this was on Holocaust Day, marking the anniversary of the liberation of Auschwitz in 1945, which is observed throughout the European Union; only by chance had the synagogue been open to the non-Jewish schoolchildren and adults who came to see—I suppose—the rootedness and uprooting of their fellow citizens.

The Norsas directed me to the Colornis, who walked me through the erstwhile ghetto, most of which had been plowed under and built over at the end of the nineteenth century to make it possible to build on its prime real estate near the *centro*.

I returned to my hotel on *Via Scuola Grande*, where surely de' Pomi had once prayed. Circles are closing.

The following day I walked silently, slowly through where the ghetto had been. Though officially Jews had only been forced to live in the ghetto twelve years after the date on Avraham de' Pomi's manuscript, there is no doubt that even before they chose to huddle together close to their synagogues and scholars, kasher butchers and bakers. Four hundred years ago there had been two thousand Jews in

Mantua. Today, a marriageable young woman, member of one of the old families told me, "There are so few Jews here, that if I wanted to marry a local *Ebreo*, it would have to be my brother!"

All evening, on the train to Venice, I relived these scenes, marveling at the majesty of the destiny of my people, its pain and its beauty. Unfortunately, there was no one with me I could tell yet.... But soon I will relate it all to Violetta.

The next morning, I strolled briefly through parts of Venice, recalling my frequent visits, renewing memories. I only had about a thousand dollars left, but wanted more entry stamps on my too-new passport. A travel agent found me a last minute routing to Zurich. I called Vi in our prearranged safe way; she was already in London, awaiting word. Another two or three days. Meanwhile, the passport would show authentic Italian entry and departure stamps, and Swiss as well.

The next morning, I headed for the airport, taking in last looks at the Venetian skyline as it dropped behind our *vapporetto*, one of the bus-boats that ply the canals. I had not seen the morning papers. As I walked towards the newsstand, I recognized the face blazoned across the front page of *Corriere della Sera*.

It was the older man I had met in the restaurant in Palermo with Captain Armerino. His face peered out of the stack of newspapers, filling half of the upper part of the latest edition. Distinguished. Gray-haired. Dead.

MAGISTRATO INVESTIGATORE ASSASSINATO IN MESSINA. COSA NOSTRA? NUOVO CASO FALCONE-BORSOLLINO

So, he had been an investigating magistrate, like the other two who had been killed by the Mafia: Falcone and Borsollino. Today, their names are attached to the Palermo Airport. What airport would they name after this newly assassinated keeper of the law?

He *had* been legitimate. In that case, I assumed that the passport he had given me was also legitimate. Maybe the passport had been part of a trade between the Canadian RCMP attaché and the Italian anti-racketeering investigators. Toronto could very well be a link in the Sicilian chain....

I spread the paper over the bar, waiting for my flight to be called, and drank a brandy, then espresso. Then another brandy. I walked over to the washroom and rinsed my head in cold water, forcing my hands to be still.

It only took another few seconds to realize that at least two official bodies could easily keep tabs on me, Canadian and Italian. Is any agency leak-proof? And probably any good hacker could probably find me as well.

From Zurich I took the night train to Milan, southward, crossing the Alps. I got in and out of Switzerland without any trouble. Thank you, Canada!

The name of the dead magistrate was Gianni Sciacca. I remembered that Sciacca was also the name of a town I had seen on a map, near the town of Corleone, of *The Godfather* fame. Another Sicilian tragedy.

I was not prepared to be any kind of tragedy. Life is everything, especially, as we say in Yiddish, "if they let you live." My next moves would have to be more careful than ever and I couldn't even trust these travel documents. Finally, though the journey was almost over. Enough. Together Vi and I will have decide what to do. I've done enough running.

As the EuroNight sleeper climbed through the mountain passes, I slept in my berth, exhausted from the inner turmoil. In Milan, I took the first train to Verona, sleeping in my seat. Weary, blurry-eyed, I found the station café and ate a full breakfast, and swallowed a strong cappuccino. Clearer-headed, I found the connection to Bolzano.

That afternoon, in the pretty little town of Bolzano, I succeeded in part one of my plan. There was a fair for the shoe trade in the modern trade center *Fiera Bolzano*. I walked through the back streets of the straggling little town, which, at a guess, had a population of about 100,000. Between one of the rivers and a concrete overpass I found some garages, some scruffy and some posh and shining. I sought out the scruffiest. Naturally, I opened with *Buongiorno* and received a stolid *Grüss Gott!* in return. Point made. I continued in my own personally invented Germanized Yiddish dialect, not too different from his swallowed and mangled Tyrolean.

I still had a few hundred dollars. I also had a gold ring and a watch. I explained to him that I needed to borrow a good used car for not more than three or four days. I'd pay him a hundred a day, in advance, and leave my ring and watch as guarantee that I'd bring it back. He didn't like it too much, and finally I had to promise him another fifty a day. I drove off in a well-used Fiat Panda, green, dusty, anonymous, and something of a curmudgeon when gearing down. I chose to head back north along the riverbank on the old slow road next to the speeding highway, and branched off at Bressanone, still stubbornly co-billed with Brixen, the German name.

I didn't have a driver's license, so I drove slowly and carefully, like a frightened old man on a Sunday. Bressanone was a beautiful thousand-year-old medieval center, with handsome buildings— residential and hotels—all around it. I checked out the Tourist Office billboard, liked the name Belvedere-Waldheim, and drove over to it. It had some vacancies. It turned out to be a pretty chalet-type pension overlooking a forest and only a few minutes from Bressanone, comfortable with simple wooden furniture and a pizzeria-ristorante on the entrance level.

I let Vi know where to meet me; she hoped to arrive in about two days, making her way as deviously as I. I had just enough money to last till she came. I passed the time catching up, writing all the things I had done recently, rereading and adding to what went before it. It was hard to telescope everything. How much had I learned as I fled? Something about myself, about different types of love, of trust and betrayal, of the innate goodness of man and the innate evil. Since I do not know what tomorrow may bring, I will write this down as a brief moral last will and testament....

When I had once spoken of the evil in us to one of my daughters, she had remonstrated, "But Abba, you taught us to believe man is good." I did, and try to live that way most of the time, but now I know more and more how evil we can be. Perhaps I had erred in not explaining that. But certainly they have learned that on their own. Either way, here's what I will tell them: the essence of my experience.

The greatest evil we can do will always be in the name of the Great Truth, the overarching theory, the Will of God, of the Leader, of the State, of the Sacred Book. It is all a form of idolatry, as is excessive egocentrism, sexual exploitation, the mad pursuit of wealth, and other crimes against our humanness. I am now a better Jew, because I see how I have practiced this idolatry in my own life, how I have served others who shared the sin. I do repent.

Repentance. What they call a return to God is a return to the humanness Creation implanted in us. Creation is a manifestation of divinity, even though a personal God who saves, rewards, and punishes, seems to be a failed hope of every child ultimately abandoned by his parents.

Life is the holy of holies.

The Sabbath is the mother of all human equality and of respect for the Other, and even for dumb animals.

Repentance, in its internalized deepest and most hidden way, is the true mercy we are granted. Love is the gift that illuminates our brief path through a world strewn with choices, dilemmas, the pull of evil, the imperative of good.

I trust that those I love will know, each in her or his own way, to find this path.

The time underground made all of this clearer, and I awaited my true love to tell her all this, face to face....

Chapter Eight

This is Vi writing. I arrived yesterday, read everything Avraham left for me, and waited all day today as well for him to show up. Now the hotel-keeper has told me that the police are en route. They had been checking on missing guests in the area, and he reported that Avraham had not returned. I have spent the day reading breathlessly and worrying endlessly.

As the sun set, I got into the back of a small Italian car with a blue rotating light on it. I don't think they were caribinieri; I can never get it all straight anyway. Polizia, polizia stradale, caribinieri... At this moment I couldn't care less. A very kind man, whose name I didn't get then (it was Ucelli, I discovered later; he was some kind of officer) and his driver, Bruno, had come for me. In very clear English, Mr. Ucelli told me that they had found a bearded man who might fit Avraham's description near the highest funicular station connecting to Santa Andrea. He had no identification on him, but he was mumbling in a foreign language—not Italian or German or French or English. They had called all the hotels—which took most of the afternoon—before they had reached mine.

"He has fallen down the mountain, or been in a fight. His body is very bruised, but he dragged himself close to the funicular station. He was dehydrated and suffering from exposure. The first passengers saw him as they reached the top. He was unconscious."

"Will he live?"

"Perhaps. Probably, even, the doctors think. We rushed him right to the Ospedale in Bolzano. The ambulance men—

you say medics???—gave him an infusion and kept him stable. We have much experience with mountaineering accidents." He patted my hand.

It was not a long drive. They didn't use the siren, but the flashing blue lights cleared the lane. The trip took about thirty minutes. It seemed endless. I was clenching my jaws and my face hurt. In a way I was outside my own body, and my head was so full of clashing thoughts and ideas. I felt nothing. My mouth was dry, my throat constricted. Exposure, dehydration. Perhaps. Perhaps. Perhaps Avraham, perhaps he will live. Perhaps.

The Ospedale had the same smell as all I've ever visited, but the nurses, the doctors, the cleaning staff, all seemed to be uniformed. It was very formal, European, old-fashioned. I was led into a private room, not very well lit, and from the door I saw a man with tubes connected to him. I walked over to the bed. Over it there was a crucifix on the wall. I leaned forward.

"This is not my husband. You have someone else here."

The man began muttering. The words were unclear, but I thought I recognized the phrasing, the cadences, I guess you'd call them.

"Is he conscious? Can I speak to him?"

A young doctor in a white coat, with a stethoscope around his neck, nodded. He had a thick accent. "Yes, but only for a few minutes. Please. He is still weak."

I leaned over the man once more. He had a gray beard, bandages around his head, and black-and-blue contusions on his face. "Atta medaber 'Ivrit?"

"Ken. Ken."

This was no coincidence: he spoke Hebrew. Why would one Hebrew-speaker be missing, and why had this one turned up battered?

"Do you know Avraham Ben-Hayim?"

"Yes."

"Where is he?"

"On the mountain."

"Alive?"

"More than I am." With that, he dropped off. They ushered me out, the officer barely restraining his curiosity.

I asked for a glass of water, and sat down heavily, drained. The doctor must have seen how I felt, and quickly pushed my head down between my knees. The blood flowed back into my head, and I managed not to faint. He took my pulse, and brought me more water. When I felt better, he asked gently, *"Who is he, do you know?"* The police officer took out his notepad.

"I have never seen him before. He is an Israeli. His Hebrew sounds sabra—native-born. I asked if he knew my husband. He said that my husband is on the mountain. He is on the mountain! He is alive. We must find him immediately. Maybe he also is suffering from exposure, dehydration. We must look for him."

Ucelli said something into a portable phone. *"We will organize a search team right away. These are Alpine specialist rescue teams. We can begin where we found the other man. Will you help us talk to him?"*

I didn't answer right away. Then I nodded slowly. *"I want to go with the team."*

"We shall see. It will take a few hours to have everything together, and we may need to wait until first light, unless I can get a helicopter."

"If the police don't have one available, hire one." My head was swimming.

Ucelli called Bruno over and spoke to him in Italian. *"He will take you back to the hotel. We need to go via Bressanone anyway. Stay in the hotel until we come for you. Rest, sleep."* He turned to the doctor who nodded and wrote out a prescription. On your way out, get this at the hospital pharmacy. It will relax you."

Again, I said nothing. I had no intention of taking sedatives or tranquillizers. Maybe they meant well. Maybe they just wanted a "hysterical woman" out of their way. I clenched my jaw. Tragedy is always around the corner at home. We are a tough breed. Women are, too. Israelis have grown calluses. We're a tough, callused breed.

When I got back to the hotel, I took a hot bath, my head swirling. I lay on the bed alternately dozing and starting awake at the ugly thoughts that I kept trying to push away. I thought I heard a helicopter. I thought I was dreaming.

At first light, Captain Ucelli came to the hotel. The owner and his wife spoke to him in throaty dialect. They had risen early, started the coffee machine, and prepared us a quick breakfast. They filled thermoses for the search team that had been out since about 3 a.m.

We drove off quickly, speeding up the mountainside. The winding road took my breath away, and the driver put on the siren because the road was so twisting and narrow. We sped through Santa Andrea as the sky began to glow and the light reflected onto the jagged Dolomites from behind us. Valcroce, towards Plose. High up. Beautiful. I couldn't appreciate it then, though.

A burst of rapid-fire Italian came through the police transceiver. I was too confused to look for words that I might be able to pick out. I thought maybe I recognized the word elicottero.

Ucelli turned around to face me. "In a few minutes we will be at the top of Plose. They have found a man there. Alive. He took refuge in a cave. We have a helicopter coming to fly him to Bolzano Ospedale. By car it would take over an hour. I think it is your husband. Soon we shall know."

Tears came, finally. The car slid around the curves, siren blaring. I felt bruised from all the emotion, all the adrenalin. I saw the man lying on a stretcher, the kind that has the pop-up legs, so it can fold down into the ambulance. Some Alpine team climbers, young, sturdy, and not too tall, stood around. They had started an infusion and he was huddled in blankets. His eyes were open. His eyes.

I looked for a place to kiss that wasn't covered by his beard. He had always been clean-shaven. I kissed his lips, and he kissed me back. His eyes lit up, and I knew he would be alright.

"A lot to tell you. But too tired. Tired."

"I can wait." I turned to Ucelli. He was speaking in dialect to one of the men. "This is my husband. Thank you. Thank you."

He nodded, embarrassed at the gratitude, but mixed with pride. We heard the helicopter coming in. They loaded Avraham into it, and I got in with Ucelli. The paramedic checked the infusion line, and asked if Avraham had any bruises or pain. "No, no, no pain, just hurts where I fell." The man said they couldn't give Avraham any water until he had been checked for internal injuries. I wished that I could take this helicopter flight over the mountains some time when we were both healthy. The spectacular view was tempting, but I kept my eyes on Avraham, found his hand under the blankets and held it. It was cold.

Four days later, he was out of danger—out of danger! I was able to start writing down the long story that Avraham told me. At first he could only do it for a short time every day. Then, as his strength returned, he would talk for hours. I made notes because he asked me to be precise in writing down what he said. He said that we would need it for the record one day.

CHAPTER 9

The morning before Vi was due to arrive, I had driven to the top of the Plose mountain. I had wanted to walk, and had bought boots and a walking stick in Santa Andrea on the way up. It was truly beautiful, sunny but chilly. Where the walking trails begin, there is a restaurant and café, with a few rooms above them. I decided to have a coffee and relax, relishing the peace and quiet and the thrusting primitive beauty.

A bearded man wearing a heavy jacket and a hat came out of the restaurant. I paid no attention to him. He pulled up a chair, sat down beside me, and spoke very quietly in Israeli-accented English. It was then that I recognized the voice and recognized the face.

"How did you find me?"

"You demand explanations from me? You remember when we met in the Prime Minister's Office decades ago? You had a lot of *chutzpah* then, too."

"Look, Manny, what the hell do you want from me? Have you come to kill me? Here!" In a pallid imitation of the brave Trotsky, I pulled my shirt open. A button popped off. "Here. Shoot me."

"Shut up, you stupid fool. Lower your voice. First, I'll talk to you. Then, we'll see...."

"Go to hell! You've made my life miserable for the last four months. I have no intention of taking any more shit from you."

"Get up, idiot! Walk in front of me. I wanted to talk to you here, but if you insist on behaving like a *shmock....*"

"At least I never betrayed my trust."

"Didn't you? Didn't you?" His dark eyes turned into burning pinpoints as his anger flared—I even thought I saw red in his eyeballs, so alive were all my senses.

We walked along a narrow path leading off to the right. At a curve on the path, he said, "Sit down," and pointed to an outcropping of rock over a steeply graded hillside covered with bushes and evergreens. He sat on a rock on the other side of the path, above me, so I was at a disadvantage in terms of both height and distance. I had to turn my head to look at him, and would never be able to gather enough force to get up from that position. By that time, I had calmed down enough to note that he was still a good tactician.

"Why have you been chasing me?"

"I will tell you."

"How did you find me?"

"I will tell you."

"Now!"

"You are in no position to dictate terms to me."

I nodded. He held the upper hand. Perhaps he always had and had been playing cat-and-mouse with me.

"I found you because the Italians alerted my former friends when you entered Italy on your new passport. One of my assistants is now high up in the Mossad. I got him to help me. He is ambitious and I promised to make sure he would have support from politicians I know. He wants the top job. He won't get it, so I helped him anyway. Then I traced you myself from Milan. It wasn't hard."

"How did you get to the politicians?"

"Listen, and I will tell you a story and you will see why you are here. And then we will decide what will happen here today."

"We?" I asked.

"You are a changeless bastard. When you were with the PM, they said you told him he had enough yes-men around him; that you chose to be the no-man he could believe…. I have a gun in my pocket. I have reason to kill you. So shut up, don't get smart with me. Just shut up and listen!"

Oh, yes, he was angry. White-lipped. I believed he did have a gun. I sat with my legs dangling over the rock-face and kept quiet.

"When we were in our late twenties, I worked in the ShaBak, and you were a *makher* in the little group around the PM. I was doing a term of specialization in VIP protection. You were friendly. Everyone was in those days. It was an intimate band. A few years later I got posted to Jerusalem with my wife and kids."

I didn't interrupt. I remembered.

"We found an apartment a few streets away from you and your wife, and one day we bumped into one another. You invited us to visit, and the four of us became friends. You were not an easy husband. There were rumors about you then. Sometimes you'd be seen with a woman in your car. Remember, it was a small town then. We knew each other's cars."

I nodded. The mood had changed subtly. "Manny, look, neither of us is so young. This is not the best place for storytelling. Let's go back to the café. I give you my word that I won't cause any problems."

"Just remember, I have a pistol. Nine millimeters, automatic and loaded, safety off. Clear?"

"Clear."

We both moved slowly and stiffly, I first, he behind me. I was right—we weren't so young anymore. It had been a long time since we'd done field exercises. We sat in a corner of the restaurant; each of us had a *schnapps* and a large coffee. He picked up the thread of his story again.

"You often had coffee in that little place on Palmach Street, in that small strip of stores. I heard you had taken time off and were writing, that a friend had loaned you a small place he had where you could write in peace. We all lived in small apartments. We all had kids around. The rumors spread. Tamara used to meet her girlfriends at that café and every once in a while she said she saw you. She told me once or twice that when you were both alone, you sometimes sat together. I figured that as long as she was telling me about it, it was all kosher. Hah!"

Now I began to understand where this was going. And I was more puzzled than ever. Me and Tamara? I bit my tongue and restrained myself.

"Then I was put in charge of running agents in the territories, *shtinkerim.* I was home less and less. The Mossad and ShaBak set up a joint team to track down terrorist connections to Lebanon, Syria, Libya, and Iran. The Mossad borrowed me. I was abroad more and more.

Every time I came home, Tamara and I fought. She wanted a husband, not a spy. I felt a thousand meters tall when I was tracking those people, and one centimeter tall at home.

"I smelled men around her. I could see that she didn't give a damn whether I knew or not. One day I saw you with her in the café. Not so kosher anymore. The years passed. I found women in Europe, lots of them. But I only loved one woman. Only one, and you stole her!"

I opened my mouth. He hissed something at me, and I shut it.

"A few years more, a few years less. You peaked in government early, and left when you left. I heard you were writing full-time. One day, one of our guys in Jerusalem called me. He said he had bad news.

"That same day I had received a letter from Tamara. She had left the house. The kids were at her sister's. She couldn't stand the non-life we had together.

"And then the phone call from someone I trusted. He had seen Tamara walking down the street with you. You were carrying a suitcase. I put two and two together."

Again I took a deep breath. Again, he silenced me with a wave of disgust.

"For almost twenty years I traveled all over Europe, and to Arab countries, to Turkey, even to Iran. I had so many identities that I had to check each morning who I was. Once you even helped me with cover, before I learned about you....

"I slept with women in every city in Europe. Six times I ordered executions. Six times I had the live bullet. When Tamara left me, I knew part of me was dead, so I didn't care. I bluffed the psychologists until I couldn't anymore. I went back to the ShaBak. They gave me a cushy job. Liaison with the Knesset. I got to know all the parties all their people, and then I befriended especially the ultra-orthodox politicians and their hangers-on. Some of them became my friends.

"Of all the politicians, I knew they were the ones who had belief. Through them, I met the real right-wingers. They were true believers. Over time, they gave me back what I had lost.

"I studied with their rabbis. I began to become observant. With time I became religious. Really religious. No more casual women, no more airplanes and hotels, no more double agents, no more phony identities. I thought I had begun to come home.

"Once I was retired, they gave me generous scholarships and grants, and I studied and tried to return to myself and my roots."

Manny's mood suddenly changed; he slumped in his chair, exhausted. I could have hit him then, run away, made a fuss, something. But I didn't. I couldn't run away from his pain.

He was very pale. "I was there for three years. I prayed three times a day. I kept Shabbat. I ate only *kasher*. And then one day, I got a phone call at home, late at night. I recognized the voice.

"Can she come to see me? Right then, immediately.

"At first I was going to say no. I waited. She waited. Then I thought, okay, you can come, even though.... And then I remembered the rule, *lo tikom, ve-lo titor!* In simple language: when you do something good, don't remind the other person that you are doing it even though they acted badly towards you.

"I tried to be the new me, my original self. I wouldn't be vengeful; I wouldn't put myself on a pedestal and put her down. I wouldn't return evil for evil. I said yes.

"Did you ever see *La Bohème* or *Traviata*? That's how corny my situation was. The spurned lover becomes the support for...." He choked. Tears ran down his face.

"What did she have?" I whispered.

"What not? Some kind of autoimmune disease that began with lupus and went on until it consumed her. I saw her drift into nothingness, a skeleton, a living ghost."

"I adjusted the morphine dose. She died without pain. It took only three months.

"We both realized what a mistake we had made, how many mistakes we had made. She knew that she could come back to me. Only me, of all the men she'd had." He remained silent for a few heartbeats.

"I wish God knew that we could come back to Him."

"What do you mean? I thought you became a believer."

"When she came back to me, I tried to convince myself that everything that had happened was Divine Providence, that it was God's will. Suddenly, though, I asked myself, does that make God a good guy or a bad guy? I started talking to the rabbis about this. They referred me to all the books. One of them quoted a great rabbi who said that the holocaust was caused by our sins—those of the Zionists and the modernizers.

"I remembered how Avraham had argued with God over every evildoer in Sodom, and here some rabbi was condemning to death a million and a half children and millions of adults—even those who had remained believers. He was consigning them all to ashes. In God's name.

"When I talked to him about that, he said that since the *zonah* had come back into my life, I was like a moonstruck child. I should throw her out, like Avraham drove out Hagar."

"He actually called her a whore?"

"*Zonah! Your zonah!*"

He was trembling. I reached out to touch him, then remembered what was between the two of us and pulled my hand back, as if from fire. He didn't notice. He was staring into the distance.

"She died. I helped her die peacefully. I held her bony hand when she stopped breathing. My children became reconciled to me when she came back. Until then, they had blamed me for the collapse of our family. We stood together at the graveside. When all the mourners left, and the *hevrah kadisha* burial group left, we stood there and we sang her the lullaby she used to sing to them, *Numi numi!* After the *shiv'ah*, I stopped praying. Finished."

He stopped, utterly drained.

I said very quietly, "Let me tell you something. Something that will make it easier for you. Something true."

He nodded almost imperceptibly. Both his hands were on the table. If he did have a gun in his pocket, he had released it. "Speak!"

"It is true I had coffee once in a while with Tamara. It is also true that I had a bad reputation. And I admit that I once considered whether I should make any suggestions to Tamara.

"But I didn't. I don't know why. More and more whenever we met—and it wasn't often—she told me how much she loved you, but how she was becoming disillusioned, how she wouldn't waste her mid-life years on you. The truth? I felt pity, I felt empathy.

"What you may have seen in my face or body language was compassion. Yes, we both know that whenever there is a male and a female there are physical attractions at play. But we kept them out of our talks because she said that she knew she could trust my discretion. Whatever I am or was, I never was a gossip. I always honored confidences.

"I tried everything I could think of to get you two back together—marriage counseling, awareness raising, all the fads. She just shrugged and said, 'You don't know Manny. He'd never agree!' I acted as a friend and mediator, and never broke my trust with you."

"Like going off with her for a weekend?"

"What weekend?"

"The suitcase weekend. The suitcase, liar!"

"The suitcase?"

"You walked down our street together and you were carrying her suitcase."

"Listen to me. I haven't thought of that suitcase incident for years. It took me time to know what you were even talking about.

"Look at me and you will see that this is the absolute truth. It is so simple that it probably sounds like a lie. I swear that this is true, without reservation, and if I lie, shoot me in good conscience."

"So?"

"So. This is how it was. You lived around the corner from us. It was a very sunny day in late spring, I remember, because I decided to take a bus to see someone at the university. I didn't have the car that day. Remember we were all one-car families then. I stepped out of my house, and I saw Tamara walking down the street, parallel to me, on the other side. I crossed over to her side, and asked where she was going. She said to the bus. Naturally I offered to carry her suitcase.

"I remember that one of us, I guess it was me, made a joke: if someone sees us now, for sure they'll think we're going off for the weekend.

"She looked away. At that moment I knew she *was* going away with someone. Her bus came first. I kissed her on the cheek and didn't see her again for many years. I heard she was having affairs, I heard she married an older man. I heard that he had died. I lost contact, and our worlds—yours and mine, mine and hers, didn't cross. I never even thought about you again until I heard your name in Crete."

Manny didn't say anything. His eyes probed mine, and then he looked away, staring off into the distance again.

Then he had me retell the story, and kept interrupting with questions. I had to repeat it. He made me describe the place, the street, the time of day. I couldn't tell him what year it had been because I had forgotten about the incident for decades.

Finally, after countless re-phrasings and trick questions to find the flaw in my story, finally he stopped. Finally, he nodded.

We ordered lunch. He ate sparsely. I still avoided meat. We drank beer with the meal. Light Italian beer. We ate in silence.

He looked at me. I thought I could even detect relief in his pale face. His straggly gray beard struck a false note in my memory of him. As must mine to him. Two impostors, making peace in the Dolomites.

"I believe you."

I just nodded, and then said, hesitantly, "But why was there a contract put on me? What can you tell me? And were you supposed to kill me?"

"Let's walk. I need air. I will tell you everything."

We paid our bill, and both of us went to the men's room. It's male bonding, peeing together, side by side. As we walked to the front door, the kitchen door swung open, and I could see a swarthy man in a white chef's jacket cutting vegetables. A *Gastarbeiter.* All of Europe is overflowing with the cheap labor imported or "permitted" from the southern countries, and from the poor lands to the east.

We turned again onto the path that we, as enemies, had followed before. Now there was the camaraderie of those who had paid their dues and could now look back at a past that contained both so much promise and so many broken dreams.

"When I was going through my crisis, after Tamara died, all my anger turned against you," Manny said. "You had a good first marriage, with wonderful children, and an excellent second marriage. You'd made a name for yourself, had an outstanding second career. People spoke of you with respect. I kept picturing you walking down the street on the way to seducing Tamara, to stealing her from me. I wanted revenge. I wanted to pull you down." The recalled anger distorted his face for a moment. I spread my arms, reminding him of my clean hands.

The sun was behind us, making everything seem longer and darker as it began to sink behind the jagged mountains. Perhaps we were looking into Switzerland, the air was so clear. It would be twilight soon.

Manny stopped, and we sat side by side on the rock where he had sat when he had held me prisoner. There was a thin sheen of sweat over his upper lip.

"I have liver cancer," he said. "My time is fixed. Soon. I just don't know exactly when. The search kept me going. Now...." He shrugged.

"Tell me why you were after me."

"A few of the rabbis came to me. I know their way of thinking. 'Even though Manny has left us temporarily, he will return. He will see we are right.' They came with their insufferable self-righteousness; God was in their vest pocket and the Halachah a crown on their funny hats. They owned the Knesset in those days, they owned the government, they owned the mayors.

"I was beyond caring. They needed someone like me. They would pay me. I would evolve a plan how to get rid of you. They never said 'kill.' They never spoke explicitly. I began to meet with them. They paid me as much as I wanted. No problem. They were lining their pockets, so why not throw me some crumbs. Especially if I could get rid of the person who was muckraking, throwing filth on them, running to journalists, paying private investigators, appealing to the High Court. You were the one man in their way; the political parties were useless."

"What happened?"

"One of the rabbis spoke out of *cheder*." He smiled thinly. "Out of *cheder*," he repeated, savoring the term. "Word got out, and someone told you to run. One person who didn't want you on his conscience. You panicked, and ran. When you ran, they had a debate, and they decided that murder would be too dangerous, might implicate them, and anyway, you were gone. Your panic helped you with them."

"Panic, maybe," I said. "But after Rabin, maybe just wisdom."

"Maybe," he said, reflectively. "Maybe. Anyway, I had been turned on to the idea of getting you, and they couldn't turn me off. I wanted my revenge for Tamara. It was my personal vendetta. My private business. But I wanted to confront you first. I wanted to see you face to face. To tell you why. And then, finish it! Finish you. Finish me.

"Then, all I saw was a tired old man: still strong, still able to run; but an old man with a dyed beard and dyed hair. And I saw me, a dying man, losing strength every day, losing more of my ability to function with each passing day. You had the shine of truth on you."

The sheen was heavier on his face, and a trick of light gave it a greenish hue. "Help me up," he said. "I'm exhausted." We started back down the path. "I believe you. I can kill an enemy. I have. I still would. But I can't kill you—"

"Look up," I hissed at him. "You may yet be tested."

"What the hell?" Manny yelled.

Coming down the rise between the restaurant and the path, one of the swarthy kitchen staff was running, waving his arms and shouting. Manny motioned me away, and poised in the way he had been drilled—feet apart, right foot slightly forward, knees bent, his center of gravity low and steady— and put his hand in his pocket.

The man kept on coming down the slope yelling. I grabbed Manny's arm. The man was yelling in an African accent, "Wait, sorr, Shalom Shalom! Israel! Israel!" He was smiling, pleased he had caught us.

"Sorr, I am hurrying, I'll miss the funicular. But I hear you speak Ivrit. I was in Tel Aviv, very nice, very nice, want to go back, but they said I'm not legal. But I like Israeli people. Shalom Shalom!"

I took out my wallet. Manny never relaxed his guard. I found a ten euro bill and gave it to him.

"No need, sorr. No, I won't take it. I am from Nigeria; we are brave strong people, we like Israelis. I am going! Shalom Shalom!"

I waved my arm at him. "Take it. Take it. Don't miss your funicular."

Manny and I both laughed. An old spy and an aging muckraker had been able to hold the line against a suspected Hamas agent. We both laughed until Manny folded over, coughing, and began to fall. I moved to catch him, and my foot slipped on a stone, I lost my balance, and slid down the incline. I tried to grab some of the brush, but the fall turned into a bruising roll and then I lost consciousness.

When I came to it was dark. I was cold, confused, and frightened. I tried to stand and couldn't, so I crawled toward a cavity in the mountainside. De' Pomi must have been with me, because it was a shallow cave, sheltered from the wind and dry. I was lucky. I slept a long time. I felt all my bones, and I thought I had some cracked ribs and maybe fractures in one arm and an ankle. But I slept. By the time I came to, it was getting dark again. I had a small backpack with me, with water, a first-aid kit, and some biscuits and fruit. I ate a bit, drank, and then I took my plastic rain poncho and managed to spread it out over a few bushes in front of the cave. I had hoped that when Vi realized I was missing, she would send search teams for me, and that they just might see the yellow color.

The next thing I remember was Vi, kissing me and crying....

It was finally over.

Manny wasn't as lucky—he was very weak, still too weak to fly home. His doctors told me that he would need another few weeks of close care, and then could be flown back to Israel, but only with a doctor in attendance. He asked me to call his Mossad people and bring them up to date. "They have me covered, he said. "They'll look after me."

Two days later a young woman, supposedly his daughter, arrived. Grazia was an Italian on her father's side, and after they moved to Israel, the father had insisted on speaking Italian with her. She even had a Tuscan accent. She had been given some medical training first in the army and then in Mossad.

Grazia stayed by Manny's bedside most the day. I supposed that her first priority was to look after him, but, given my new-found suspicions, could she have been there in case the medication might bring out things better left unsaid?

For me, what was most important was that Manny dictated an affidavit, properly witnessed by Captian Ucelli, Rabbi Daniele Bemporad of the *Seminario Rabbinico,* and a rabbinical student the Rabbi brought along. It was a full and damning statement, duly witnessed for both a state and a rabbinical court, an iron-clad time bomb. If it ever found its way to being published it would land a few well-known rabbis in jail, disgraced for life. I phoned Sandor, the rebbe, and explained the contents of the affidavit—without names.

When I find someone I trust in the government, I will have him deal with it... perhaps.... Or maybe I will see these rabbis face-to-face, and make sure they know that I will destroy them if they don't stop. Or maybe both.

Vi and I needed a break, though, we needed to stay away from all of this. We needed to nurture ourselves as the adrenalin of flight began to drain out of our lives.

After I was released from hospital, Vi and I went back to the Belvedere. We called the children, who had known something was very wrong, without knowing what and why. They had worried about us just as we had longed for them. Soon we will see them all.

Right now, though, we deserve the rest. We need to be together. We hadn't gone through such strain since the Yom Kippur War. Or was it since the Scuds? Or was it the intifadas?... And this had gone on for months.

Now together, we at last had respite, peace and quiet. I began writing again. We took walks, did whatever we wanted, ate whenever we felt like eating, drank the good Italian wines whenever we felt like drinking. We were free agents.

The consulate in Milan issued me a new passport—in my own name.

I felt a thousand years younger. Vi's face and eyes no longer broadcast worry, fear.

We were together. We were us again.

EPILOGUE

He brought me to the banqueting house,
his banner over me was love.
Stay me with flagons,
comfort me with apples,
for I am sick with love.

Song of Songs, 2:4–5

There was a waning moon earlier tonight; its reflection dimly separated the green pine trees, now shaded black, and the blacker heaviness of the mountains rising behind them. I have gone out onto the porch, and the gentle luminosity of the fading moon and the starry night moves me deeply. A soft still wind stirs the boughs below, and a soft still voice stirs my heart.

We are going home.

How great the luck that guided me in this way, through my two intersecting journeys. Everything, as usual, can be explained rationally. But I can still marvel at the wonders all of this has wrought for me, this Avraham, restored to the beauty and value of life as soft and luminous as the moon, stark and harsh as the sun, with its treasured privacy, and the love that illuminates it… and the miracle of Avraham de' Pomi, resurrected from the dust of a Cretan mountain village.

Logically speaking, of course, I should never have run, but, just as logically, I could not fully trust the agencies of the state. Police, secret services—all have been in some way subverted; some openly for the usual bad and boring reasons, and some secretly, in the most subtle and perilous way. Too many have been infected with ideological viruses. All people in public service have, to a greater and lesser degree, ideological leanings and preferences. In a decent system, the believers in the extreme ideologies—left or right—are cast out. But state norms have changed. What was beyond the pale yesterday is today's common ground, and tomorrow's cliché.

Sandor, the Rackover *rebbe*, told me that Manny's affidavit had created a stir among "his friends." In Halachah, the testimony of a dying man is incontestable. They wanted my promise never to reveal any of it.

Now they are the pursued. I am not sure whether I want to be the pursuer.

Manny is still alive, but his bitter and unhappy days are drawing to a close. Vi and I have been to see him twice. We are fully reconciled. He has been generous enough to wish us well. His new-found "daughter" is with him every day, and will eventually fly back to Israel in an ambulance plane with him. They've arranged a hospice for him.

I have called Ariadne. It was a sweet call, full of tenderness and resonances of the Greek poems and songs she taught me. We will correspond by email. Violetta said to me, "I know what this poetry and friendship must mean to you. More I don't need to know."

She is, as usual, right. I am here with her, richer with poetry and music.

It's true that love begets love, penetrating the many bands and subtle substructures of our souls and our bodies, *psyche* and *soma*, and these cannot be separated into warp and woof. I have been blessed with love at different times, in different ways. And now, I am renewed and can give rebirth to my creative self, long buried under fact, conventional lies, and accepted truths, stunted by ambition and ideals.

My renewal will first be Violetta's, and then will embrace all whom I love. Life has its hard times ahead; surely the precarious days will come. Their pounding steps echo in every breath and every heartbeat. Inevitable, tragic, natural. Until then, I will tend "mine own vineyard." Violetta and I will make each day a one of joy, a day of light.

I have paid my dues. We have paid our dues. It's time to hand over to the next generation.

The moon is dim now, the stars brighter, and soon Vi will call out for me. I will look just for a moment at the Book, and find the words with which I want to close.

We now belong only to those we love, come what may. There is no more room for rancor.

Who knows how much time we have?

> *We shall sustain ourselves with flagons,*
> *be comforted with apples;*
> *for we are sick with love.*

> *Sostenetemi con focacce d'uva passa,*
> *rinfrancatemi con pomi,*
> *perché io sono malata d'amore. Cantico dei Cantici 2:5*

Avraham Ben Hayim
Alto Adige/Süd Tirol
January 23, 2009

AFTERWORD

Everything in this story exists in the realm of the possible. The modern tale, that of Avraham Ben Hayim, reflects part of the present-day reality in Israeli life, but is fictional in all its characters and situations. The places where the tale unfolds were all personally and carefully researched.

The renaissance tale of Avraham de' Pomi is based on historical reality. Great Jewish philosophers, linguists, doctors, and rabbis thrived in the Italian cultural and academic setting of the time. In the story we refer to Rabbi Leone da Modena, who practiced over thirty professions, and in addition to his rabbinical decisions, was world famous as one of the great orators of his period. The doctor and professor of medicine (also a rabbi) Davide de' Pomi did certainly exist; my hero, Avraham de' Pomi, is his imaginary nephew. Solomone de Rossi, a musician in the court of the Duke of Mantua had great influence on the development of music in Europe, and also pioneered the introduction of Baroque music into the synagogue service.

They represent for me an ideal Jew, one who is totally at ease in his Jewish identity, who is familiar with Jewish texts and structures his life in harmony with them, and at the same time is thoroughly worldly and rooted in the classical wisdom of his time and in its worlds of thought and beauty. Even though the Italian Jews in this period were often rebuffed by their Christian neighbors or persecuted by Church and secular authorities, they were fully open to the learning and wisdom of their Gentile compatriots, and able to enjoy the cultural and artistic richness of their native land.

The tale of Avraham de' Pomi is written as though translated from an Italian Hebrew manuscript 400 years old. The Hebrew version of this part of the book is actually in the style of the period and place. The English text attempts to convey that sense. Footnotes have been added to direct inquisitive readers to the sources cited.

To the best of my knowledge the Duke of Mantua did not have lands in Crete. I assume that his heirs will not bring suit against the government of Crete for the fruitful valley I awarded him. In spite of this lapse, my descriptions of the island are relatively exact, and references to its history are basically factual, though not in every detail. Although we do know that there were people of Slavic origin in medieval Crete, there is no record of a Bosnian Moslem settlement in that period, nor of any known Moslem settlement at that time. A noted scholar assured me that had there been, he would have found some record of it. This is known in academia as *argumentum ex silentio*—proof from silence. You might say that I have broken the silence and created such a "fact."

In my search for the realities of the era of de' Pomi, I am deeply indebted to the scholars whose books and studies brought to life for me the history of the Jews of Italy. Among them are Professors Cecil Roth and Moses (Moshe) Avigdor Shulvass, both of blessed memory, and Professors Reuven Bonfil, David Ruderman, and Shlomo Simonson. I also consulted basic works on the Renaissance and Baroque periods and studied the Hebrew and Italian writings of some of the figures of the time.

In Mantua itself the gates to Jewish existence of then and now were opened to me by members of the Norsa and Colorni families, whose ancestors would have surely known the heroes of this tale. I note their help and warmth with gratitude and affection.

My interest in Italy dates back to my adolescence in Toronto where I was fortunate enough to learn ancient languages and classics. I visited Italy frequently over the years with growing fascination. My more recent visits to Greece captured my heart, especially the wild beauty of Crete. Two individuals there who became my friends introduced me into the life of the people of that magnificent island.

Maria K. helped me understand the realities of today while keeping an ear attuned to the echoes of the past. She helped me open to the modern language and poetry, to Greek and Cretan music, and explained the role of family history and its link to land, and identity.

Nikos Stavroulakis is a wide-ranging intellectual, historian, archeologist, artist, and writer whose personal history is that of the eastern basin of the Mediterranean. I first met him in Hania in 1999 when he completed the rebuilding, restoration, and rededication of the synagogue that had been built by exiles from Spain over five centuries ago and had been desecrated and destroyed by the Nazis.

Directly and indirectly, these two drew me into the great and sometimes tragic history of their homeland and kindled my imagination and writing. To both I owe an immense debt of gratitude.

I wrote this book both in English and in Hebrew. The first English text was edited by Andrea Knight, and has since gone through a number of permutations. The Hebrew text, *Ma'aseh bi-Shnei Avraham*, was published by Carmel Books, Jerusalem in 2008.

This final version has been edited (and produced) by Heidi Connolly, who worked with perceptiveness and ability. I am happy to record my gratitude to her for her talent and warm identification with the book.

This edition, like the Hebrew, is dedicated to Violetta, and the *maven* (he who understands) will understand.

Jerusalem
January 23, 2013

About the Author

Avraham Avi-hai was born in Canada and immigrated to Israel in 1952. He has been a journalist (*The Jerusalem Post*; Canadian Broadcasting Corporation), a top-level civil servant in the offices of early Israeli Prime Ministers David Ben-Gurion and Levi Eshkol, and an advisor to the legendary Mayor of Jerusalem, Teddy Kollek. He served for ten years as World Chairman of United Israel Appeal—Keren Hayesod.

Avi-hai holds degrees from the Jewish Theological Seminary and Columbia University in New York. He was a founding dean of the Rothberg International School at Hebrew University of Jerusalem, and is Member Emeritus of the University's Board of Governors. He has taught there, at York University in Toronto, and at the University of Rochester in New York. He speaks English, French, Yiddish, Hebrew, and German, is familiar with medieval and modern Italian as well as modern Spanish, and has studied Ancient Greek and Latin. He made many visits to Italy and Greece to research the writing of A Tale of Two Avrahams.

Dr. Avi-hai and his wife Henrietta live facing the Old City walls of Jerusalem and are often joined there by three generations of offspring. Dr. Avi-hai can be reached at 2avrahams@gmail.com.

Made in the USA
Lexington, KY
17 November 2013